DART

ALCO LAMMERS

For Lilly

CHAPTER ONE

ED MOVED ASIDE to let a woman, whom he didn't recognize, pass him on her way to the bar in a hurry. As she did, her purse brushed his shoulder. She turned around to face him.

"I'm sorry, I didn't mean to be so rude," she said.

Confined to a wheelchair, Ed often found himself isolated in crowded social gatherings, so any attention, however fleeting it might be, came as a welcome surprise. "No big deal," he said, trying to sound cheerful, "sometimes you just really need a drink."

The woman laughed. "Isn't that the truth?" For a moment she looked as if she was going to leave it at that, but then she changed her mind. "I'm Hannah. Hannah Simmons, pleased to meet you. How long have you been with Sure Trust?"

Ed shook her hand and laughed. "Longer than I care to admit," he said. "Nice to meet you Hannah, I'm Ed Sutherland. I take it you're from out of town?"

It was a fair assumption; Sure Trust Insurance had closed their offices in this city many years ago. But for some unknown reason, likely rooted in nostalgia, they still held their annual regional convention here. This year they switched venue to this less fancy hotel to save on cost.

"First time here," Hannah said. "I've always skipped this one until now. It's too far of a drive for me."

"Yeah, I'm a visitor as well. I used to live here though."

Hannah offered to get them both drinks and Ed accepted. The room was quickly filling up with people. When Hannah returned with the drinks, the noise of the crowd had swelled, making it much harder to carry on a conversation. Without talking much beyond some general remarks about work, they couldn't make their drinks last, and it seemed this encounter with Hannah would be short-lived after all.

Sure enough, as she put her empty glass down, she said, "I need a cigarette, so I think I'll pop outside for a bit."

Ed nodded. Fearing it was a long shot, he asked, "Would you mind if I joined you? I can't hear myself think in here."

"Sure." She gently pushed the wheelchair out of the room, toward the elevators. Once outside, on the sidewalk in front of the hotel, Hannah lit a cigarette and offered one to Ed.

"Oh no, thank you, I don't smoke."

Hannah shrugged and pointed across the road. "Do you know what all that is? It looks a bit gloomy. It's what I see when I look out the window in my room."

"Yeah, me too. That's the old university."

Hannah raised an eyebrow, blowing smoke out of the corner of her mouth. "They had a university here? I don't think I've heard of that before."

Ed made a gesture to the mess across the street. "The Northern Maritimes University, or NMU. My father used to work there in the physics lab. It's that building there, closest to the road, just inside the campus perimeter."

It looked severely damaged, with some of it already collapsed. The remaining part was boarded up.

"It was quite the outfit. When the university closed, the buildings were abandoned. All investors vanished, along with several tech companies that the lab had attracted to the area. Nobody wanted to clean it up, including the city."

Hannah waited for Ed to continue, but he remained quiet. Maybe he was trying to remember something, so she gave him some time.

"This is why I don't like coming back here," he finally said in a much lower voice now.

Hannah exhaled another puff of smoke at Ed and asked, "Why was it closed? Did something bad happen there?"

Ed nodded and gazed across the street. "At the time, the physics lab was under renovation," he said. "They were installing some type of new machine in there. A guy named Shim had invented it, or designed it, something like that, I'm not sure, and my father worked for him. The main lab needed to be expanded to make space, so that's why most of the building was under construction."

He paused and tried to get some fresh air, in between the clouds of smoke coming from Hannah.

"A crane was lifting a huge cement bucket when a cement truck came flying through the fencing and crashed straight into the crane support. The truck driver was going way too fast, with a full load, when some idiot crossed the road in front of him without looking. The truck swerved, avoiding the pedestrian, but then had to correct again because of a car parked across the street. The driver, now also trying to get out of the way of another car approaching him head-on, stood no chance of staying on the road. As soon as he hit the crane, the whole thing started tilting and swinging and the bucket came down. It went through the roof of the main physics lab. All hell broke loose in there. There were fires, thick smoke, and dust everywhere and concrete pouring into the lab. It was an absolute disaster. When the smoke cleared and the dust settled, almost everyone in that room was dead, including Mr. Shim. And my father."

Hannah stared at him briefly and said, "I'm so sorry. That is just so awful."

"Yeah. And I was there that day. My dad had taken me to the lab for the first time to show me around. I think they were installing some part of Shim's machine that day; I can't remember exactly. I was just a kid. I do remember Shim and my father joking with each other about a tennis ball. Dad did that a lot at home too. A few months before the accident, he brought that ball into the lab and placed it on some sort of table that was meant to support the machine. I believe he did that specifically for the purpose of joking about it. I don't know why it was funny to them, it all went over my head."

Ed paused again as some people passed by, on their way into the hotel.

"Nice evening," one of them said.

Assuming that it was, Ed had to think it was slightly diminished by Hannah still blowing smoke in precisely the right way to skillfully enshroud him in a smelly grey mist. She was blissfully unaware of the nuisance she was causing, and silently waited for him to continue.

"Before the crash, almost everyone had gathered around a whiteboard. They were discussing some details of the machine that I could make head nor tail of. It seemed to me people were just taking turns drawing meaningless lines and arrows on the board and arguing about whose lines were better. I needed to use the bathroom, but the ones nearest the main lab were closed, because of the renovation, so it ended up that I had to go to the far end of the building. It is why I am still around today. The cement came down precisely where they were all gathered. My toilet break saved me but left me without the use of my legs. Hence this god-damned chair."

Ed looked up at Hannah and said, "You know, I'm going to need another drink soon."

Hannah agreed and told him to stay put. To Ed's relief she extinguished her cigarette and went inside.

Ed hadn't talked about this incident in a long time. Not two months after the accident, his mother, who had been struggling with depression before, took her own life. Ed eventually ended up in a foster home, in another city. By then, the university was already in financial trouble. Inevitably, NMU closed its doors, and many companies that supported it, or depended on it, went down with it. The local economy went into gradual decline, and the once flourishing city became a shadow of its former self. Many residents moved away to find new work, and with the students also gone, local business activity dwindled in all sectors. Nowadays the city is suffering from an aging population, high unemployment and too many vacant buildings to count.

Ed sighed. His desire to continue his conversation with Hannah had waned. He wheeled himself back into the hotel and, with the help of a hotel clerk, made it to the elevators before Hannah returned from the upstairs bar. Back in his not necessarily wheel-chair-friendly room he looked out the window at the old campus once more.

If it hadn't been for one man crossing the road all those years ago, what came next would have been trivial. Instead, it would be a familiar, but embarrassing ordeal getting out of this suit and tie, out of this chair and into bed. Three long and boring convention days were ahead.

Chapter Two

"So, professor, what can I do for you?" Lora moved her phone to her other hand and picked up her notepad. She had returned home from the lab and nestled herself in a comfortable chair, with a cup of tea and a book, in her favorite room. Her study, which she habitually referred to as her home office, held the middle between a library and an office. Not exactly the middle of course, it was leaning quite heavily toward the former. All walls, except the window side, where her desk was located, were lined with bookshelves, well-stocked floor-to-ceiling with mostly works of fiction. On one of the long walls, the shelves were interrupted to make a spot for her chair and a little side table, currently holding her tea and a few books she had on the go. More books were stacked on her desk as preselected future reading. On the floor some small piles were starting to form as well, even if that was strictly against her own policy.

"Well, I am curious to know how the last day went." On the other end of the connection was the famous, retired professor Dr. Shim. He was referring to the last day of experiments Lora was running at the university's main quantum physics lab before moving on to the next phase of her project. The second phase had been important for the data it generated, but its results wouldn't be particularly exciting until the third and final phase was completed.

"It was the same routine, with the same outcome. As problematic as Phase-B may have been initially, we concluded it without a glitch, so far as we can tell," Lora said. "The data looks good, but nothing is certain until the end."

The doctor felt proud. People told him all the time he had struck gold when he found her and by now, she was like family to him. "Well done, Lora. Well done indeed."

"Thank you, David. But there is no time to lose. If I am to get this wrapped up before the convention, we need to get Phase-C up and running as soon as possible."

David Shim held somewhat of a celebrity status, and due to the extensive media attention that his work had received over the years, he was now mostly known as simply Dr. Shim. Even some of his close colleagues could be forgiven for not knowing him by his first name. He joked sometimes that his first name was in fact Doctor. Lora, who obtained a doctoral degree as well, as did most of her coworkers, preferred a more personal, first-name based approach, at least among her equals. Of course, she generally respected Dr. Shim's preference when referring to him or addressing him in public.

"Has a decision been reached regarding the target object?"
Lora chuckled. "Yeah. We're finally going to use the tennis ball."

"Ha-ha, are you sure about that?"

"I know, I know… bad luck. But Phase-C will be the last time we're using the machine in this configuration. That ball was specifically put there to be used in an experiment. I think it is time for it to finally fulfil its purpose."

"I'm sure Gary is pleased with that. I think that might keep him from retiring for a few more years."

"I hope so. He can be a little rough around the edges, but I don't know if I can run this project without him."

"Yes, he's a good man," the doctor said. He considered Gary to be one of his most respected colleagues and counted him among his best friends. "And what will you do if it doesn't work?"

"Then we will proceed as we have for the other phases. Pick random stuff until something sticks."

"I see. You'll let me know when you run it for the first time, will you? I'd like to be there for it," the doctor said.

"Oh god. I haven't told you, but Ian is planning on making it into a bit of an event. He wants to invite a bunch of people to witness the first run. You will most certainly receive an invitation."

Ian Byrne was the physics department chair. This put him in charge of everything that went on in NMU's Everett building, where most of the university laboratories, including the quantum physics lab, were housed. Despite his traditionally elected position, Ian was in effect installed by private investors, about a year after the start of the experiment that eventually propelled Dr. Shim to fame. Ian was notoriously obsessed with rules and regulations, which admittedly had kept everything running smoothly, but caused Lora and everyone else who worked there a lot of frustration. Lora had suffered many headaches resulting from arguments with Ian about lab rules, funding and hiring. She estimated that she came out victorious less than half of the time. But when it came to Dr. Shim attending the first run of Phase-C, there would be no argument. Ian, just like everyone around here, fostered a deep respect for the doctor.

"Before anything else, I need to get my new assistant up and running. A student named Randy Fletcher," Lora said. "He was the only survivor after interviews."

"Poor kid. I hope you can make him last," Dr. Shim said, laughing affectionately.

Lora blushed. "I don't mean to scare them, David. I'm just not very lucky with them. I need the extra pair of hands, that much is clear, but it would be nice if they came with half a brain attached."

It remained quiet on the line.

"Anyway," she continued, "I will see him in the lab tomorrow."

WHEN THE DOCTOR FIRST CAME to work at NMU, before Lora was even born, he was in the final stages of developing his first theory. Within a year of his arrival, he proposed an ambitious experiment, to be carried out using a machine that he would have purpose-built for the task. It imbued his peers with abundant skepticism. But the doctor had a unique talent for selling his ideas. And it wasn't an idea that was hard to sell, because, if the machine worked in the way he had predicted, it held the promise of grand commercial opportunities and endless practical applications. Before long, he was attracting the attention of more than just unconvinced peers. In fact, the majority of interested parties were potential investors, sponsors and even commercial companies interested in helping him realize the device. There were so many offers that the university, at the time often struggling to make ends meet, decided to partially privatize their physics labs. It turned out to be a very lucrative move, despite the fiscal nightmare that accompanied it. Even the resulting loss of access to most government funding couldn't prevent the labs from quickly growing to be among the most advanced and well-funded in the world.

Attempting to minimize disruptions at the lab during the development of the machine, an off-campus location was secured by the university and the investors, specifically intended for building custom lab equipment.

To the disappointment of the investors, the doctor's machine could not produce the results he had hoped for, and within a year after beginning tests, Dr. Shim abandoned the project and his theory in favor of a new, more elegant, and arguably more promising idea. Even though some had lost their faith in him, he had no difficulties securing funding from remaining and new investors. With money pouring in from all directions, the university put up little in the way of opposition. New and existing companies were setting up offices and factories in the area, eager to be part of the action. The doctor had everything he needed. Together with an almost entirely newly hired crew of scientists, engineers, and specialists in a variety of fields, Dr. Shim began work on his second machine, which would take all of seven years to build, at the off-campus location.

Once the machine was finished and tested successfully, it was moved and installed into the quantum physics lab at NMU, which had been substantially renovated for the purpose. It took another year to get it ready for the experiment, which subsequently ran uninterrupted for eight years, led by the doctor himself.

Lora first met Dr. Shim nearer the end of that project, first for a year as an honors student under his supervision. He had immediately taken a liking to her. She then left NMU, and the country, for some years to pursue her PhD, but eagerly returned to the lab, much to the delight of Dr. Shim, to assume a more permanent position.

With the project in its final stages, the doctor started gathering ideas for follow-up projects that could be run using his extraordinary machine. One proposal that focused on future commercial opportunities was unanimously chosen, and the investors were already lining up to support it. Most of that happened while Lora was away, but upon her return, she proposed an idea of her own, which immediately resonated with the doctor. Her idea, unlike all the others he had evaluated, was one of pure research. A true mission of discovery, that was exactly what he found had been missing from his own career. He had been so preoccupied with pandering to investors, appeasing the leadership of the university and negotiating deals with suppliers, that he felt science was sometimes pushed into the background.

Dr. Shim's last official act before retiring was to present the results of his experiment at the annual Physics Advances convention in the city. During that presentation, all those present in the room knew they were witnessing history in the making. Dr. Shim's machine, even more so than the experiment itself, was revolutionary. There was no doubt that it was going to radically change the world. The doctor returned from that event a celebrity, as well as a retiree.

The university appointed a new lab leader, who immediately failed to impress anyone. Meanwhile the doctor tried to convince them to give Lora's proposal a chance. He warned that the lab was at risk of turning into a production facility controlled by the investors, rather than remaining a place of fundamental research. In the same breath, surprising everyone, he claimed to have found a sponsor for Lora's project. Somehow, the doctor had sold one single investor on the idea, even though there was no known profitable outcome. As the officially selected follow-up project was estimated to require several years of preparation time at an external location, Lora's idea was finally greenlighted for three years. Soon after, at the recommendation of Dr. Shim, Lora was appointed the new lab leader at the prestigious quantum physics lab of the Northern Maritimes University.

Chapter Three

A SECURITY GUARD OPENED the door and let a nervous looking student into the lab. Lora watched him search the room for her. When he finally saw her, she raised her hand and waved him over.

"You are in the right place!" she said. "Come in."

Before he met her for his interviews, Randy had heard of Lora through some of her published work, as well as by reputation. This university didn't rank very high on the world stage and as such, public information was in short supply and mostly controlled by the university itself. Studying at this school might not impress anyone, but if you worked in the Everett building, in the quantum physics lab, you belonged to an elite. This lab had produced some remarkable results, the most famous of which were Dr. Shim's. Randy could feel the history of the room. Lora too, remembered how she felt when she first walked into this place, so she left him some time to gawk.

"So, Randy, what do you think is going on here? What are we doing here?" Lora asked out of the blue.

"Um… Well, you're expanding on the work of Dr. Shim, as I understand it."

"Very good, that is precisely what I told you during your interview."

Randy got more nervous. He found Lora immediately intimidating. It had been made very clear to him that most of the work currently going on here was kept quiet, where possible, because premature information from this quantum physics lab had previously led to dramatically distorted stories in the media. The university, and more so the private investors, since made it a strict policy that the lab could only publish research that was advanced and complete enough to avoid the worst journalistic sci-fi stories. Not everything that happened here could potentially blow up a planet.

The lacking response prompted Lora to try a different approach. She asked, "Why don't you start by telling me what you know. What do you know about The Shim?"

Randy relaxed slightly. "It's that machine over there, built by Dr. Shim," he said, pointing to a large plateau with multiple machines suspended above it. He had hardly taken his eyes off it since he sat down by Lora.

"You're almost giving him too much credit. David Shim wasn't some lonely genius putting together the next big toy for scientists. He had a big team working with him," she said.

"That's right," admitted Randy. "He had over fifty people working here over the course of his career."

Lora nodded. This student had read the Wiki page. That was a good start. "Continue," she said.

"Okay. The Shim is described by most people as a teleportation device of sorts."

"Sure. But you're skipping all the good parts now," Lora said.

"I know, but I was under the impression that you already know all this," Randy said, attempting to joke.

Lora smirked and let him talk.

"The Shim can take any object that is small enough to fit under the beam and move it from that one definite position to a different position that is randomly selected from two options, the two cohesion pods of the machine. The way I understand it is that the beam projects a rapid succession of simulated random environments onto a target. If such an environment happens to match a specific configuration, it produces interference which effectively brings the whole object, including the projected environment, into the equivalent of a quantum superposition. The object then occupies two distinct locations, inside of the two coherence pods, simultaneously until they are opened. At that point the object will appear in only one of the two pods. To an observer, it looks like the object was teleported."

Lora nodded slowly and said, "That's not bad at all. You are making it sound simple. I like that. I may choose to make you our representative for the media."

Randy smiled. "That sounds good to me. I always prefer simple explanations—" he said, until he was interrupted.

"I was kidding, we do *not* talk to the media!" Lora looked so serious that Randy couldn't tell if he was already in trouble, until she finally smiled again. "You certainly glossed over some things, but I think you got the gist of it. I will do my best to keep it simple for you today as well. What do you know about my work, despite the hush-hush?"

"Dr. Shim left when the machine was fully operational, and all initially planned experiments were successful. So, when I hear that you are trying to expand on his work, I wonder what there is left to expand on. Obviously, I don't know exactly what it is because there has been no information from this lab. I had to sign an NDA before I was even allowed an interview when I applied."

Lora cringed but decided to keep quiet.

"I think you are probably trying to allow even larger objects to be transported. Dr. Shim has always said that the device cannot be used on living organisms, so maybe that is also a focus."

"Let me stop you there," Lora said, shaking her head.

The one thing everyone knew was that her work was being kept secret. How was he supposed to answer her question then?

"Have you ever seen The Shim in action?" Lora asked.

Randy sat up and said, "No, I've never been in here before. I saw a video in class once. It was bad."

Teleportation was rather easy to market, as it turned out, so there were many ideas for practical applications out there already. As revolutionary as The Shim was though, it was still too bulky, too slow, too expensive, too energy consuming and too limited for practical use outside the lab. It remained, to the satisfaction of both Lora and Dr. Shim, still purely a research tool that existed only in this lab. That would change soon enough, Lora knew, but until then she loved being one of the few scientists in the world who had access to it.

Even so, Lora's remaining time with the machine was limited. A slew of potential investors was pushing for her to wrap up, sitting on their money for the more lucrative opportunities that lay beyond and for which preparations were now in their final phase as well.

"Follow me," said Lora as she got up and started her way toward The Shim.

Chapter Four

IN A RELATIVELY NEW PART of the city, characterized by modern buildings, hip stores and urban dining experiences, a statue stood moderately tall in a small park. You might expect it to be a statue celebrating the achievements of a former mayor, or of the city's founder, honoring a locally praised hero, or memorializing a tragic victim. Sometimes, a statue merely exists for its aesthetic value, as an expression of art adding visual interest to its environment. But this truly unique example was different. It was the statue for Dart. It was commissioned by himself, sculpted by himself, and erected by himself, to commemorate himself. That may be unconventional to those unfamiliar with Dart, but the citizens of this fine city have embraced it. For the most part. Most of the time. Dart describes himself as a superhero. He is shrouded in mystery.

His first job, as he prefers to call his rescues, was a high school fire. Three students were trapped inside, with the fire department still minutes out. Dart, then a civilian, just happened to walk by, carrying a wet green blanket. He wrapped it around himself, entered the building and brought out one of the teens. Without too much hesitation, considering the danger he was exposing himself to, he then went back inside and brought out a second. He left the scene when fire trucks were pulling in. The next day, newspapers headlined "Two Teens Rescued from Fire by Caped Superhero" and, somewhat less sensational, "Exceptional Bravery Saves Highschoolers". The third student, who sadly perished in the fire, was barely mentioned, and as such didn't take away much from the praise Dart received. When he read the papers, he knew instantly that this was now his calling. He would be a superhero and his job would be to save lives. He never revealed how he came to be carrying the wet green blankets that day.

He also never explained why he chose the name Dart. A background article about Dart in a local business magazine some years ago proposed two theories on the origin of Dart's name. The first explanation, which seemed plausible enough, was that Dart happened to have a name pin already in his possession, with the word Dart pre-existing on it. He pinned it to his costume and called it a day. The second theory suggests that the name was a variation on his real name, touching on the strong example of Bart, or a reference to his place of birth. The magazine failed to dig deeper into his identity leading some to suggest, unsubstantiated, that Dart had a hand in the contents of the article.

One of his proudest moments came when a toy manufacturer offered him a deal for an action figure based on him. The initial excitement made way for disappointment when the first toys started appearing in stores. Dart spent the following months fighting the manufacturer in court to stop the toys from being sold.

The final versions on the shelves were very unlike the demos he had been shown earlier, and even more unlike him. Even worse, they had used a different, and in his opinion offensive, name on the box than was printed on the action figure itself.

Dart has been described by people as slightly overweight and not particularly muscular for a superhero. Despite that, it would be a mistake to think of him as weak. He packs a good punch. People trying to unmask him, which was an annoying occurrence especially during tourist season, invariably came away with a few bruises and no new information.

He generally wins the fights he is in, in part because of what he likes to call risk management. Dart chooses his battles carefully. He has allegedly foregone some potential rescues to protect and preserve his ability to do his job. A broken Dart, he reckons, will not rescue anyone's life.

No special superpower has been attributed to him, except by himself. He is on record saying that his superpower is to be in the right place at the right time all the time. His mode of operation is to simply wander the city streets until he senses trouble, then hang around until something bad happens so he can step in to save the day. He has claimed to possess a sixth sense for finding people in distress.

Over the years he earned a level of respect and a decent reputation with citizens. This is explained easily, as despite his strange and often ridiculed appearance, he has managed to save a few more lives since the high school fire. In one job he saved two people from being run over by a school bus, admittedly resulting in slight injuries among the children on the bus. In the same year he also saved a child from drowning in a fountain, although not too many people know about that. Dart bravely risked his life when an old man was being mugged. He had pushed the mugger in front of a speeding car. And as the driver wasn't wearing a seatbelt, Dart was presented with the opportunity to save his life as well, by promptly calling the emergency services. Less spectacular, but still very much appreciated, was his rescue of a man choking on his lunch.

Because saving lives didn't happen every day, he spent a lot of time doing small, good deeds in the streets, which he thought could help him keep his generally favorable reputation. He had helped countless people crossing roads, managed to single-handedly stop a bar fight, prevented several car thefts and one time even helped a young man propose to his girlfriend.

The business magazine article had ended with the question if, with such an impressive track record, Dart could have any flaws. It didn't definitively answer that question, instead offering the suggestion that nobody is perfect.

Chapter Five

Surrounded by control consoles, wires, buttons, and levers, The Shim sat as what was clearly the most important thing in the room. Randy felt that he was a couple of computer science courses short of being qualified for this.

"It's a tool," Lora said. "Don't worry. You'll get the hang of it. You'll be working this thing so much you'll end up bored with it." She walked back and forth between two consoles and started pressing buttons and turning dials. "The most important control elements are the big red emergency stop button right here," she explained as she slammed her hand on the button, "and the big levers on the wall there." She pointed behind Randy. "Those will turn this thing on and start the experiment." She walked toward the plateau and pointed to a small control box with some buttons and a couple of joysticks. "This is where we can manually control the position of the pods and the beam, and where you can open and close the pods. We don't really use manual positioning anymore, because in our upcoming experiments that is almost surely not going to work. It was fine in Dr. Shim's days, or during Phase-A. Once the whole system is calibrated, which I'm sad to say we have to do in preparation for almost every run, we can start The Shim with the leftmost lever." She pointed again and waited for Randy to confirm that he saw it. "My expansions, added for this experiment, are activated with the two levers to the right of it." She grabbed the manual control box and started repositioning the beam. A large piece of equipment that looked like a cross between an oversized gun and the exhaust of a spaceship, slowly moved across the ceiling with a satisfying hum. A red targeting laser projected a crosshair on the plateau, indicating the position of the beam. It was initially positioned over what looked like a tennis ball, placed in a circle marked on the plateau. She centered it on a different, empty circle elsewhere on the surface, closer to the edge. "You can actually do this from the consoles as well, but this is way more fun," Lora said with a grin. "What do you carry in your pockets?" she asked.

Randy checked all his pockets and then pulled out his cellphone.

Lora laughed. "How original. You are aware that you can't take pictures in here, are you?"

Randy blushed and asked, "Am I not allowed to have this?"

"I don't really care," Lora said, as she shrugged, "just don't let Ian see you use it in here." She looked around as if to check they were alone. "I think you will find that most people here ignore the cellphone policy," she said, pointing out her own cellphone she carried in her back pocket. You'll also find that trying to secretly take a picture in here, will get you thrown out of this building so fast your picture will be blurry."

Randy was quiet again.

Lora continued. "I will teach you the calibration procedures today. When we do it together it should take only half an hour or less. Honestly, it's the main reason why I requested an assistant."

Randy nodded.

Lora took his phone from him and turned it off. Then she placed it in the empty circle on the plateau, directly in the cross-hairs. She walked back to the console and briefly typed on a keyboard. After pushing a few more buttons and adjusting a dial, she walked over to the other console to check the screens. "Lucky for you," she said, as she continued toward the levers, "The Shim is all calibrated and ready to go right now." She pulled down the lever. A deep humming sound emanated from above the plateau and a broad purple beam started forming over the phone. Lora came back to Randy and said, "Now comes the boring part. It takes anywhere from a few minutes to half an hour for the beam to find a suitable environment. If you blink, you might miss it. Keep look-ing at the phone. I'll be right back."

Lora walked away to help one of her data analysts, who was having trouble accessing some of the archived logs from Phase-B, while Randy remained fixated on the brightly lit phone.

When Lora returned ten minutes later, nothing had changed yet. She stood beside him and said, "I've seen this many times al-ready, but I still hope to catch the moment every time."

This time, The Shim needed only just shy of twelve minutes. For a moment, the phone seemed to glimmer before it simply dis-appeared from within the beam. A few faint sparks of soft light and then… nothing. The beam slowly faded away and the hum died down. A subtle chime sounded from the console. The circle on the plateau was empty. "Did you see it?" Lora asked.

Randy nodded and said, "I did. It disappeared. I knew it would, but it is very strange to see it happen before your own eyes."

Lora shook her head and tried to be more specific. "Did you see the lights?"

Randy looked puzzled. "You mean that faint sparkle before it disappeared?"

Lora beamed a smile. "Good boy. Yes. Most people don't notice it the first time. That little twinkle is called 'shimmering'! Remember it well. Your phone 'shimmered' out of existence. David Shim hates it when people call it that. We call it that all the time! It's basically policy. Shimmering, or shimming if you're in a hurry. You will also call it that. Understood?"

Randy just nodded.

A tad disappointed with her audience's lukewarm response to her humor, Lora continued the demonstration. "Okay Randy. Where is your phone now?"

Randy pointed at the two pods labeled one and two and said with some confidence, "The phone is in both of those."

"Well, yeah. Sort of. Kind of in a way. But do you know where *you* are?"

Randy looked around and answered, "I'm in physics heaven."

Lora laughed. "Okay cute. Try again."

"I'm in the legendary Everett building of the Northern Maritimes University standing next to the equally—"

"Correct!" Lora called out. "So let me reinterpret what you just said in a way Dr. Shim would approve of. According to him, your phone is now spread out across roughly two large slices of the multiverse. In half of all the universes where we just did this experiment, your phone has moved to coherence pod one, and in the other half it is in pod two. The multiverse isn't vague about where the phone is. Only *we* are. That is because we don't know in which universe we are. So, until we open the pods, we can't tell where the phone is."

"That is what I said. You're just using more words."

"Yeah, but doesn't it sound a lot cooler this way? We need it to sound cool. That's how we please Dr. Shim."

Randy nodded.

"Dr. Shim has made it very clear to me that if I explain what The Shim does, I am to do it in terms of the multiverse. Get used to it," said Lora. "Let's open the pods." She went back to the small control box and pressed a button. Coherence pod one made a brief hissing sound and then lifted off the surface. Underneath was nothing but the plateau floor and an empty circle. "As you can see, the pods can be moved away from the plateau without disturbing what's under them. That's one of our modifications to the original. They used to have closed bottoms and a door." She pressed another button, and now pod two opened, revealing Randy's phone neatly centered in another circle on the plateau. Lora picked up what looked like an extended squeegee and used it to retrieve the phone from the plateau like a croupier using a chip rake at a roulette table. She handed the phone to Randy and said, in her best magician's voice, "Randy, is this your phone?"

Randy chuckled. He confirmed that it was and turned it back on, fearing it wouldn't work. The phone was in fact unharmed.

Lora went back to the console and pushed a few buttons. "Looks like calibration is still good, but it will take a few minutes before we can do this again," she said. Randy knew that every time this experiment was done, the outcome would be completely random. There was no way to predict which of the two pods the target object would appear in. Dr. Shim's team had performed a very large number of these experiments, leading to a statistical result that confirmed a nice equal distribution. "Why don't we take a little break and go get ourselves a treat? Do you know Delany's, just off campus?" Lora asked.

"Everyone knows Delany's."

"Good, then you won't have to spend too long studying the menu when we get there."

It only took five minutes to walk over to Delaney's and as Randy settled in a seat at a table by the window, he asked, "Do you really believe that all these universes you talk about are real?"

There was no one else in the restaurant and Lora was over at the bar ordering Randy a coffee and herself a tea. As she came back to sit across from Randy, she answered, "It doesn't matter what I believe. I do agree with the doctor that it becomes easier to understand what The Shim is doing for us. It just works as a simple way to explain it. When you see what we did to expand the machine and the experiment, you'll probably come to see it the same way. However, if you have a different way of understanding this stuff, then that is good enough for me too. One day, if we have more time, I would love to argue with you about it. Make sure you come prepared."

Randy stayed quiet for a while, looking as if he was pondering the universe he was currently in, slowly sipping his coffee.

Meanwhile, Lora turned her attention to the man behind the bar again and called to him, "Hey Neil, I'll take the usual take-outs with me. Jarod's been on my case about the coffee again, I cannot disappoint him."

The bar tender laughed and answered, "Right away."

Randy looked at Lora and said, "So, about those expansions, what could you possibly improve on The Shim? Why isn't everyone using teleportation yet?"

Lora adjusted herself to a more comfortable sitting position. "An important thing to know about The Shim is that it is limited in its abilities. We have just spent twelve minutes, and an obscene amount of energy, to move your cellphone three feet to the right."

Randy chuckled. "That's true," he said.

"Besides, building one of these things is a very large undertaking, not unlike building a particle accelerator or a nuclear fusion reactor. You can't just have one at home. Not yet anyway." She paused. "The Shim can move objects, but only if they are relatively small. The machine cannot move things that are larger than about twenty centimeters in any dimension. The machine is big enough that it should be able to move things three times that size, but it just won't. Personally, I think it is just some problem with the design and not something fundamental. Not too long ago we all used to think it was impossible to move anything other than atoms and some molecules, now we're moving phones. The Shim also can't move anything that is itself already moving, so whatever you put in that beam needs to sit perfectly still relative to the beam."

"Hmm," Randy said, as if he just realized something. "I suppose that explains why Dr. Shim said it can't move living organisms."

"Exactly! But it's not just living organisms. A ticking clock, or a mechanical wind-up toy won't make it through either. The moving parts will just stay behind, and you find a partial clock, or toy, in the pod. With living things, all parts are moving, and so they are unaffected. You can put a rat in the beam, and it will just sit there. Nothing happens to it. I mean, it might be annoyed and squint at the bright light."

Randy said, "I didn't expect you experimented on animals in there. Isn't that against NMU policy?"

Lora grinned. "We've tried to kill every kind of animal that fits under the beam, but we never managed to so much as tickle them." Randy didn't really appreciate the humor. "Besides animals and moving objects, we also have a hard time with low viscosity liquids. If we put a glass of water under the beam, the glass will transport, but the water stays behind. That's one that the investors would love to see fixed."

Randy asked, "And what about electronics, don't the moving electric charges cause trouble?"

"Electronics seem to transport fine, as you've just witnessed. We have seen strange malfunctions if a device is on while going through, but usually it just needs a power cycle to work again. That's why I turned your phone off before we put it through. Wouldn't want to accidentally modify one of your photos or delete an important message." Lora got up from her chair. "We should head back to the lab." She went to the bar to pay the bill and pick up her take-out order. "You can carry that," she said, handing him a double tray of hot drinks.

Randy thanked her for paying for his drink. He felt that he still hadn't learned much about what Lora's research was about. He asked, "So, are these limitations not the subject of your research? Aren't you seeking to improve on The Shim?"

"We wouldn't mind finding solutions for those issues, but it is not the focus of my research," she said. "In fact, that's what the next project will spend time on. I'm doing something a little more interesting than that. Deeper. Subtle. I will show you."

CHAPTER SIX

W**HEN LORA AND RANDY ENTERED THE LAB,** they found Jarod at Alice's desk. When Jarod saw the tray of hot drinks, he abruptly cut his conversation short.

"Randy, these two hard workers are Alice, our main data analyst and Jarod. He's someone who drinks coffee. Not sure what else he does," said Lora. She introduced Randy to them and handed Jarod and Alice their drinks from the trays.

Jarod told Randy to put the trays down so he could shake his hand. "You must be Lora's latest victim," he said. "But at least she isn't making you drink the radioactive sludge that comes out of our coffee machine. I swear, if this lab ever explodes, it will be because of that grueling—"

"Okay," Lora said to cut him off. She turned back to Randy. "Jarod leads the electronics lab, back there, so he isn't technically part of my team. Why I am even bringing him coffee is a mystery.

But he's in here so often, I think he just likes my lab better than his own."

"Dude, listen," Jarod said, making a defensive gesture with his arms, "this lab is just a room I walk through to get to mine. Nothing more."

Everyone laughed, and Randy felt instantly at home among these people.

"I'm about to show Randy the expansions on The Shim," Lora said.

"Oof! You should have brought yourself an extra shot of caffeine, kid. I've been on that tour," Jarod said, feigning a yawn. Then he smiled. "No, man, I'm kidding. I helped put those things on there, and it is some impressive hardware."

Alice turned her monitor so that Randy could see it. "The Sharpener spits out more data in an hour than we can process in a week. Impressive isn't really the first word I would pick," she said, also smiling.

"The Sharpener?"

"It's the first of two Phase-B expansions we installed," Lora explained. "This one consists of two parts, one on each of the coherence pods. They provide information we use to adjust the beam in very specific ways. The effect is that of sharpening the target object. You know, in the same way some quantum gates can sharpen qubits."

"Woah! The tour has started!" Jarod said.

Randy already looked puzzled. "Are you suggesting that you can somehow manipulate the object after it has disappeared from the beam and before you open the pods? You're saying you can preselect which pod it goes to?"

"Yes, exactly."

Alice clapped her hands. "You found a fast learner, Lora. Please don't kill this one, I think we should keep him!"

Jarod almost spit out his coffee. "Randy, man, watch out for these two. They're witches!"

Randy chuckled, but he was too intrigued by what he just heard. He asked Lora, "So, the machine can teleport something to a known destination now, instead of a random one. Do you still need both pods?"

"Yes, the manipulation occurs after the transport. It's very fast, but we still need both pods. But that's not the interesting part."

"It isn't?"

"Oh, trust me," Jarod said, "it is!"

Randy saw how Jarod was getting on Lora's nerves, so he chose not to respond.

"We pick which pod the object will travel to, but we make that choice randomly, using a trick Gary taught us. If you assume this will be equally true in all participating universes, what does that mean, you think?"

"Well, um…"

"No pressure," Alice said, theatrically looking at her watch.

"I think that if they all picked randomly, then half of them would pick pod one and the other half would pick pod two."

"Right," Lora said. "So, after the experiment, the multiverse looks very similar to what it would have looked like if we didn't use The Sharpener. The target object is still evenly distributed. But there *is* one major difference. The scientists all saw what they expected to see, instead of a random outcome. The people are different."

Randy looked almost disappointed. "Okay… So, how is that more interesting than teleporting to a preselected pod?"

Jarod laughed. "Hah! Told you."

"During Phase-A we ran The Shim without any extension, similar to the experiments that Dr. Shim did before. This was meant to set a baseline and collect reference data. In Phase-B we installed the two expansions and ran a series of experiments with The Sharpener. We achieved a perfect result. The target objects we used all ended up exactly where we wanted them. In Phase-C we will activate the second expansion, called The Slicer."

"That sounds aggressive," Randy said. "What does it do?"

"Nothing. It doesn't work," Jarod said, grinning.

Lora sighed. "Well, I guess that's technically accurate. So far, no one has successfully programmed The Slicer in a way that works. But I will. *We* will. I have run simulations throughout Phase-A and Phase-B. I'm decently confident I cracked it."

"The real problem is," said Alice, "that The Slicer will crap out even more data than The Sharpener and we don't know exactly how we are supposed to use it to prove that it even works."

"Right," Lora said. "That's part of why we're doing this. To find out if we can somehow see the difference between running with and without The Slicer."

Randy was confused. "But what is it supposed to do?"

"Its purpose is to limit the type of environments that the beam can project onto the target, based on criteria that we program into it. That turns out to be extremely tricky. But if we do it well enough, The Slicer will essentially cut slices out of the multiverse to isolate them from the rest."

Randy had appropriately replaced his already confused look with a more confused one. He was beginning to think he might have picked the wrong job to apply for.

"Alright, I am going to leave you to it. There is work to do and I'm already running behind," Jarod said. "Thanks for the coffee, you probably saved my life. Randy, it was great talking to you. I'm sure I'll see you around."

Alice made a similar announcement. "Yes, I must also get back to it. Robert has something planned for his work tonight, so I need to get home a little early today. I get to spend the evening babysitting our two-year old."

"You can't say I didn't warn you," Jarod said. "The kid will inevitably take over your life." He turned to Randy and added, "Alice is our most recent parent on the team. I am a little further along, with two young teens and a rabbit."

"Hah, nice," Randy said, as Lora started to lead him away, toward The Shim. "It was great to meet you, Jarod and Alice."

When they reached the machine, Lora pointed out the parts that hadn't been included in the original design. It wasn't very meaningful to Randy, as he had never seen The Shim without the expansions on it.

Randy said, grinning, "Alice is married to Robert, is she?"

He received a deathly stare from Lora. "If you value your life, mister Fletcher, consider carefully what will be the next words out of your mouth," she said. "Unless you think you can tell me an Alice and Bob joke that I haven't heard before, your best option is to zip it."

"Point taken. So, what is it you hope to achieve using The Slicer?"

"Imagine if we could take a slice of the multiverse that contained only our universe, and those where the tennis ball is present at the same position as in ours, but in a different environment. We're looking for somewhere where their ball isn't part of this experiment. It might be because there is no lab there, or The Shim is missing, or I am, or all their scientists are replaced with illiterate dinosaur-cow hybrids. The ball is what matters."

"That sounds impossible."

"Yes. But my hope is that with The Slicer, we can limit the beam to environments compatible with there being a ball but no experiment."

"Okay. But why? What does that give us?"

"If we run the experiment with The Sharpener, so that we can preselect which pod the target object will travel to, and use The Slicer to limit ourselves to universes where the ball is not in the experiment, what do you think we get?"

There was just silence from Randy.

"It means that, after the experiment runs, the ball will be in the position we selected in all participating universes. Anything else would be dropped from the slice. If all this works as expected, we will have moved the target object exactly where we want it, not just in our universe, but also in those other places where the ball exists, but the experiment doesn't. Our challenge is to prove it."

"You are putting a lot of faith in the physical reality of these other universes."

"I told you to get used to it. If you can explain what The Slicer does without invoking other universes, then be my guest."

Randy didn't feel like arguing over how to interpret her own work. "Why the tennis ball? What if you replaced it with something else?"

"The origin of the tennis ball is a story for another time, maybe. We need to get moving. But replacing it wouldn't really make a difference. If you put a teacup, then The Slicer will have to find universes with a teacup and no experiment. If it's possible, and if it is configured correctly, it will find it. Let's get you up to speed about these controls. We'll do a full recalibration and alignment, and then run The Shim with, and without, expansions. Not using the ball though, that's reserved for the first official Phase-C run."

Lora saw Randy look at the ball on the plateau.

"Don't ever touch it," Lora said, unexpectedly sternly.

"I wasn't planning on it," Randy said. There was a good chance that wasn't entirely true.

"Once we start the experiment, it is vital that the target object is never disturbed. We want to always know exactly where the ball is in the whole slice, which is possible because we put it there. If I was to move the ball by hand, I would have made our universe different from all the others in the slice, precisely where it matters. The position of the ball. The Slicer would simply drop all of them, leaving us with just our own universe. That ends the experiment, because that's not a valid slice. After that, it would be impossible to repeat or continue the experiment. We would have to start over from scratch, starting with figuring out a suitable configuration. So, just don't even think about it!"

"I promise, I won't touch the ball." Randy suddenly laughed out loud.

"What's funny?"

"I just realized. You're going to confuse a lot of people in those other universes, when you start moving their stuff around."

"Ha-ha, yes. I think we better not use car keys or socks as our target objects. Another reason to stick with the tennis ball."

They both laughed.

"Alright," Lora said. "Let's get you seated at one of these consoles. There is a lot to learn."

CHAPTER SEVEN

DART JUST CAME OUT of a heated debate with two teenagers who he had caught red-handed in the act of applying stickers to a stop sign. There was no reasoning with these two and when one of them childishly started calling him names, like *Dartman Fartman*, he overpowered the boy and tied him to the defaced stop sign using one of his own shoelaces. The other one took off, no doubt straight to his mommy's house. Dart called the police and explained that he had apprehended a vandal for them to come pick up.

Business had been slow so far. There just weren't too many people in distress today. Earlier he walked along a patio where he saw a child, a young boy, who apparently spilled his ice cream cone on the ground. The boy was crying, and the parents seemed uninterested in doing anything about it. Dart thought he could fix it by buying a new ice cream cone. When he offered it to the kid, the parents laughed at him, and said he shouldn't have done that.

They could have just said thank you.

Next thing he knew, the boy chucked his new treat on the ground, depositing it approximately beside the first.

"Oh Dartman," the mother said, still laughing, "we know you mean well, but Nathan here really does not like ice cream. Never has. I'm so sorry."

Dart flinched. "I'm sure you know my name is not Dartman."

"Well obviously," said the woman. "That is not a real name!"

Dart made a considerable effort to let this one slide. "Why did you give him ice cream if you know he doesn't like it?" he asked.

The father had recovered somewhat from laughing at Dart now. "We didn't," he said, "The restaurant brought him a free one." The man pointed at a sign on the sidewalk that advertised free ice cream for kids on the patio, with the purchase of an adult beverage.

"Thank you, Dartman, it was a nice gesture, but—" the mother said until she was interrupted.

"I am Dart. Not Dartman, but just Dart," Dart said. He turned around and started walking away. "And I paid for that stupid ice cream cone!"

Presently, Dart was walking past the train station. It was one of those places that he frequently liked to check up on. Especially the bus terminal in front of the station was bustling with people almost all hours of the day, so it warranted his attention. Today though, things were rather quiet here, as they had been everywhere else in the city. Dart sensed no trace of danger. Maybe now was a good time to take a break. If he kept walking in the direction he was going, he would eventually end up in the university district, where he was quite appreciated by a very specific group of very nice people. They were the security guards who worked the entrance of the Everett building on campus.

One summer, years ago already, Dart had walked this same route, from the bus terminal to the university district. The NMU campus was quiet that day, which was how it usually tended to be in the middle of the summer when schools were out. That didn't mean there was no one there. Especially those who worked on sponsored projects in the labs were here year-round, and there were always some students around who were following a summer program or worked on school projects.

The Everett building, which housed the most important of the labs, had recently had a string of problems with unauthorized persons entering the quantum lab, in one instance causing significant damage to equipment. It was the result of a sensationalist publication about a research project conducted in the quantum lab. The university had to spend a great deal of time and resources debunking the information, as ever more fantastical stories proliferated, spun off from that one article. It was a losing battle, and soon the more skeptical members of the community wanted to see for themselves that the lab hadn't created an artificial black hole that could swallow Earth, and that they weren't trying to cover up a radiation leak that made students sick. And that, in fact, no aliens were being dissected in there. Even some of the students at the university became convinced that the labs were hiding some great secret. Their relatively easy access to the lab caused the most disruptions, which was especially exasperating for the private investors funding potentially commercial projects. When at last someone damaged new equipment that had been recently donated to the lab by a local tech company, the investors, sponsors, and some of the lab employees asked the university to take measures to control more strictly who could enter the quantum lab. Even though all the labs in the Everett building were supposed to be accessible to qualified students, the quantum lab became off limits for anyone who didn't have immediate business there. Guests, visitors, and students were allowed in only by invitation, and if the department chair greenlighted the visit. To enforce the new rules, an external security firm was enlisted. A keycard system was installed so access to the building could be limited to authorized personnel and students, but that didn't stop the persistently inquisitive from tailgating their way in.

That was when the decision was made to bring in security guards. At first, a single guard would be stationed outside the Everett building, tasked with ensuring that everyone who entered used their key card. After suffering through a few technical hiccups with those cards, and people sneaking in when the guard wasn't paying attention, it was eventually decided to put a permanently staffed security desk in the foyer. The key cards were now limited to only those who worked in the quantum lab and some staff. Everyone else, including students who worked in other labs, had to be let in by the guards. Visitors and guests had to name the person who invited them and sign a registration form.

In the summer, when it was quiet, the guards would often spend time outside the building, usually on the bench near the entrance, especially around lunch time. That was when Dart happened to walk by on that faithful day. He didn't know the specific guard – their faces changed with every shift – but he had noticed some of them hanging around by the bench a few times before. This time, he sensed something was off. He felt that strange tingle that indicated some sort of danger. It was a feeling he trusted, so he slowed his pace and watched carefully. The guard was sitting on the bench, and it looked like he had his hands around his own throat. He made no sound. It did not look normal. Dart decided to rush over to the bench and got there just as the guard dropped his hands in his lap and started sagging sideways. The man was choking on something and was just about ready to lose consciousness. Dart knew exactly what to do. The Heimlich maneuver was one of those things every self-respecting superhero should know how to perform.

As Dart hoisted the security guard off the bench into an upright position, a second guard emerged from the building, carrying his lunchbox, and whistling an unrecognizable melody. It took the new guard a moment to register what he was seeing. It looked to him as though the green superhero, the one he had seen on TV sometimes, was wrestling his colleague. He dropped his lunch, grabbed his baton, and rushed over, ready to end this fight. But when he got there, Dart had just managed to dislodge whatever it was that had blocked his coworker's throat.

"You saved my life," the rescued, but embarrassed guard said to Dart, while still making throat-clearing noises. Then, to the newly arrived guard, "I thought for sure I was going to give up the ghost to a god-damned turkey sandwich! He saved my life!"

"It's what I do," Dart said, introducing himself.

Ever since, Dart was a legend among the security guards. Often, when they saw him walk by the campus, they would wave him over for a chat. Sometimes they even invited him inside the building, offering him coffee, which he greatly appreciated. They had good coffee there, although none of the guards he had met so far ever drank it.

At the far end of the foyer there was a small seating area consisting of a sofa, two comfortable chairs and a coffee table, situated near two wall-mounted TV screens and a large tree-like potted plant. One screen was always showing the news, the other displayed information about the university. Dart liked to sit there sometimes after he had completed a job successfully, just to watch the coverage. He wasn't technically allowed inside the building, so he could never stay long.

This being such a slow day, that's where he would go now. Hang out with the guards and hopefully have a coffee.

CHAPTER EIGHT

LORA WAS THE FIRST to arrive in the lab, which was not her usual style. Today was the first time that Phase-C would run. As there would be guests, she went around the lab making sure that everything was neat and tidy. Sensitive documents needed to be locked away, unused computers had to be turned off and the ever-increasing mess left behind by the electronics guys needed to be covered up. She only got to enjoy fifteen minutes of alone time, and then others started arriving. Jarod came in with a double tray of drinks and went straight to her.

"Your tea, boss," he said.

"My hero," Lora replied. Moments later the door opened again. "David!" she called out as Dr. Shim walked in the door, accompanied by a small group of others.

"How is it looking?" he asked.

"Perfect." Lora scanned the lab. "Where's my helper?"

Jarod replied, "I saw Randy outside, busy with his phone."

When Randy came in the door, he was in a big group. As per Ian's instructions Lora had invited nearly everyone who worked in the building, a few representatives of the investors and some of her colleagues at the university across multiple disciplines. In all, she expected around forty people. It wasn't normal procedure to allow an audience to witness the start of a new experiment, and she wasn't keen on it, but Ian had insisted that the investors needed some form of confirmation that she was on track with the project. Lora was sure some of them were only here to find out how she was still here hogging the machine of their dreams. Phase-B had already tested their patience and now Phase-C was about to start. Everyone was gathered in a large group, about as far away from The Shim as they could be. Lora took a sip of her tea before putting it down on a desk and stepping onto a footstool to ask for everyone's attention.

"I will not be keeping you long this morning," she said. "Before we begin, I need to make sure everyone is on board with the rules. You will gather around The Shim quietly. That means, walk there slowly, one by one, and keep outside the marked lines on the floor. Keep chit chat to a minimum. Don't touch anything. The target object is the tennis ball, voted in unanimously by my team. The initial position was chosen by Gary. The selected destination is pod two. On the first run, the position isn't as critical as it will be for successive runs, but we do ask that you try to keep all disturbances to a minimum. Leave all your drinks here, and please turn off your mobile devices. We do not generally worry about interference from phones, but we also don't normally have so many of them around."

Ian frowned and made a mental note.

"Once there, I will simply start the experiment without further announcements. We'll first activate the two expansions, The Sharpener and The Slicer, and then the beam will come on. A typical run is expected to last between thirty minutes and two hours. If you have witnessed a Phase-B run before, you are not going to see anything new today. You are free to watch for as long as you wish. To see the target object *shimmer* out of existence," she said while winking at the doctor, "you will need to watch it carefully for the duration. You may step away at any time, and return at any time, keeping in mind the rules. Once the run is complete, we'll open the pods to see the result. At that time, you are kindly asked to leave the room quietly so that we can begin preparations for the next run, hopefully tomorrow. If you have questions, please ask them away from the machine." Lora waited for the crowd to quiet down again. "Alright, if everyone is ready, let's head over to the machine. Single file. Dr. Shim, please lead the way."

Lora stayed back with Randy until the crowd had settled in place. She was very confident that the first run would be successful, because it would be essentially the same as any Phase-B run. For her, the interesting part would be to see if subsequent runs would also be successful. She was happy with the current programming and configuration of The Slicer, based on careful simulations she had been running throughout Phase-B.

Randy appeared nervous.

"You'll be fine. Let's do this," Lora said, as she started walking to The Shim with him in tow. The crowd was nice and quiet. A few soft coughs, an occasional whisper, some general noises of shuffling feet and rustling of clothes was all she could hear. Lora was pleased. Randy took place at one of the consoles and Lora went to the levers on the wall. With everything well prepared, Randy only had to push a few buttons. He looked over the screens and raised his hand with a thumb up. Lora pulled down the two expansion levers one by one. A slight wave of whispers went through the crowd. Many small lights blinked on, all over the machines suspended above the plateau. The red laser crosshair was centered precisely over the tennis ball. Randy walked over to another terminal, entered something on a keyboard and raised his thumb again. Lora grabbed the beam handle and firmly pulled it down. The deep hum of the beam impressed the crowd. There was a sound of soft voices and shuffling feet coming from them. Someone let out a muted "wow!" Randy looked around with his index finger in front of his lips. Purple light colored the crowd, as the beam engulfed the tennis ball. Lora came back to the console and stood beside Randy. They looked over the screens and appeared pleased. After a short while, a few of her usual crew members began quietly breaking out of the crowd to walk back to their stations. They had seen this show many times before. None had made it far when an unexpected thud sounded from behind the crowd. The purple light disappeared instantly, and the room noticeably darkened. Most of the small lights had turned off, but the tennis ball was still sitting in the same spot on the plateau. The crowd immediately started making a lot more noise. There was some laughter as people joked about the apparent failure. Soon people started moving around and voices began to fill the room. Lora waved both her hands above her head to draw their attention. She too now made the shush gesture. The crowd obeyed. She said, in a low voice, and with an irritated look on her face, "What the hell, Randy?"

Randy was frantically looking over the screens, adjusting dials and pushing buttons. "Looks like the safety on The Sharpener tripped," he said. "It's reporting a power spike, too. It's unclear."

"Great." Lora waved Jarod over and told him to check it out. She noticed Ian in the crowd, mouthing swearwords at her, while trying to calm the investors. It took her some effort not to flip him the bird.

Randy said, "It ran only two minutes and twelve seconds. We got nothing, no useful data. The good news is that The Slicer shows no errors, and probably found its slice right away."

The crowd started wandering off to the other end of the room, where they could talk. Jarod was back at the console only fifteen minutes after he had left and had both good news and bad.

"It's a faulty relay in one of the control computers for The Sharpener," he said. "It's just dumb luck, man. The fix won't take long, but The Shim needs to be taken offline completely to reset the safety."

Lora shrugged. "Do it," she said to both Jarod and Randy. Jarod left them again, and Randy started the shutdown procedures. Lora knew shutting down would mean they'd have to recalibrate, which would take at least thirty minutes in addition to the repair time. She walked over to the crowd and stepped back onto the footstool.

"Ladies and gentlemen. We're having some minor technical difficulties. Unfortunately, it will be about one hour before we can try again."

When Randy finished the shutdown, he came over to Lora, who said, "Let's go outside for a few minutes and get some fresh air."

Chapter Nine

E D'S DAY WAS SUPPOSED to start at eight in the morning, on the first day of the convention. After going over the program, he had decided that the morning events were not relevant to him. It was something about how to conduct yourself in various situations with clients. For Ed it was impractical to visit client sites or homes. He worked from home and was rarely in direct contact with clients. That gave him time this morning to clean himself up and enjoy breakfast in his room at leisure. He briefly thought about Hannah, whom he had rudely ditched yesterday, and thought he should make sure to buy her a drink before the end of the convention. What if she was some kind of bigshot at the company? He checked his phone for any pressing matters, but so far, his inbox remained exceptionally quiet, and no one had called him. Putting the phone down on the desk, he switched it out with the remote control for the TV. He wasn't dressed yet and was sitting in his wheelchair with just his underwear and a hotel bathrobe on. This was not an uncommon outfit for him. Getting dressed was always a bother, so at home he often didn't. It was necessary only when he went out, but that didn't happen too often anymore. His groceries were delivered to his door, and anything he needed, he could just order online. He turned on the TV and then noticed the mini fridge. "Please don't be empty," he said, realizing full well that it was still morning, and started maneuvering his chair to get to it.

A bright flash of light, and a sound that held the middle between electric crackling and the sound of bubble wrap being popped, suddenly came from below his wheelchair.

"What?" he said.

There was a blue glow below his seat, and what looked like electric arcs spraying around him. Ed tried to get away from the chair, but he found himself unable to feel his seat. He looked down at himself. He wasn't even in his seat, he saw now. Instead, he appeared to be hovering just above it, rising from it. The blue glow, forming a nearly opaque sheet, expanded around him until he was completely enclosed in a roughly spherical space. More lightning-like arcs shot back and forth and ran along the inside surface of the sphere, almost as if he were inside one of those plasma globes some people kept in their homes as a decoration. Some arcs crackled around his body, but he couldn't feel them. He kept rising until he was high enough that the sphere was clear of the wheelchair entirely, his arms flailing to no effect. Ed yelled for help. He couldn't see out of the sphere and remained suspended in the middle of it. A sudden extreme pain shot through his back and down into his legs, a wholly unfamiliar sensation. Then, in an instant, the sphere disappeared, and he dropped to the ground. A few of those electric arcs fizzled out around him.

Everything was different now. He was sitting on grass, outside. "Where am I?" Ed looked around at what appeared to be a park of some sort. He saw trees, neatly groomed grass, and the back of a bench with a garbage bin by a path. The wheelchair was nowhere to be found. "Help," he whispered, not yet sure if he needed it. He felt very strange. He tried to sit up more and saw a few people around him, all at some distance. No one had seen where he came from, apparently. A man wearing headphones was slowly walking on the path in his general direction and was looking at him without much interest. Ed felt his forehead to check if he was hallucinating. "Sunglasses," he whispered. He didn't even bring sunglasses on his trip, did he? But he found a pair on his face now. He took them off, but that blinded him, so he put them back right away. He looked at his arms and chest. His clothes were also unfamiliar. A red blazer over a black button shirt. Ed was pretty sure he didn't own a flamboyant jacket like that. "I need help," he said again, a little louder this time, still without trying to attract attention to himself. The man with the headphones, now a little closer, was still looking at him but probably hadn't heard his plea. Ed leaned over to grab one of his legs to adjust it. As he reached over, he clearly saw his leg move toward his hand before his hand even touched it. He *felt* it move.

In the same instant he also registered another bright flash of light, almost as if it was inside his head this time. For a moment after, it went dark. Vision restored gradually over a few seconds. "No, no, no!" he exclaimed. He was back in his wheelchair, pointed towards the fridge. *What was that?*

"Did I faint?" he asked out loud. He wheeled back to his phone and looked at the time. "If I did, it wasn't long."

He tried to remember everything he just saw. Where had he been? Who were those people? It didn't feel like a dream or an old memory. For a few minutes he was there, as sure as can be, but he had not recognized anything, or anyone, while he was. He remembered how it smelled, the sound of the cars behind him and the soft warm breeze in the air. Surely, he had never visited that place before, but now he had. The unfamiliar man with the headphones had seen him, looked at him directly. Who was he? "My leg," he said. He rubbed his hands over his thighs. *Nothing.* Nonfunctional atrophied quadriceps sat motionless under his hands, not registering, not responding in the slightest to his touch. He wished he had been there a little longer. *How do I get back there? How did I get there to begin with?* The bright blue sphere had not left any trace. No burns, no stains. Nothing in the room seemed to have been moved, marked, or changed. He tried to reenact the scenario from the beginning, turning to the TV, then to the fridge, but this time he reached the fridge just fine. And, of course, it was empty.

Chapter Ten

As the Everett building was right on the edge of campus, it was a very short walk to the city park, directly to the left coming out of the gate. Randy and Lora walked beside each other going over what had just happened during the initial Phase-C run.

Usually, Lora would be walking here by herself, because she found that most of her colleagues weren't interested in lunchtime strolls. On days like today, when the weather was nice, she would have brought a book and sat on one of the many park benches to read, eat and take her mind off work.

Ahead of them, in the grass behind one of those benches, a group of people had gathered around a young man.

"Huh, that's Ganesh," Randy said. "I see him during math lectures sometimes. He stands out in class, asking a lot of questions."

It looked almost like the group was preventing Ganesh from moving. Was he being harassed?

"Let's see what all that is about," Lora said, stepping off the path onto the grass. When they got closer, she could hear Ganesh speak.

"Ninjas? No! It was nothing like that! He was just sitting here, clear as day. I don't think he was doing anything. Next thing, he wasn't! Sitting there, I mean. There was no transition, no puff of smoke. He just vanished. Instantly erased. Gone."

Lora asked, "What happened here?"

One of the others said, "He claims he saw a guy disappear into thin air."

"Thin air? Who was it?"

Ganesh shrugged and said, "I don't know. Some rando in a red suit, sitting right here in the grass."

Randy greeted Ganesh with some sort of secret handshake unfamiliar to Lora. "Had a few too many drinks last night?" Randy asked, surprising Lora with this rather direct approach toward someone he claimed not to know very well.

"Does your girlfriend know about your new girlfriend?" Ganesh responded, looking straight at Lora.

Ganesh didn't drink and wished he had not said anything to begin with. It was obvious that his story wasn't credible, and now he was stuck with all these people and their opinions. "Alright people, I am done here." He put his headphones back on and just walked away, leaving the group and all their questions and comments behind.

"Girlfriend?" Lora said.

Randy sighed. "Don't ask."

"Ah," Lora said, suddenly feeling awkward.

After the otherwise uneventful break, and a longer than expected recalibration of The Shim, Lora's audience was gathering around the machine once again. There were noticeably fewer people now, but the important ones, those with the money for future projects, were still there.

Randy and Lora activated the experiment and soon the reduced crowd was once again staring at the brightly lit tennis ball. Even the most dedicated watchers walked away from The Shim after about forty minutes. Some were hanging around in other parts of the room, while others had left entirely. Lora went around to remind those who remained in the room that the only way for them to see the actual moment was to continue looking. She asked Gary and Randy to keep an eye on things and let her know if anything changed. She was going over to Delaney's to eat lunch. By herself.

ACROSS THE STREET from Delaney's were apartment buildings lining the road all the way past the university and the park. In between the buildings were narrow alleys that allowed the inhabitants, who were almost all students, access to the back doors of their homes. A strange blue glow emanated from the alley between the two buildings directly opposite Delaney's restaurant. Initially a faint glow, it quickly grew brighter and seemingly larger. Electric arcs were spanning the distance between the two walls and racing randomly across the surface. Then, suddenly, after only a few seconds, the light disappeared.

From the alley came a surprised sounding voice. "How in the… Are you kidding me?"

Someone walking on the sidewalk, just then passing the alley, peered in and, sounding concerned, asked, "Are you alright sir? Do you need help?"

The voice from the alley hesitated. "Yeah, I might. I seem to have misplaced my wheelchair…"

The pedestrian had to check if he heard that right. "A wheelchair?"

"Oh god!" the voice called out, sounding somewhat hysterical. "My legs! I can move my leg!"

The pedestrian got a little nervous now. "Do you want me to call someone?"

"You know what?" the voice asked, more calmly, "Thank you, but I think I've got it from here. I'm fine, actually."

Ed, still sitting on the ground, wiggled his feet and stared at them in disbelief. *Please don't flash, please don't flash.* He tried to move his legs and they did exactly what he wanted. *It doesn't even feel weird.* Repositioning himself, he already knew, before trying, that he would be able to stand up. The anticipation was building rapidly, almost too much to handle.

Here it comes!

Ed stood up. *Just like that!* He was standing on his own two legs for the first time since he was eleven years old, and it felt wonderful. It felt normal. And completely natural. His knees buckled and he had to lean against the wall, but this wasn't because of his legs. There was *nothing* wrong with his legs. He was flooded with emotions. *Why is this so easy?* It just worked. "Oh god," he whispered. He straightened himself and took a careful first step. "I can walk again," he said, as tears started rolling down his cheeks from behind those weird sunglasses. He said it again, his voice cracked, "I can walk again!"

The alley was somewhat dark compared to the street, so he took his sunglasses off. Instantly, his eyes were stinging. He wiped his tears and looked around, but he could hardly see anything. The sunglasses went back on, and his vision went back to normal. He carefully took a few steps toward the end of the alley and stopped. That over-the-top red jacket he was wearing was going to draw a lot of attention, he thought, so maybe he should remove it. The sunglasses were bad enough. As soon as he tried to swing the jacket off his shoulder though, those strange electric arcs started forming across the fabric. *No!* Panic seized Ed's brain. *Please don't take me back! Not now!* He straightened his jacket and the crackling stopped. Relieved that he was still standing, Ed realized these sizzling arcs were unlike the arcs he had seen while he was in the blue sphere. These new ones *hurt.* They caused an unpleasant burning sensation that would undoubtedly worsen the longer he exposed himself. He carefully tried again to take the jacket off his shoulder, but the same thing happened. Maybe the jacket somehow protected him. *I can walk. I have magic visors and a magic jacket that I can't take off. Who am I?* He straightened his jacket once again and decided that it suited him rather well. It was time to go for a walk. The mere thought thrilled him. Today might just turn out to be the best day of his life.

He stepped out onto the sidewalk and looked around. *Where am I?* Nothing looked familiar, so he had to just pick a direction and start exploring. He turned right.

LORA HAD ORDERED A BOWL of soup and was trying to read some news on her phone. When she came in by herself at odd times, like today, Neil, the bartender who worked here most during the daytime, knew that Lora was looking for peace and quiet and that he shouldn't try to socialize with her. He had spent hours talking to her on other occasions, but today was not the day for it. He was behind the bar with nothing much to do, as Lora was his only customer at present. The only sounds in the restaurant were some soft background music and occasional clinking sounds from Lora's spoon in the soup bowl. He looked past her, out the window, but besides the occasional car driving past, there was very little to see, unlike earlier today. He watched, while also keeping an eye on Lora's progress with the soup. When she was finished, he walked over and asked how it was.

"It wasn't the worst thing you've ever put in front of me," she said with a smirk. "Thank you, Neil."

He smiled, took the empty bowl, and looked outside again.

Lora noticed his gaze and followed it. She saw nothing out of the ordinary. "What are we looking at?" she asked.

"Oh, nothing."

She gathered her things and then followed Neil to the bar to pay her bill.

"Earlier, before you came in," Neil said, "I thought I saw some kids setting off fireworks across the street, in between the apartments there. But then, a few minutes later, this strange looking fellow, an adult, stepped out from the alley by himself. He looked rather lost if you asked me. He went that way, toward the city." Neil pointed out the direction as he handed Lora her receipt.

"Any idea who it was?" Lora asked. Neil knew an awful lot of people, so it was a fair question.

Neil shook his head. "Never saw him before. Or anyone like him. He was wearing a rather dreadful red outfit."

"Hm, I just heard a similar story this morning."

Neil looked out the window again. "I don't think he belongs here, to be honest."

E D WAS WALKING THE STREETS of this strange new place and loving every second and every detail of it. Now that he was paying closer attention, some things he saw along the way began to look familiar to him. He just passed a small church that remarkably resembled the one that was close by the hotel where he was staying.

A little before that, he had seen a store with the same name as a store near the hotel. It looked different, but not exactly different. He picked up the pace now and was closing in on an open space ahead. It looked very familiar indeed.

When he reached the end of the street and looked across to the wide-open square, he gasped. "Hemingway," he whispered. He crossed the street and stepped onto Hemingway square. This looked precisely like Hemingway square in his hometown. *There's the old library. What the hell is going on?*

He crossed the road and sought out a bench near the edge of the square, by a tree. There were only a handful of people around, most of them just walking across. As soon as he sat down, he noticed for the first time there was something in his jacket pocket. He pulled it out. It was his cellphone. *How did that get here?* Ed unlocked the device, which on its screen indicated that there was no signal available. He opened a map application, which worked fine, but the phone didn't have any data or GPS reception, so it couldn't show him where he was.

Ed looked over at the old library and decided that's where he needed to go next. With some luck, he would find a map and newspapers there to help him figure out where he was. He returned his phone to his pocket and started to get up when a bright flash of light blinded his eyes.

When his vision returned, Ed was back in his wheelchair looking at the TV in his hotel room. "No!" His first thought was to look around for his phone. It was still sitting on the desk, being charged, just as he had left it. He wheeled himself over to it. This time he had been gone for more than an hour. *How? What did I do differently this time? Why did it end?* "I walked! Oh man, I have got to get back there!" he said out loud. The rush was still there, making him feel giddy and excited. He had missed lunch, and part of the afternoon program of the convention, but he didn't care. He needed to stay right here in case it happened again. It *had to* happen again.

LORA GATHERED THE REMAINING GUESTS in the area away from the machine one last time and took her spot on the footstool. "Alright, everybody. As you can see the target object has disappeared," she began. "Did any of you catch the moment?"

A few hands rose, including one of the investors, a man she recognized as Jim Ferguson, the one investor who was sponsoring her project. And Ian. This was good.

"If you saw the faint flickering lights just before the ball disappeared, you get extra points."

There was some faint laughter.

"We'll gather by The Shim one last time, where Randy and I will open the pods. If the experiment was successful, the ball will appear in pod two. Please suppress your understandable and appropriate desire to applaud when it does."

This time she got a little more laughter.

"I'm sorry there won't be any more to see. We will need to run our additional experiments before we can confirm that Phase-C produces a result different from Phase-B. Those experiments may start as early as tomorrow, but it's quite possible it will take a little longer than that."

She looked around for Randy to make sure he was ready. She found him standing back, just finishing something on his phone.

"Alright, let's head over to The Shim one more time! This time around, it is more important that nothing is disturbed, so please walk carefully, be quiet and stay well outside the lines. Move only if you are ready to leave. Do that quietly and slowly as well. Here we go."

Randy said to Lora, as she stepped off the footstool, "You're really good at that."

"At what?"

"At addressing this crowd."

Lora laughed. "I know most of them quite well. Wait until you see me at the convention." If everything went as planned, she would be presenting the results of her project at the Physics Advances convention just like Dr. Shim had presented his, three years prior. Then, finally, the relative secrecy surrounding this project would be over. She lowered her voice. "I get that it is none of my business, Randy, but I think you are risking your life messing around on your phone with Ian in the room," she said. She smiled but sounded serious.

"Yeah, I'm sorry. She keeps texting me…"

Lora followed Randy to the consoles and took the control box for the pods. When she pressed the button for pod two and the familiar hiss sounded, the pod raised and revealed the tennis ball as expected. The crowd made a slight approving noise but stayed nice and quiet otherwise. Lora opened pod one as well and it presented empty.

Attendants made their way out of the lab soon after, quietly, according to Lora's instructions. As they left, Lora worked at the consoles with Randy, securing data and running diagnostics. Meanwhile, Gary was going through the lab with a broom and a dustpan, picking up disposable cups and other waste left behind by the crowd, muttering something about pigs in a pig stall.

Lora said to Randy, "Do you remember what your friend in the park said?"

"Ganesh?" Randy laughed. "He is not my friend."

"Whatever."

"Look, he was just joking about—"

Shaking her head, Lora interrupted him. "No, no. The other thing," she said.

"Oh. Yeah, I think he said a man had vanished into thin air. A man in a red suit?"

Lora turned to look at him. "Yeah. So, today when I was out to lunch, Neil said he saw a guy wearing a red suit. I guess he didn't completely disappear after all."

CHAPTER ELEVEN

GARY AND DR. SHIM had been good friends since the development of The Shim began. In some sense, Gary reckoned, Dr. Shim had saved him. A few years before he met the doctor, Gary and his wife Rebecca had been in the final stages of deciding to have their first child. Rebecca had been struggling with depression from a young age and was frequently without work and on medication for that reason. In their decision, they would have to consider the risks of abandoning that treatment for the duration of her pregnancy.

At the time, Gary worked in a small lab that specialized in performing tests of mostly radio-active materials targeted for both medical and military applications. For Gary, this job was conveniently close to home, so that he could be there at a moment's notice if his wife needed him. That was the main reason he wasn't already looking for something more challenging to do.

One time, Gary woke up in the middle of the night and stumbled, still half in a dream he couldn't quite shake, toward the bathroom. He turned on the light and stood with his eyes closed in front of the mirror, waiting for his eyes to adjust. It was unusual for Gary to interrupt his sleep like this, as it was Rebecca who would often go to the bathroom at completely random times during the night. She was able to do it without turning the light on, he knew, but Gary had an anxiety about stubbing his toe, and preferred to see what he was doing.

When he was done, he noticed two pills sitting on the edge of the wash basin. *She must have taken them from the container but then forgot to take them.* While washing his hands, and then drying them, he thought for a minute about what he should do with the pills. Either throw them out or put them back in the container. Small decisions like this, he habitually made in what he and the coworker who had suggested it to him, jokingly once defined as the ultimate way to solve any problem. Don't just take one option, but instead do both.

To this end, every morning when he came into the lab at work, he looked at the screen of a computer that was monitoring the decay in some material currently being tested. If the number of detected nuclear decay events was an even number, then, for that day, if he encountered a decision point, he would pick "no". If it wasn't a yes-or-no question, he would use a similar criterium that fit the situation. It could be the lowest number, or going left, or down, or whatever sorted lowest alphabetically. If, on the other hand, it was an odd number, he would pick the other option. This way, he reasoned, his decision was ultimately tied to a quantum level event, with every possible outcome realized somewhere. Whatever his decision turned out to be, he imagined that somewhere in the grand scheme of things, some other version of him would take the other path. At least then, some version of him was bound to make the right decision.

But in the middle of the night, it was a little hard to remember if he had seen an odd or even number that day. "Even," he whispered, and then thought about what that meant. He went with the alphabetical sorting of "container" or "throw", and so ended up taking the container from the medicine cabinet and replacing the pills. Undoubtedly, to him, somewhere he was now flushing them down the toilet as well.

The next day, the last workday of the week, Gary returned home earlier than usual because he and Rebecca had planned to go out for supper to celebrate a breakthrough. If it was possible, they were going to have a baby. As soon as he came in the door an uneasy feeling washed over him. He went straight to the bedroom, before even removing his jacket and found Rebecca in the bed, which wasn't unusual. She had grown into a habit of taking late afternoon naps. When he tried to wake her though, she was not responding. Immediately he noticed the empty pill container on the bedside table.

An ambulance arrived on short notice and rushed her to the hospital. Gary spent four agonizing hours waiting, until finally the news came that Rebecca had passed away from numerous complications resulting from an overdose of antidepressants.

Gary, consumed with guilt and shame for not seeing the signs he thought were so obvious in hindsight, quit his job, and isolated himself, entirely avoiding contact with people. When he emerged, bitter and estranged, after more than a year, he was able to resume his job but found no pleasure in it. It wasn't until he met Dr. Shim, who visited the small lab in search of materials he thought he needed for a machine he was building, that his life changed for the better. Gary, who was as much an engineer as he was a physicist, became interested from the first conversation. The doctor had a knack for inspiring people in that way. When he was offered the chance to work with Dr. Shim in one of the most advanced labs, to build a machine that promised to change the world, he didn't hesitate. Being of similar age, a friendship developed quickly between them, and Gary remained at Dr. Shim's side at NMU all the way until the doctor retired.

Near the end of the project, when Dr. Shim brought Lora into the lab, Gary was just as impressed with her as the doctor was. After his retirement, Dr. Shim offered Gary, who didn't feel ready to retire, the opportunity to remain at the lab and become the new lab leader. But Gary knew that he wasn't leadership material. In the end it was Gary who suggested to Dr. Shim that he should make Lora the new lab leader, and that he would be honored to work on her team to help her perform her experiment. The expansions to The Shim that she had proposed were nothing short of brilliant, and he wanted to be there when they were built. The doctor wasn't the only one who came to see Lora as a member of his family, even though Gary would never say anything to that effect out loud.

CHAPTER TWELVE

ED HAD MISSED, or rather ignored, a few work-related phone calls during the first two days of the convention. When he finally did call the office, it turned out that somehow, they found out he hadn't attended any of the convention presentations so far. They were not amused. Ed lied that he hadn't been feeling well and had met with some difficulties finding help getting around the hotel. He added that he was feeling nostalgic for being back in his hometown and asked if he could have a week off, following the convention. Of course, he would pay for the extra hotel nights. Had they said no, he would have made up some family emergency, but they accepted his request and even agreed to take care of the taxi ride home after his time off.

None of this meant that Ed would now start participating in the convention events. He was too preoccupied with his random involuntary forays into a strange new world. Nobody should see him vanish, he figured, so he remained mostly out of sight. What if someone moved his wheelchair while he was gone? Where would he return to then? Would he fall to the ground? He also desperately wanted to know if there was a more controlled way to get to this other, most appealing world where he could roam unaided. Sadly though, the last day of the convention, as well as the first two days of Ed's vacation passed without a transition. Ed was nervous. Why would they let him walk in their world only once, for about an hour, and then take it away from him?

The following day his luck finally changed. There were two transitions, both into alleys across from Delaney's. The first one, in the morning, only lasted a little over half an hour, and the second one, in the afternoon, for about an hour. During this time, he went back to the library and found a map of the city. He sat down in a quiet area and compared it to a cached map on his phone. Soon enough he realized that, even though the two maps were different, there were many similarities. The streets in this other-worldly city were laid out almost the same as in his hometown. The city was larger here, and more built up, with many more businesses and expansive residential areas, but if you could overlay the two maps, you'd find that the major structures were in the same place and carried the same names.

Two more transitions occurred the next day, following the same pattern. He spent the time walking the city, recognizing more and more of the streets and he couldn't get enough of it. Using his phone, which still didn't have signal here, he began taking pictures of places and people, hoping he could compare them to the places and people back home. Perhaps that would reveal some clue as to what this place was. But when he was back in his hotel room and picked the phone up from the desk, he was disappointed, but not too surprised, to find that none of the pictures he had taken were there. The phone was exactly as he had left it.

On the fifth day off work, he made another two trips. Unlike the previous two days, when he found himself in one of the alleys across from Delaney's each time, now he was back in that unfamiliar park he saw on his short-lived first trip over. His phone still didn't have reception of any kind, so he turned it off and returned it to his pocket. The park was nice and well maintained, but it gave Ed no clues about where it was in relation to Delaney's. Ed wanted to explore the surrounding area. As soon as he left the park, he recognized the street immediately. His jaw dropped as he looked at the Northern Maritimes University campus, situated just next to the park, bustling with activity. He could hardly believe it. The Everett building looked magnificent, as if it was built yesterday. *This is where it all happened.* Turning around to look across the street, he found the hotel, where he was staying, wasn't there at all. There were only apartment buildings. *This is so weird.* It was almost as if he had traveled back in time, but at the library he had already established that the date and time in this world were the same as in his own. He felt some anxiety about seeing the university, especially that physics lab. Could he go inside? Of all the buildings on campus, the Everett building was the only one with a somewhat concealed entrance, requiring a footpath to be followed from the main campus road, around one side of the building to a set of glass sliding doors. Ed observed from the sidewalk that there was significantly less traffic in and out of this building than any of the other ones. He watched a few people going in and coming out through the doors. There were none he recognized. Somewhat to his surprise, access to the building seemed restricted to specific individuals. *Why? Shouldn't they at least allow students in there?*

A young woman came out of the door, closely followed by a taller man, probably a student. They walked briskly, passing Ed as they exited the gate he was now reluctantly entering.

"Hey there," the woman said, "Are you lost?"

Ed acknowledged that he heard her with a wave of his hand and a nod of his head but decided not to answer the question. He was obviously drawing attention to himself with this exorbitant outfit. Maybe it would be better to minimize direct contact with people in this world, at least until he better understood the consequences of such interactions.

When he started down the path toward the entrance of the Everett building, it became clear that he wasn't getting in without some sort of invitation or access pass. There was a security check inside. Ed decided to go back to the park and walk some more.

Waiting for the next transition was becoming more difficult. On the sixth day since he took time off from work, Ed was in his wheelchair, watching TV, anticipating the moment he would be on his feet again. Seconds felt like minutes while waiting, with daytime TV doing nothing to make it go quicker. His plan for the day was to further explore the university, but when the blue light finally came, it brought him to an unfamiliar place. The university was nowhere in sight. He landed on the sidewalk of a busy street, and he couldn't see any familiar landmarks. People were walking by in both directions, ignoring him. He checked his phone, but as usual there was no signal, no navigation, so he turned it off. With a new environment to explore, Ed began what had quickly become his favorite thing to do when he made the transition out of his chair. Walk. Occasionally he stopped to look around for something familiar, but there was nothing. *This might not even be the same city.* The street was heavy with traffic and there weren't many side streets. After a while, across the street, he noticed a gate that looked like it might lead to a green area behind it. Just then, a woman stepped out of the gate and, for a moment, looked directly at him. Ed recognized her immediately as the same woman he saw yesterday at the university. *Hey there, are you lost? What are the chances of that?* She didn't stand there long, before walking in the opposite direction Ed was going. There was nowhere nearby to cross the road. Instead, he decided to keep going. To his disappointment, after only forty minutes of walking, and still with no clues about his location, he was back in his wheelchair. It remained the only transition for the day.

The next day was the last day he could stay at the hotel. Ed had already spent a lot of money on this extra week of hotel nights, and he couldn't afford to prolong it by much. Since he had never transitioned from anywhere other than this hotel room, he was afraid that leaving might end the phenomenon. On the other hand, he was afraid that he might transition during travel. Then where would he come back to upon reentry? So, he made some arrangements. He called the office and asked if he could be picked up at nine this evening. So far, no transitions had happened at night, so that would minimize one risk. Next, he booked one more night for his room, with no intention of using it, other than to wait for the taxi. He would spend all day outside the hotel, to see if a transition would occur. Hotel reception kindly arranged a wheelchair taxi to take him to the old city library. Once there, he found himself a quiet spot, and remained there reading through some magazines. By lunchtime still nothing had happened. Was his hotel room some sort of portal?

Half an hour later though, his wheelchair was empty once again. This time he found himself straight across the street from the university campus, in one of the alleys between apartment buildings, approximately where the hotel should have been. Out of habit he checked the phone, then turned it off, and decided he would explore the campus in areas where he was allowed to be. The first person who talked to him was a student commenting on his outfit. He disregarded it, but the student then asked for his name.

"Visitor," Ed said.

The student didn't pursue it any further.

It occurred to Ed that, since he didn't know anyone in this world, no one would know him either. His identity was, in effect, a secret here. He could be anyone. For the time being, that might be a good thing.

When Ed returned to his wheelchair, he was back in the library exactly where he had been. The magazines were still on the table in front of him, except for one that had fallen to the ground. No one had moved his chair, and there were no concerned faces. Satisfied that neither his absence nor his return had been noticed, he made his way outside where he waited for the taxi.

Just before arriving at the hotel, the taxi would pass by the NMU campus.

Ed looked out the window. "It looks a lot more decrepit than last time I saw it," he said to the driver. This was true in a few different ways. He told the driver to pull over, took out his phone and asked if the driver wouldn't mind taking a few photos of the campus through the fence. "My father used to work there," he explained.

Back in the hotel he watched some TV, had supper, and finally, at precisely nine o'clock, got into the van that would bring him home. A few hours later he was asleep in his own bed.

Early the next morning, Ed woke up still feeling exhausted. He worked himself into the wheelchair and then called in sick for work. After making half an effort to clean himself up in the bathroom, he didn't bother to get dressed. He sat himself in front of his TV with a cup of coffee and spent the day waiting in tense anticipation, craving the blue sphere, yearning to be taken away. Thankfully, he was afforded that privilege twice a day for the next few days. This was nothing short of an addiction now. Learning to accept his limitations had been a big part of his life growing up. He didn't accept any of that now. Landing back in his wheelchair after a walk was like reliving the day that he lost the use of his legs the first time. Each time, he would go, in an instant, from standing on his own two feet, feeling the ground pressing up at the soles of his feet, to sitting in this god-damned wheelchair feeling nothing at all. One moment he was walking, feeling his feet land with every step, feeling his pants slide around on the skin of his legs, the wind blowing in his face, and the next he couldn't even wiggle a toe if his life depended on it. It was cruel.

At night, he would lay awake going over what he had learned about the new world so far, keeping track of it in a journal. His phone was set to silent, always charging on his desk, and he ignored all calls and messages that arrived on it.

On one of his visits, he had collected names and phone numbers of people, and memorized them, because anything he stored in his phone would disappear during reentry. Knowing that a lot of the places he found in the new world were similar to those here at home, he wanted to find out if any of those memorized people existed in duplicate. He was only able to keep eight people and phone numbers in his mind, which he wrote down immediately upon his return. It was surprisingly easy to find all of them online. One was no longer alive, apparently due to a car crash over two years ago, but the rest were still around. When he tried to call the phone numbers, only one actually rang, and the person who picked up wasn't the person from his list. Apparently, most people existed, or *had* existed, in both places but they didn't have the same phone numbers.

During his visits he spent a lot of time in the area around the university, because that was where he usually entered the world. He knew that he could learn more about this place if he spent more time at the library, but he felt reluctant to waste too much of his time sitting down when he had the use of his legs. One thing he did learn was that the machine that his father used to talk about had been fully realized here and should exist in that building. He learned that the crew that built and ran it, under the leadership of Dr. Shim, who was somewhat of a celebrity here, had left the university when the doctor retired. That would explain why he didn't see any familiar faces entering or leaving the Everett building. One reliable occurrence was seeing the woman he had seen that first day he found the university, and then again in that one-off strange place. He had observed her coming out, and going into, the building a few times now.

Chapter Thirteen

After returning from one of his expeditions into the un-known, which he had spent simply walking for the duration, the TV had a hard time keeping Ed entertained. That changed abruptly when programming was interrupted for breaking news. The images on the screen were surreal and initially there were no comments. Just a helicopter view of an area in some small town in the United States. The banner underneath read "Castle Appears in Coldes Haven". A baseball stadium and many surrounding buildings had disappeared. In their stead was now a structure, similar in appearance to a medieval castle. It was of enormous proportions. On closer examination it didn't seem to be an actual building, but more a solid, rocky object with that distinct shape. There was nothing resembling an entrance and anything that looked like a window, was only an indent, not an actual through hole, as if deliberately sculpted in that way. There was no obvious way into this thing. Even when seen from the helicopter, it was so large it filled the entire screen most of the time.

Finally, a voice began narrating, saying that the structure had appeared in an instant about an hour prior. Most people there had only noticed it after it was already there. A few people had described a moment of blue illumination and others had mentioned sounds they described as muted pops and an electric buzzing. Whatever this thing was, it had almost silently replaced everything in one area, without causing any damage to surrounding areas. Not even a tremor was felt.

Ground level images were shown where the castle walls, or whatever they were, protruded from the ground, rising high into the air and cleanly cutting through asphalt roads, paved sidewalks and even a building. The wall intersected a storefront window, with the visible half of the glass still perfectly intact.

"As of now, at least 129 people are missing," the narrating voice said. "Mostly those attending a minor league baseball game at the stadium and those who lived in the disappeared buildings. It is possible, and expected, that this number will rise as it is unclear at this time how many people were out on the streets or visiting the area."

The helicopter flew closer to one of the many towers. *This thing is massive!* As the view shifted from one tower to the next, the camera caught a glimpse of two flying animals. Birds, maybe? It was difficult to get a sense of scale against the unnatural backdrop. *That ain't no birds!* The voice faltered as the camera zoomed in on one of the animals landing on a tower, at first with some difficulties getting a sharp focus.

"These images coming to us live from Coldes Haven, there appear to be two… well… are those dragons?"

Dragons!? Ed flicked through a few other channels. Most of them were now showing similar images. As of today, fire breathing dragons are real. And why not? After what he had experienced throughout the past few weeks, dragons seemed perfectly reasonable.

Two days later, Ed was stuck in front of his TV all day because his coveted daily reprieve from the chair did not come. Programming was still dominated by the castle of Coldes Haven. When something exceptional like this happened, there was always an inexplicable abundance of so-called experts on the topic, ready to comment. Should the dragons be captured, killed, or protected? Could we extract their DNA for research? Do dragons pose a health risk or fire hazard? What should they be called? The word dragon was apparently not good enough anymore, resulting in suggestions of unpronounceable names reminiscent of dinosaurs. And what about the castle-shaped monolith? Should it be explored, demolished, or exploited for tourism? Could the missing people, now numbering almost two hundred, be inside? For Ed, none of it was relevant. What he needed to know was why there were no transitions today. The craving for his daily time out of the chair was making him feel sick.

He noticed his phone was, silently, receiving a call, but he didn't answer. It was the office, no doubt wanting to know why he wasn't answering his calls, emails, text messages or even his doorbell, which he had also been ignoring several times in the past few days. Out of boredom he opened some of the regular mail and soon found a letter from the office informing him that his position would be terminated if he didn't report in, as apparently discussed in a prior phone call Ed didn't recall having. He cursed, in part because that would be what might be expected of him in this instance. But the job had never interested him much. Losing it was not the end of the world. It would be a lot of trouble to go through. He would have to check his eligibility for disability benefits from the government.

Why is there no magic today? The day progressed at an agonizingly slow pace.

"Why are you doing this to me?" he yelled at the TV. He slammed his fists on the armrests of his wheelchair, before grabbing them tight and letting out a frustrated scream.

By the end of the afternoon, Ed knew that it just wasn't going to happen today, as it never had this late in the day. He realized he hadn't eaten anything and considered calling in a pizza. Instead, he decided to get back to bed.

After another virtually sleepless night, Ed was back in his chair in front of the TV. He sat there for hours and was getting very worried that nothing would happen for a second day. He ordered in lunch but when it was delivered, he didn't feel like eating. Finally, in the early afternoon, the blue glow came. Ed stretched out his arms to embrace it. *Take me away!* He closed his eyes and waited for the noise to stop and make way for the sounds of a new world.

Traffic.

He opened his eyes and found himself in one of the familiar alleys between apartment buildings across the street from Delaney's restaurant. As soon as he began walking, he noticed how hungry he really was. He decided to cross the road and go get something to eat.

CHAPTER FOURTEEN

THE EVENTUAL SUCCESS of the first Phase-C experiment, in front of a live audience, was a great motivator for Lora and her crew. But before the start of subsequent experiments, Jarod led an effort to make a few upgrades to the system, in hopes to avoid any further mishaps with the safety on The Sharpener. This meant that for three days, no runs with The Shim were possible.

It gave Lora some time to work on her presentation for the upcoming Physics Advances convention, which was something she preferred to do at home. Her study, or rather her home office, was a cozy, warm space, where she could relax or work with equal ease. It was almost the opposite of a lab.

Back when Dr. Shim gave his revolutionary presentation at the same convention years ago, he presented everything from simple slides. Lora wanted to do things a little differently this time. Inspired by the reactions she got from people who attended the

Phase-C demonstration, she wanted to give the convention audience a live view of the lab, as the experiment was carried out, possibly for the last time.

After the upgrades to The Shim were completed, the experiment resumed. On the first try, the tennis ball successfully made the trip from the location where it was left behind during the demo to coherence pod one, as preselected. Lora was satisfied that they were now collecting useful data from The Slicer. The plan was to run at least twenty-five experiments sequentially, finishing well before the convention date. That would leave the team some time to collect and process the data, and perform preliminary analysis on it, hopefully with enough of a result to present it at the convention. The first run of the day had been relatively fast, so they did another, equally successful, move in the afternoon. In fact, on three consecutive days, two successful runs per day were achieved.

Whenever The Shim was performing its magic, Lora liked to go outside and walk in the park, or to Delaney's, often by herself and sometimes in the company of Randy. Once, when she walked with Randy, they had seen the mysterious man with the red jacket for themselves, hanging around the campus gate. She even said hello but got nothing back.

Lora had asked Gary and Randy to run the next experiment without her, as she would not be in the lab for a day. Instead, she was visiting the convention center to discuss her idea for a live video stream, and whether it was technically feasible. The center was a good hours' drive away. As traffic was lighter than she had anticipated, she got there twenty minutes early for her appointment, giving her time to get some fresh air and stretch her legs. Not too familiar with this part of the city, she didn't venture too far from the building, not wanting to be late for the meeting.

Across the street, a small distance away, she noticed a cute look-ing green area, edged with a hedge and a nice cast iron gate. What she found when she got there was disappointing. Spoiled with daily access to the park by campus, she thought this one was too small to even be called a park. It would take her less than a mi-nute to walk through it. Near the other side of it, she took a mo-ment to look at a statue that looked terribly out of place here. *It's hideous.* Lora couldn't tell what material the monstrosity was made of, but it reminded her of *papier-mâché*, painted a shade of green that somehow clashed perfectly with the surrounding veg-etation. It depicted, Lora thought, a somewhat corpulent man in a onesie. The pedestal upon which it stood much taller than it deserved to, had the word "Dart" chiseled into it. There were plaques all around the statue with too much text. Lora knew the name, Dart, and remembered seeing him on occasion, but had never heard of, or known about, this atrocious effigy that dese-crated this already lacking park. There was no way she was going to read the plaques, just no way, and so she resumed her walk. When she emerged from the other side onto the sidewalk of an-other busy road, across the street from her, she saw the man in the red suit staring back at her. *What are you doing all the way out here? Are you following me?* There was too much traffic to cross the street to go ask him, and she didn't want to be held up too long, so once again, she resumed her walk, now back in the di-rection of the convention center.

In Lora's absence Gary and Randy successfully ran the experi-ment, but only once. On the second try, there were calibration errors that took them most of the day to solve.

After that, the days began to blend into each other. Every day, the goal was to start the experiment as early as possible, and then run another one in the afternoon. Lora tried to walk outside at least once a day during a run and almost every time she would see the stranger in the red suit somewhere. She joked about it with Randy, suggesting that she might have picked up a stalker.

Randy was getting into his own now and was becoming a respected crew member. Compared with her previous assistants he had turned out to be a much more valuable addition to her team. She did worry that he spent maybe a little too much time in the lab with her, but when she asked him about it, he always insisted that his schoolwork wasn't suffering from it. Even Ian, who at first had been on Lora's case about Randy's speedy appointment as her new assistant, now seemed pleased with the progress being made thanks to that extra pair of hands, and, apparently, an acceptable brain to go along with it.

If Lora wasn't going for a walk, it was because she wanted to stay with The Shim and watch the ball disappear. There was something about the shimmering that kept her fascinated with it. It was that feeling of seeing magic happen. If the trick is performed well enough, then, even if you know how it works, it still looks like real magic. The Shim was by all accounts a very skilled magician.

Phase-C, unlike the beginning of Phase-B and much like Phase-A, it seemed, was proceeding without a glitch. It was going so well that she afforded most of her crew a day off on the thirteenth day of the series, allowing once again for some minor maintenance on The Shim.

She spent most of that day at home working on her convention speech, but also took some time to drop by the lab to make sure the run scheduled for the next day would go as smoothly as before. Of course, she checked in with Jarod and his colleagues, bringing him his much-needed coffee.

"Dude! I really hope, one day, I will see my family again before my kids forget what my face looks like, you know?" Jarod said.

"I'm sorry, Jarod. I didn't mean to—"

"I am joking with you! Don't worry, I made sure they'll never forget me. You go enjoy your well-deserved time off, while me and my friends here give this rust bucket an oil change."

The weather was perfect, so she seized the opportunity to go for a long walk around the park, half expecting, and maybe hoping, to see the man in the red suit again. In that case she would ask him what his deal was because the initial comedic quality of his timing was turning into something creepier now, she felt. Some students in the park recognized her and she talked to them for a while. Eventually she grabbed a bite to eat at Delaney's and then returned to the lab to wrap up. *I suppose the man in the red suit has a day off too.*

If everything continued the way it had before the break, Lora reckoned her project would finish with time to spare. In the morning, armed with a tea, she addressed her crew, complimenting them on a job well done so far. Then she took Randy to the consoles by The Shim. The work done for the maintenance had caused some misalignments that needed to be corrected before the experiment could resume. Lora got to work, pushing buttons, turning dials, and calling out numbers to Randy, who then repeated them, and confirmed them on his console. This machine required very few manual adjustments, so realigning the beam was at times akin to a pre-flight check on some futuristic spaceship. Call a number, push a button. That didn't mean it was fast. It took all morning. By lunchtime, Lora asked Randy if it would be alright with him if they postponed eating until the machine was running. Randy begrudgingly agreed, saying he had a planned meeting for lunch in the park.

"Anyone I know?" Lora asked.

"No."

"Okay." A silence followed that begged to be broken. "Well, let's try to get this thing running quickly."

Randy left immediately when the beam came on. Lora waited around a little longer to make sure there weren't any glitches with the upgraded hardware. When she was satisfied that it was working correctly, she looked around for anyone to accompany her to Delaney's for lunch, but most had already had their lunch, or were out now, so she was on her own again. She grabbed her book and purse from her backpack and considered going for a walk before heading to the restaurant.

Outside she found Randy and a young woman she didn't know, engaged in what looked like a very lively discussion. They were by the gate, so Lora had no choice but to walk by them. As she approached, the discussion suddenly went quiet.

The girl pointed Lora out and said, loud enough for everyone to hear, "Is that her?"

Lora generally considered herself to be a nice person, but there was an evil streak in everyone. There had to be. Internally, she felt a burning desire to emphatically wave at Randy and maybe even say hello, just to see what would happen. Instead, she behaved, and picked up her pace to pass the bickering couple as quickly as possible and without causing a scene.

"Oh my god, you're embarrassing me," she heard Randy say behind her. "You know she is my boss, right?"

The thing about this rumor that seemed to be haunting Randy, Lora thought, was that no one besides Randy had mentioned anything to her. So where did Randy pick it up? In any case, the polite thing for Lora to do now was to avoid the park just in case Randy was still going there. She decided to walk the sidewalk instead, starting across the street in the opposite direction from where the restaurant was. She'd go for a while, then turn and walk back, past the park and campus, and cross again to Delaney's for a late and lonely lunch.

Chapter Fifteen

A S SOON AS HE OPENED the door to Delaney's and stepped inside, Ed was immediately happy with what he found. *Nice place!* He walked up to the bar and sat on a bar stool for the first time in his life. With a satisfied grin on his face, he ordered a drink, something fancy, and asked to see the lunch menu.

The bartender, while making the drink, said, "Haven't seen you in here before, I think."

Ed laughed. He spread his arms and looked down at his red jacket. "I think you would remember me."

The bartender agreed, laughing as well. "Well, enjoy sir," he said, as he placed the drink in front of Ed. "You are most welcome here. Are you here on business?"

"Visitor. Just visiting, I mean." Ed said. *A visitor from another dimension.* He smiled and held the glass up to the bartender, then took a small sip. It was good, but there was so much ice. He set it back down and considered putting his fingers in and picking one or two ice cubes out, but also thought about how that would look. There was a napkin that he could use. He looked at it, then back at the ice in his glass.

"What in the hell!?" Ed jumped off his bar stool and put both of his hands on his head, his mouth wide open.

Behind him the door opened, and Lora entered.

"Hi Neil," she said to the bartender, but her eyes were immediately drawn to the man in the red suit standing at the bar, looking as if he had just witnessed a murder.

Ed pointed at his drink and asked, "Did you see that? Did that really happen?"

Neil shook his head. He didn't see anything strange.

Lora didn't know if she wanted to get involved and went to sit down at her regular table by the window. She watched the man in the red suit sit back down at the bar.

Ed stared at his drink, with one of the ice cubes now sitting next to his glass. *I didn't touch that.* He had wanted the ice cube to be next to his glass, sure, but he never did anything about it. Then, without any contact, one of the ice cubes – the one he was considering removing – had magically jumped out of the glass. *Not jumped.* It vanished from the glass, then appeared next to it, right where he would have put it, in an instant.

The bartender came over to ask if he had made a choice for food, but he hadn't even looked at the menu yet.

Ed ventured to make a guess. "A grilled cheese sandwich would be alright."

I wanted the ice cube out and now it's out! Ed looked at his glass again and wondered, half joking, if he could make the glass jump off the coaster by just making a wish.

Lora had ordered a salad, and was eating it while reading her book, occasionally checking her phone for messages or the time. She couldn't really keep her mind on the story in the book. A character in her book was, Lora was expected to believe, afraid for her life after she had heard unfamiliar footsteps in her house, and so, inexplicably, armed with nothing but a lit candle, she opened the door to the basement and proceeded down the stairs to check why the power just went out. *Does being fictional make you stupid? Just get out of there already!*

Besides, the man at the bar intrigued Lora and she was considering going over to say hello. Right then, there was some noise at the bar, and the man with the red jacket was up again.

"I spilled my drink, I'm sorry," he said to the bartender. He turned around to look at Lora. "I am sorry," he repeated, with an awkward smile. He paused for a second. "Hey," he finally said. "It's you again."

Lora gestured for him to sit at the table with her.

"I have noticed you around lately," Ed said.

Lora chewed for a moment, nodding, then answered, "I was about to ask you if you are following me."

Ed smiled. "Do you work at the university?"

"Yes, quantum lab. What about you?"

The bartender came over with the grilled cheese sandwich and Ed dug right in. "I'm famished," he said. "Quantum lab, huh? So, you're a physicist." *Good.* "What do you guys do in there anyway?"

"Well, I am leading a follow-up study to the research done by Dr. Shim. Are you familiar with his work?" Inevitably, Lora thought, she would end up trying to explain her research to someone who didn't understand it, while also trying to avoid details due to her non-disclosure agreement with the university.

Ed said, "Sure. The teleportation guy."

"Right."

"So, what are you studying?"

Lora decided she wasn't going to answer that. "It's kind of a secret. To prevent misinformation in the media, I'm not allowed to say too much about it yet. Soon though."

Ed looked disappointed. He was making quick work of his lunch. "Not too bad," he said about it, wiping his lips with a napkin. "I heard something about a tennis ball. Is that the one you're working on?"

Lora put her fork down in her bowl and studied the stranger's face. Those sunglasses weren't letting her read him easily. "I'm sorry," she said, "but where did you hear that?" The tennis ball was a bit of an inside joke. It was not a secret under NDA, or anything like that, but it was certainly not public knowledge.

"My father. He was a quantum physicist, until he was killed in the construction accident at the lab."

Lora was confused. "What lab?"

Ed adjusted himself in his seat. He began telling Lora about the incident that put him in a wheelchair as a boy and that had killed his father, along with nearly everyone who worked in the lab, including Dr. Shim. He gave dates with all events. He explained how the university is now closed, and that he had been staying in a hotel across the street from the ruins just recently. He went into detail about his suddenly gained ability to transition into this alternative reality. "For a few hours a day, on average, I get to walk around here, dressed like this." He straightened his red jacket and touched his sunglasses. "When I pop back into my room, I'm back in the wheelchair, sans jacket and glasses. It's quite a setback each time, going from whatever this place is, to being paralyzed from the waist down. I sit there and pray that it will happen again." He paused briefly. "Now," he said, "seeing as you're a scientist, what do you make of all this? I wouldn't mind learning how I ended up here, or how I could stay permanently, with my legs working."

Lora had made a few weak attempts at interrupting him as he was telling his story, without success. It was the most fantastical thing she'd ever heard, easily outdoing the book she was reading. It made no sense whatsoever. "The lab is right there. I've been there almost every day since Dr. Shim took me in. As far as I know, no serious accidents occurred during construction."

About three years into construction of The Shim, when only the plateau had been set up in the lab, and all the machines were still in workshops and at external companies, a major renovation of the lab was underway to make more space. As far as Lora knew, the required construction on the building happened without incident.

Lora continued. "And last time I checked, Dr. Shim was very much alive."

Ed, in anticipation of her response, had already brought out his phone. *No signal.* He brought up the photos he took of the campus during his stay at the hotel and showed them to Lora.

Lora stared at the screen in silence. Her face gave no hint about what she was feeling. She was looking at photos of the Everett building, no question. It looked like the building had partially collapsed. The remaining part, which included most of her lab, had its windows boarded over. Another picture showed a wider view of the abandoned campus, with all the buildings in a deplorable state. Everything was overgrown with shrubs, grass, and moss. A third image showed an old newspaper headline about the incident.

Lora had been in high school when construction on The Shim was finished but she had never heard of this accident. She had so many questions. How did this man know about the tennis ball? Where did he get these photos? She wanted a moment to herself. "I'm sorry," she said, suddenly getting up from her seat and half running to the bathroom. Ed sat by himself.

When she returned, Lora hesitated to sit back down at the table, but Ed wasn't done with her. He needed to make sure that this scientist took him seriously enough to look into his situation. He took Lora's fork out of her bowl and placed it on the table in front of him.

"Remember," he said, "how I spilled my drink earlier?"

Lora sat and nodded. She was about to take her fork back, but before her hand could even reach it, the fork was already back in her bowl. Ed had willed it to be there, and now it was.

To Ed's satisfaction, this time Lora's face very much told him how she felt. She was suddenly white as a sheet. Her hand still hovering over the table on the way to where the fork had been, her eyes wide. She whispered, "It shimmered… that's impossible."

Ed didn't know what that meant, but he assumed it was her scientific description of what he had just done.

When people saw an object disappear in her lab for the first time, they often didn't notice the shimmering effect, but *she* never missed it. Lora saw the faint, but unmistakable sparkle before her fork vanished from the table and reappeared in her bowl. She saw the shimmering many times before, but never expected to see it outside of The Shim, without the beam.

"I only found out I can do that today. That's how I spilled my drink earlier. I certainly can't do that where I am from."

Ed was satisfied that he had grabbed the scientist's attention in full now, but it seemed she had lost her desire to talk. He waited a while and then tried to ask if she was alright. She responded by getting up and gathering her things. She thanked Neil and brought her mostly empty bowl to the bar, saving Neil the effort of picking it up at the table. It looked like she was in a hurry to leave now.

Behind her, Ed said, "Damn, I forgot my wallet."

Lora told Neil to add his meal and drink to her bill and then turned around. She realized that neither of them had introduced themselves. She asked, "Hey, who are you anyway?"

"Visitor." He smiled.

Lora looked like she was waiting for more.

"When I am in this world, I go by Visitor. It seems fitting."

"Okay, that's not weird. Visitor. It was nice talking to you, but I have to get back to my lab now. With how things have been going, I'm sure we'll be seeing each other again."

"Can I come?"

"Sorry, but we don't allow visitors in the lab at the moment." She walked out the door and said, "I'm Lora, by the way." She felt like her head was spinning and needed some air. The whole world seemed to have gone crazy just now. She quickly walked back to campus.

Randy waved Lora over as soon as she came in the door. "You missed it by ten seconds," he said. The tennis ball was gone from the plateau, and Randy opened the pods. Another successful run.

As they were attempting to get the machine ready for the second run of the day, which it appeared to be resistant to, Lora could not keep her mind focused on the work. "I'm sorry, Randy, but I'm not feeling the best. Maybe it was my lunch," she said. She announced the cancelation of the second run to her team and went home.

The next day Lora had to sit with a few of her crew, most of them data analysts, to go over some perceived anomalies in the data of the previous run. Meanwhile Randy and Gary tried to get the experiment running, but The Shim was still not cooperating. It took them, with help from Jarod and eventually Lora, all morning and most of the afternoon to get up and running. Luckily the run only lasted thirty-five minutes this time, and everyone ended up going home at a normal time.

Chapter Sixteen

D ART WAS WATCHING the street in front of the city's largest hotel. He just happened to walk past, as a man with three stuffed suitcases of luggage was clumsily coming down the five steps by the front entrance. Dart thought about helping him, but he changed his mind when the man began to yell at a woman behind him.

"You think you could do any less to help?"

The woman, wearing a long brown coat and a scarf, as if she was confused about the season, looked down on him from the top of the stairs. "Eat me!" she yelled back at him.

Dart decided that this might be interesting, so he slowed down to watch. Both the man and the woman noticed him immediately, no doubt due to his green superhero outfit, but they were too busy with each other to care. One of the suitcases tumbled down the last two stairs and the woman laughed loudly.

"Five days!" she yelled at him. "You can't even do five days away from your stupid computer? Can't spend five days alone with your wife?"

The man scrambled to the bottom of the stairs and yelled back, "Jeff only calls when there is a real problem. I must go. If I lose this job, there won't be any more of these trips!"

The woman threw her hands in the air. "There aren't any trips now! This is the first time in six years we've even left town!"

"I know! I'm sorry."

"Five days. And you're going home on the first day!"

Dart wondered why this man thought he needed three suitcases for a five-day trip.

The man looked at his watch, desperately wishing his taxi would show up early. "Look, I'll make it up to you."

The woman didn't believe him. "I might not even come home!"

"Excuse me, sir," someone, who had snuck up on Dart behind him, said. "We need you to move."

Dart looked around. The woman was wearing a headset and held a clipboard. She pointed across the street, where a news crew was setting up their gear. "We're shooting some footage of the hotel for a segment in tonight's show, and we'd like to have the sidewalk empty," she said.

There were many others on the sidewalk, Dart noticed, so it was obvious to him that he was being singled out for his appearance. It didn't bother him. Not much, anyway. Across the street he saw the crew unloading equipment from a van. Looking at him from near the van was Natalie Reed, one of the reporters for the evening news on Channel 56. Dart wouldn't mind meeting her sometime. He apologized to the woman with the clipboard and walked toward the hotel, saying he would remain hidden behind a pillar.

A taxi pulled in and stopped by the suitcases, now neatly lined up at the bottom of the steps.

The disgruntled wife came down and changed her tone. "Please just call them and say you can't make it. They're not going to fire you for not responding to one call in sixteen years."

The man shook his head. "You don't know that. And I can't afford to find out."

The taxi driver finished loading the suitcases into the trunk and opened the door for his passenger. The man got into the car without looking at his wife. Something bad was about to happen. Dart could feel it. It was a familiar tingling sensation in his neck. He trusted this feeling enough to start walking toward the taxi, in defiance of his promise to stay out of view of the camera. The woman stood by the open taxi door and bent forward into the car. Dart couldn't hear what she said, but he still felt he would be needed soon. The woman got back up and the door closed. Almost immediately, the car started moving and Dart saw what he had come for. The woman's coat was caught in the door and as the car started rolling it pulled her with it. She jerked forward and then fell to the ground with a scream. As she fell, Dart sprinted forward and threw himself on the hood of the taxi, yelling, "Stop!" He was just in time to prevent the woman from being dragged along with the car.

"What the…?" the taxi driver yelled as he stopped the car.

Dart pointed to the rear door. "How did you not see her?"

The rear door opened, and the woman scrambled to her feet the moment her coat was released. She was unharmed but for a few scratches. "Unbelievable!" she said as she turned around, climbed back up the stairs and rushed into the hotel.

The man in the rear seat quietly grabbed the door and closed it again.

Meanwhile, Dart got back on his feet as well. He shook hands with the taxi driver.

"I guess that taught me not to talk to the passenger while driving. Nice outfit, by the way. And thanks."

Dart laughed. "That's my job. It's what I do."

As the taxi pulled out, Dart looked across the street, and sure enough, he found the woman with the clipboard running toward him again.

"Mister, mister! That was very courageous of you! I think you saved that woman's life!"

Dart shrugged and said, "That's exactly right, I did. It's what I do."

The woman looked him over and said, "There's a live news bulletin starting in just about ten minutes. Would you care to be interviewed on live TV? If you don't mind…"

Dart beamed a big smile and said he would like nothing more as he introduced himself properly.

The woman with the clipboard dropped him off with the crew. "Everyone, this is Dart. He's a real superhero today!" In a lower voice directed at Natalie, she added, "If there's nothing else you need from me here, I need to get to the crew on Holborn Avenue. They're waiting for me."

Natalie thanked her and looked briefly at Dart and his costume.

"Hi, I'm Dart. It's so nice to…"

Natalie had already turned away and was now talking to her cameraman. The woman with the clipboard got in her car and drove away in a hurry. Dart stood awkwardly waiting until Natalie faced him again.

"Are you ready? We'll be on in about two minutes," she said. She gave him a reassuring look. "Relax, you'll be fine. Don't worry about the extra equipment. We came here to shoot footage for an extended piece, not to go live in the middle of the afternoon. Hence that big microphone boom instead of our familiar handheld. Take a few deep breaths."

Dart had to admit he was a little nervous. He had given interviews before, but this was the first time he was going to be on live TV immediately after a successful job. With no one other than Natalie Reed!

"Alright," she said, "I will first introduce the scene to the viewers. Then I'll talk to you, and the camera will move over here. When you talk, you can look at me, or at the camera directly. This is not a movie, there is no fourth wall." She turned away again and said something unintelligible to the cameraman who handed her a bottle of water in response. She took a quick sip and positioned herself in front of the camera.

"Twenty seconds," a new voice suddenly said, seemingly out of nowhere.

Dart made sure he was turned precisely in the direction where the camera would be and adjusted his name tag, so that it would be clearly visible to the viewers. He cleared his throat.

The mysterious voice started counting down, "Five, four, three," then silence.

Natalie looked directly into the camera and started, "I am standing in the street where moments ago a woman narrowly escaped certain death. With me here is… um… Dartman, who selflessly saved her life, in an impressive act of what can only be called genuine heroism."

The cameraman moved to the second position to put Dart into the frame. But Dart looked directly at Natalie and tapped his finger on his name tag.

Natalie continued. "Dartman, like a superhero, you risked your own life to save another today. Can you tell us what—"

Dart interrupted her. "Dartman… Really? I told you who I am, didn't I? I am wearing a name tag for god's sake! I mean, if there is something wrong with your hearing and your eyes, you may be in the wrong profession, Natalie!"

The cameraman went back to his first position, returning Natalie to the center of the screen.

Natalie was still looking at Dart and was lost for words. "I… I uh… What?" She made an aggressive throat-slicing gesture with her hand, signaling the end of the interview.

Dart wasn't finished and pushed her out of the way, taking her spot in front of the camera. "I am Dart! Not Dartman. I've made this quite clear before we started this," he said, sounding angrier now. "It shows no respect, no respect at all, to get this wrong. And this is not the first time! You people always get it wrong!"

The mystery voice in the background said, "We're off air, no one can hear you."

Dart yelled at the camera, "No! Put me back on!"

The microphone boom retracted. The camera had already come off the cameraman's shoulder and was now pointed at the ground. Both the boom operator and the cameraman shook their heads at Dart and started back to the van. Dart grabbed Natalie's arm and demanded again to be put back on air.

Natalie hissed. "You touch me again and I will bury you."

Dart briefly evaluated her threat and then shoved her again. "Far worse things will happen to you if you don't put me back on and correct my name on air! I will not have this Dartman nonsense perpetuated by incompetent dimwits like you. Do your job or face the consequences!" Dart felt like he was boiling inside. He used every ounce of restraint that he could muster, even as he thought these people did not deserve it. These were supposed to be professionals. Sure, it was possible that they got a name wrong sometimes. Once. Maybe twice. But this had happened so many times now, he couldn't take it anymore.

"Put me back on, now!" he yelled. He started toward the van, where the sound guy was just lifting in the last piece of equipment. Dart snatched it out of his hands, threw it at him and then pushed him into the van, following him in. Natalie could hear loud noises from inside the vehicle and wasn't sure what to do. She heard Dart swearing and breaking things inside. A loud scream emanated from the van. She took out her phone and started calling the police. Dart emerged with the camera and stomped back to Natalie, angrily knocking the phone away from her.

He shoved the heavy camera in her hands, almost pushing her over, and said, "I am not kidding! Put me back on."

Natalie felt she could be in danger and just bolted to the van, hugging the camera, and then jumped in the back. "I think we have everything we need, Dartman," she yelled from inside. The cameraman exited the back of the vehicle, ran to the driver side door, and got in. "I'm sure we'll see you on the news for more than just saving a woman tonight, psycho freak!" yelled Natalie at Dart with newfound courage. "Oh my god, what did he do to you?" she then asked, directed at someone inside.

Dart exploded with rage. He charged at the van, which the cameraman had some trouble starting. He ripped open the door and shoved the cameraman hard. "Move over, asshole!" Dart said. He punched the man on his chin and made it clear there was another one coming. The cameraman climbed over the center console into the passenger seat and tried to open the door to get out the other side. It was locked, and Dart had already managed to get the van started and began accelerating fast.

"All I want," he said through his teeth as he fastened his seatbelt, "all I ever want, is some respect. Respect for my work and respect for my name! It isn't much to ask." The van was speeding through traffic. Dart's voice rose higher as he continued. "Yet here we are! You screwed up a perfect opportunity to advance both our careers. You had a good story here! Emmy material, or whatever awards news people get off on. But, no, you screwed it up and, next thing I know, you're threatening to ruin my reputation." Dart sped out of the city into an industrial park and continued his rant. "You wonder why people don't trust the media anymore? Well, it's because you can't be trusted! You are vermin! You can be sure I won't let you destroy what I have built. I saved that woman's life. *Dart* saved a woman's life! That's Dart, like it says clearly on my name tag. And *that* is what people need to know. If you can't tell that story, then what purpose do you even serve?"

Natalie, who was in the back, said, "Please, we need to get to a hospital, Lennie is bleeding."

Dart, the only person in the van wearing seatbelts, slammed hard on the breaks, sending everyone else careening forward. Natalie's head slammed hard into an equipment flight case just beside her.

"Who the hell is Lennie!?" Dart screamed. The cameraman beside him sat slumped in his seat, bleeding profusely from his head, after slamming it into the windshield. "This guy?" Dart asked, shoving his passenger once again.

Natalie was feeling her face with her hands and moaned softly. There was a big gash across her cheek that was bleeding as well.

A voice out of nowhere said, "Lennie… the sound guy."

Dart whipped around to see where it came from. A young

woman sat crouched in the far corner of the van, holding her wrist in her hand, clearly in pain. Dart had never seen her before, but he recognized the voice. "It's miss nobody can hear you," he said, laughing hysterically.

Lennie, the sound guy, was laying on the ground, with a rapidly swelling black eye, and bleeding from a wound on his upper leg.

"Lennie had it coming," Dart said, "I beat the crap out of him."

Natalie found her voice. "He needs help."

Dart turned facing forward again. "You all need help," he said, and stepped on the accelerator.

"Where are you taking us?" Natalie wanted to know.

Chapter Seventeen

When Ed returned home from lunch with Lora, he felt good. It had been a nice long excursion into the other world, and, even if he had spent too much time sitting down instead of walking, he had learned a few things. He was confident that he had won the scientist over enough for her to keep talking to him. Hopefully she could help him figure out what was happening to him and how to make it more permanent.

It wasn't until later in the next day that he made another transition. He had planned to use some of the time to explore the park and get some walking done, but his visit was cut unusually short, coming in at just over half an hour. That didn't mean it wasn't an eventful day though.

Ed's journal of notes about his journeys into the alternate reality was filling up quickly but today's short walk wouldn't add much to it. He went online to order in supper and then made himself a coffee to enjoy while waiting for its delivery. He turned on some music and had his supper at the dining table, which he didn't very often do anymore. The food was good, the music was great, so he made it last.

When he finished, he took his more familiar position in front of the TV. Unsurprisingly, the news channels were still talking about the castle. They seemed to struggle to come up with something original to say about the topic. One channel was showing diagrams to indicate the true size of the dragons compared to various well-known objects and animals. The animals were estimated to be juveniles and expected to grow up to twenty-five percent larger. An apparently renowned expert was talking about estimated body mass, wingspan, and the amount of lift they could generate. In principle, he said, with much confidence, it should be possible for up to three adults to ride on its back. Ed laughed. Another channel was focusing on the castle. A few people had already successfully climbed to the top of the structure, on the opposite side of where the dragons lived. The surface on the top, they claimed, was the same as the walls. Of course, you could already clearly see that from the abundant helicopter and drone footage that was now available. The dragons hadn't shown much interest in anything other than the monolithic structure itself. They didn't venture far from the tower they occupied. *What do they eat?*

Ed changed the channel for something more entertaining, turning off his brain to voluntarily consume whatever they were feeding him. Halfway through the evening his phone rang, silently, but as usual he ignored it. The persistence of the caller eventually got his attention and when he saw who it was, he picked it up immediately.

"Mom?"

After Ed had left the city, following the accident at the lab and his mother's death, he first moved in with his aunt, one of two of his mother's sisters, the only one still in the country, and her husband, an uncle who was violently against that idea. So violent in fact, that Ed didn't last six weeks before he was taken away by child welfare at his own request. With considerable luck, he ended up in a welcoming, and at the time rather well-off foster family. Soon after though, his foster father, a banker named Brock Fisher, struck bad luck when he was diagnosed with Crohn's disease, promptly followed by the loss of his job. Treatment for his condition was generally successful, but he never recovered from it emotionally. The times ahead were hard. There were frequent squabbles between him and his wife, Emily. Selling their home provided a way for them to survive for many years in a smaller house, even with both Brock and Emily not working. Ed took considerable time to warm up to them as he was himself struggling with his newfound disability. The Fishers never officially adopted Ed, but he had eventually come to see them as his family. Oddly, he had grown into the habit of calling his foster father by his first name, while calling Emily "mom". She never called this late at night.

"Mom? What is wrong? Why are you crying?"

"It's Australia," Emily said. "The darkness took him."

"Australia? Mom, please, I don't understand," Ed said, his voice trembling. He didn't understand, but he felt that it was not going to be good once he learned.

"They just called. He was one of the first to be identified," Emily said, with a squeaky voice and in between sobs.

Ed sat silent, listening to her cry, not knowing how to ask for clarity. These moments. These were the times when he cursed his disability. Why couldn't he just jump up, get into his car, and go to his mother. It was only a twenty-minute drive from here. She needed him, that much was clear.

"Eddie?"

"I don't know what it means, mom. Did something happen to Brock?"

Emily quieted down a little bit, attempting to suppress some of her despair. In a tone of voice that sounded much more like herself, she said, "Don't you watch the news?"

Ed could hear Emily sniffling, breathing irregularly. She was having a very hard time staying silent. The sound was cutting into Ed's soul. Why couldn't he think of something to say now? Was Brock dead? How?

"I... I can't," Emily cried, suddenly hanging up the phone.

Quietly and slowly turning back to the TV, Ed grabbed the remote and pointed it, hesitating for a long moment before changing the channel. What was he going to see?

A map of Australia appeared on the screen, with a circular area marked centered to the north-east of the city of Perth. The banner at the bottom of the screen removed any doubt about whether he was looking at the right thing. "Unusual Darkness and Bodies in Western Australia." A police representative in Perth was talking to a reporter when the map was removed. Ed turned up the volume.

"...bodies have already been found, and the phone hasn't stopped ringing since it began. The bodies are all nude or nearly so and appear to have been severely mutilated. Most of them have countless broken bones, bruises, and some traces of skin burns. Identification is difficult and slow at this time, as all the bodies we've seen until now belong to people elsewhere in the world. We're matching them against missing person reports filed in the last four hours, from everywhere..."

Other channels were showing similar reports. Hundreds of bodies were being found within the area indicated on the map. Only hours into this new crisis, hospitals and morgues were already overwhelmed. Bodies were being retrieved using all manner of large vehicles and taken to makeshift processing facilities for identification. It was the most gruesome thing Ed had ever seen. Simultaneously an enormous number of people were being reported missing all over the globe.

One channel that wasn't showing these nightmarish scenes was instead focusing on a different aspect of the events down under. A science journalist, a woman Ed recognized from a TV show he sometimes watched, even if he couldn't remember her name or the name of her show, was explaining the inverse square law that describes how light intensity falls off with distance. Not something, Ed thought, that would normally hold the attention of the viewers for very long.

"…but in the affected area, the light has changed. And not just the light, gravity as well. Normally, if you double your distance from a light source, its intensity decreases to one quarter. Over in Australia it now reduces by a factor of eight instead. The inverse square law has turned into an inverse cubed law."

The woman, thankfully, looked like she was finished talking, but the young and very nervous looking reporter didn't catch on and waited for more, keeping his microphone in front of her face. Ed didn't see why. If she said anything else, it would only make things worse for him. But Ed wasn't going to change the channel to see more dead bodies. He needed this distraction before he would have to come to terms with the possibility that Brock had died in Australia today, without ever going there. That, for the second time in his life, he had lost his father.

"The intensity falls off with the distance to the power of the number of spatial dimensions less one. So, this seems to indicate the presence of a new spatial dimension."

Ed was right. This was worse.

"So... where is this extra dimension?" the reporter asked. He was so far out of his depth that it could at least be a little entertaining from here on in.

"We don't know. It's not visible. The only clue to it is the change in falloff for light intensity and gravity."

"Oh, so... Okay. So, that means..."

Ed laughed, despite everything. *You go, reporter guy! You're doing great!*

"It means lights look dim. The lamps in your house, car headlights, traffic lights, streetlights and even the sun. They dim faster than normal as you move away from them. And gravity falls off more quickly with distance as well, so you can—"

Ed could feel himself get dimmer too and turned off the TV. He would pour himself a drink, a beer maybe, or something stronger, to calm his nerves, and then call his foster mother back. Brock, so it appeared, was dead. It was beginning to sink in. *I liked the dragons better.*

CHAPTER EIGHTEEN

RANDY HAD SCHOOLWORK to do today, so he could not come to the lab. For Lora this meant she was doing all calibrations of The Shim by herself, as Gary also wasn't available to help this morning. Perhaps unsurprisingly, the beam was misaligned for no obvious reason, which was typically something that was much easier to fix with an extra pair of eyes and hands. Regardless, it was going to be a quiet day at the lab. There were a few data analysts present, but unless they ran into problems, they usually didn't need much attention from Lora. Ian wasn't in either, which seemed to be the norm as of late. It wasn't until after noon that Lora got The Shim ready for the next run, which meant it would be another single run. There were no irregularities when she started the experiment, so she grabbed the lunch she had packed and made her way to the exit to go for a walk in the park and eat there.

On her way out she found Naomi and Matvei, the only two cleaners with direct access to the Everett building, and one of the security guards, standing by the wall-mounted TV screens. The guard was holding a remote control that he had used to turn up the volume on the news.

Naomi, when she saw Lora, said, "Honey, I swear, this city is going down the drain."

Lora half joined them in front of the screen. It showed a burnt-out vehicle parked in front of what could be an abandoned warehouse or factory. "What happened?" she asked.

"They killed Natalie Reed, and her entire crew!" Naomi said, sounding genuinely shocked. "You know, the Channel 56 reporter?"

Lora had no idea who that was. "That's terrible," she said, watching the screen quietly for a moment longer. "I'm headed out for a walk."

The weather had changed since this morning. It was heavily overcast, and the wind had picked up. She barely made it off campus when she started to think she might just go back inside. Then she heard her name.

"Lora! Is that right?" The still mysterious man in the red suit came running toward her on the sidewalk, from the direction of Delaney's.

"Yes, you got it," Lora said. "Visitor…"

"What are the chances of us meeting again so soon?"

Lora wanted to say something funny about statistics but thought better of it. "You are stalking me. Don't you have another world to go back to?"

"I have. In fact, I haven't been here since shortly after you left me at the restaurant last time. Just a few minutes ago I came back, not far from there. And it looks like I caught you on your lunch break once again."

Lora held up the lunch box she was carrying. "Cold leftovers." It was beginning to rain. "Great. So much for my walk in the park." She started walking back to the Everett building and Visitor followed her.

"That park," he said, "is a parking lot for the hotel across the street in my world."

"You really believe all this, don't you?" Lora asked.

"What, my life? Yeah, I take it quite seriously."

When they reached the doors, Lora waved her key card to open them. She really shouldn't invite him in, it was strictly against policy. But this man was interesting. He knew things about this lab that he shouldn't know. Seeing as Ian wasn't here, what harm could come from letting him in just this once?

"Come in," she said. The TV in the foyer had been turned back down and Naomi and Matvei had resumed their work elsewhere in the building. The security guards were still heavily debating the news among themselves. "He's with me," Lora mumbled as she quickly passed them.

"This is very weird," Visitor whispered, following Lora into the lab. She led him in the direction of The Shim, but he was moving slowly, falling behind when the machine came into his view. He put one hand over his mouth and stroked his chin as he scanned the room and took it all in. So many feelings were competing for his attention.

Recognition. Everything looked different than he remembered, but it also looked familiar. He knew where the bathrooms were, without having to ask.

There was an uneasy feeling. Fear, maybe? He had memories of walking into this room as a boy, but no memories of walking out, or ever again after that. Until recently.

He felt a sense of wonder, seeing the machine that his father told so many stories about, but never got to see realized. Even his father's tennis ball was sitting on the machine, being zapped.

Grief, of course. This was the room where his father died.

Lora was sitting down at a mostly empty desk, a short distance away from the consoles by the machine. When Visitor reached her, she said "I'd offer you coffee, but I really wouldn't recommend it. I don't drink coffee myself, but I've heard some frightening stories about what comes out of the coffee machine in this place. Most people avoid it."

Visitor said he was fine and continued to observe, staring at the purple glow.

"What's the deal with the visors? Do you ever take them off?" Lora asked.

He turned to face her. "The light in your world," he explained, "is different. It isn't brighter or whiter, but it just seems harder to see with. If I take my glasses off, it's as if I can only see silhouettes but no details in anything. A bit like someone maxed out the contrast. It hurts my eyes."

Lora held out her hand, asking if she could see them. "You can sit down, you know?" she said, pointing at a second chair.

"I much prefer to stand," Visitor replied. "Lately, I enjoy standing up a lot, if you can imagine." He handed over his glasses. "What is also strange," he continued, with his eyes tightly closed, "is that no other sunglasses seem to help. I tried a bunch of them at a store down the street on previous visits, but all they seem to do is dim the view. I still see only silhouettes and no details. And it still hurts."

Lora, after briefly trying them on, handed the glasses back to him and said, "They look like regular sunglasses to me."

Visitor put them back on and turned his head to look around the lab once again. "This is impressive," he said with a sigh to indicate he didn't really know much about what he was seeing.

"It's something…" Lora said, smiling. "Do you wear those glasses in your world?"

"No. They *are* my glasses, but I don't even have them on me most of the time, and I honestly don't even know where I last put them. Whenever I come into this world, they are on my face. My phone is like that too."

"Your phone?" Lora laughed, not knowing exactly why. "Listen," she said while getting up from her seat. "I am going to check on my experiment. I'll be back in a few minutes. Stay here and don't touch anything, I will know."

When she returned, Visitor asked if everything was alright.

"I've been looking for patterns in the signals to better predict how long it will run. I just had to make sure we're recording it correctly. For now, anything from thirty minutes up to two hours is possible. It would be nice to know in advance."

It surprised Visitor that she finally shared something about her experiment, beyond what he already knew. Lora had pointed out to him before that this project was shrouded in secrecy. Yet, here he was, sitting in her lab. She didn't seem worried about it.

"Running this thing is becoming routine, so I have time for little side projects like that. Anyway, you mentioned your phone?"

Visitor pulled out his cellphone and showed it to Lora. "No signal here," he said. "Like my sunglasses, this thing always comes with me. Earlier today, I left this phone at home, face down, on my desk. When I come into this world, the phone is in my pocket. It seems these are the only two things I can bring." He handed Lora the phone.

Lora said, "Those, and your jacket, right?"

Visitor nodded. "Oh, yeah. But not really, I—"

"Huh, I have the same phone as you," Lora said, turning his phone over in her hand. "I wonder why it doesn't work."

"It works fine at home. Here, even though the screen works, and it will run apps, take pictures and charge and all that, there's no connectivity of any kind. Not even GPS. It does something else though…"

"Hm. Follow me," Lora said. "We're in a lab, we can figure this out while I wait for The Shim to finish. And I have just the guy for this."

Visitor had more to say about the phone, but for now he just followed her. She asked around for Jarod, but it appeared he, like everyone else today, was nowhere to be found. She brought Visitor into a much smaller room packed wall-to-wall with electronic equipment. He saw soldering stations, wires, magnifying glasses and parts cabinets, along with a lot of things he didn't recognize, all organized while still looking like a giant mess.

"Our electronics lab," Lora said, "but nowadays it functions more like a repair shop for the quantum lab." There was no one else in the room. Lora opened a device that half looked like a microwave oven, tapped a few times on the phone's screen and then placed it inside.

"That's not going to fry my phone, is it?" Visitor asked, looking somewhat concerned.

"Nah, it just measures." She punched a few buttons and peered at a screen mounted off to the side. She frowned and kept adjusting. "This thing is completely dead," she said, pointing at the screen. "I should be seeing something, but it's as if your phone doesn't have a battery."

"Maybe it's in airplane mode," Visitor joked.

Lora smirked but kept her eyes on the screen, changing a few more dials and punching more buttons, but nothing changed. She took the phone out of the box and asked Visitor to unlock it and do something with it. "Run a game… anything."

"It won't retain anything I do here," Visitor said. "If I take a picture, or type a message, it's all gone when I get back home. The other way around works fine, as you know." He handed the phone back with an internet browser opened.

She placed it back in the box but found the same result. "Nothing. I can't even tell it's there."

At that moment, Jarod walked into the room. "What are you doing in my lab?"

Lora grinned and said, "Just the man I was looking for! I'm trying to figure out why this phone isn't working."

Jarod looked at her puzzled. "A phone?" He looked at Visitor and said, "Oh, hey man," to which he received no more than an almost imperceptible acknowledging nod.

"Yeah. Just curious that's all," Lora said.

"I really don't have time right now, I can take a look at it later, if you want."

"Sure, that would be great. We'll check back with you later. Thank you, Jarod."

Lora took Visitor back into the quantum lab, handing him back his phone.

A security guard opened the entrance door and for a moment Lora worried that he was letting Ian in, but it was only Randy.

"Hey Randy, I thought you had the whole day off."

Randy explained he was stuck on his schoolwork and figured he might be of more use in the lab. Lora asked him to check The

Shim. "You can collect the data from yesterday's run and prepare it for the analysts," she said. "I'll come help you when I'm done showing this visitor around." Randy looked at Visitor, slightly disappointed, but said nothing. When he was out of earshot, Lora turned back to Visitor. "The other day," she said, feeling silly, "how did you really move my fork? You really believe you have some sort of psychokinetic ability?"

Visitor seemed to appreciate the question. "When I sat at the bar," he said, "I was convinced that it was just that. Pure mind-over-matter control. Sadly, I was back in my wheelchair soon after you left, and that was it for the day. Next day, I tried it many times, but I couldn't move anything. At first, I thought maybe it only works in that restaurant, but then I remembered something. I have this habit of checking my phone for signal every time I come into this world. There never is any, so I usually just turn it off and put it back in my pocket. On that day, I was very hungry, so when I entered your dimension straight across from the restaurant, I went there without ever checking my phone. I didn't touch it until I showed you the photos."

"Universe," Lora said. "You said dimension." She was worried that she knew what was coming next but didn't feel ready for it.

"Whatever. It only works if this phone is turned on and close to me. If I turn it off or put it at more than an arm's length distance, I can stare at forks all day without them moving."

There it was. Lora threw her hands up in defeat. "Nice bit of research," she said. "Are you somehow pranking me? Who else is in on this?"

"I promise, I am not trying to be funny. I am dead serious. I am a serious guy. Once I knew, of course I tried moving all sorts of things. But my superpower, if I can call it that, turns out to be quite limited." A pen appeared out of nowhere, just above his open hand. It fell into his palm. Lora looked around to where he was looking. He had taken it, effortlessly, from a pen basket on the console behind her. "I can move small things like this," he said, handing her the pen. "For some things, even when they are small, it just won't work. Larger stuff won't budge at all. If this is a superpower, I'm afraid I will not be saving the world with it, unless I can somehow train to become better at it."

Lora slowly shook her head. "Can you move animals?"

"I don't know, I haven't seen one yet," Visitor said, looking somewhat surprised.

"I mean, can you move something that is already moving?"

"Hmm. I think you may have a point there." He paused for a moment to think, as a mischievous grin appeared on his face. "I found out the hard way that I cannot unbutton shirts or drop pants. In fact, I got escorted out of a store for staring at someone's—"

Lora rolled her eyes. "A serious guy, huh?"

Visitor bit his lip.

"Look, this is fascinating, but I can't process it. What you are doing looks very much like what our machine is doing. I see you do it, and I still don't believe it. You seem to be carrying a portable version of The Shim, with expansions, in your pocket. That is impossible."

Visitor shook his head. "I don't think my phone is a teleportation device. I am doing it with my mind, whatever it is. The phone is a prerequisite. It facilitates, somehow. Here," he said, handing over his phone. "You try it."

Lora took the phone and turned around to look at the pen basket.

Behind her, Visitor took some extra distance and said, "Just concentrate on one pen and envision where you want it to be."

After almost a whole minute of watching Lora stare intensely at the pens, one hand clenched around the phone and the other stretched out in front of her to catch the pen, Visitor began to laugh. "It only works for me. I hope that doesn't come as too much of a surprise. For me, it's as easy as breathing. I guess you'd have to be from the right dimension for this to work."

Lora didn't think any of this was funny. Sounding tired, she sighed and said, "Not dimension. Universe."

Something popped up on one of the screens on the console while a soft chime sounded. The purple glow of the beam dimmed, and the lab got noticeably quieter.

"It finished," Lora said, getting up from her chair. She felt relieved that something normal had happened.

Randy came rushing in to see the result.

"I picked pod one this time," Lora said as she grabbed the control box and pressed a button. Pod one hissed, then moved. Underneath, the target object was revealed as expected.

Randy raised his hand at her and exclaimed, "High five!"

Lora looked around to see if no one was watching, and then loudly slapped her hand on Randy's. "I think we have this all figured out now."

"Yes, we are getting pretty good at this."

"According to Dr. Shim," Lora said, smiling, "we will soon be famous."

"Awesome. I want to be played by Tom Holland in the movie!" Randy joked.

Lora laughed. "Nice. Knowing my luck, I'll be played by Amy Adams. Not a fan." She looked around the lab again and realized that there was in fact no one else watching. "Where did he go?" she asked.

Randy shrugged. "I don't know. But I don't think he belongs here," he said.

"Damnit, I still have his phone!" Lora went off to look for Visitor, but he was nowhere to be found. On her way back, she went by the electronics lab and gave the phone to Jarod, asking him to check it out if he had a chance sometime before the next run of The Shim.

"Without a trace," she said to Randy upon her return. Visitor had to be back in his own world now, as unbelievable as that whole idea still sounded. She took a deep breath and said, "Well, back to work. It's early enough that we can recalibrate this thing for the next round. Then we go home."

Chapter Nineteen

Ed was home, back in his wheelchair, contemplating his latest visit to Lora's world. He had to admit it was fun talking to the physicist, watching her slowly lose her faith when he showed her an image she could not process or told her things she had no explanation for. But he wasn't learning much about his plight. Could she really help him understand why this was happening to him? And, more importantly, could she help him out of this wheelchair more permanently?

Coming back from her world into this more familiar but bleaker reality, there wasn't much for him to do but spend the rest of the day watching TV. He certainly wasn't going for a walk now, was he? As he grabbed the remote control, he noticed his phone was missing from the desk. *That's strange. Was someone in here?* He looked around the desk, on the floor, then around the room until he suddenly remembered.

I left my phone in another dimension.

He smiled as the thought corrected itself.

Universe.

Could he still transition without the phone in his possession? This was something new to worry about, but he quickly decided he wasn't going to. He turned to the TV. There was nothing he could do about it now.

On the TV screen Ed was surprised to see images of the NMU ruins. Apparently one of the buildings had collapsed. In and of itself that should surprise no one. Those buildings had all been deteriorating over many years, as he had witnessed himself on his last visit. It was certainly not worth putting in the news. Pointing the remote, he turned up the sound.

"…say the earthquake, which to this moment has not subsided, has a magnitude of five point two on the Richter scale and is localized to just one small area on the former university campus site. The collapsed building, which has been out of use since the university closed over…"

Ed listened, while looking through his journal. Only two days had passed since the devastating events in Australia. The death toll of that catastrophe was still rising, now reaching nearly a thousand, with many more missing persons reports still pouring in from around the globe.

Meanwhile, several more castle-shaped monoliths had been discovered in England, in South America and even one in Antarctica. In contrast to the castle of Coldes Haven, the new structures had not claimed any lives, owing to their remote locations. Their towers numbered far fewer and were not circled by mysterious flying creatures. It was estimated that the enigmatic formations must all have appeared at or around the same time.

Both these disasters, Ed noticed, occurred while he wasn't present in this world, beginning on his sixteenth absence when the dragons first appeared. Was that a coincidence?

Over the next hour, dozens more earthquakes across the world were being reported. Each of a similar magnitude but varying greatly in scale. Over in Europe three city-sized areas were affected, the largest in Poland, and two smaller but more powerful ones in Germany and on the French-Belgian border. Many smaller earthquakes, some barely larger than the footprint of a single house, were also found throughout Europe, from Scandinavia down to Iberia. The news quickly expanded to the rest of the world. The biggest earthquake found so far, located on the Arabian Peninsula, covered an area the size of Luxembourg in Saudi Arabia, near and slightly across the border with Qatar and was shaking the ground with a magnitude of six point one. According to experts the area is known to have one of the lowest incidence rates for earthquakes in the world, making this event seem like an impossibility. Thankfully, the area was sparsely populated, unlike those in Europe where casualties were expected but not confirmed yet.

"…well over an hour, making any one of these the longest lasting earthquakes ever recorded. With mostly moderate magnitudes, it is especially the long duration that is causing damage. For comparison, the longest recorded earthquake in history until now, lasted only just about ten minutes…"

It never seemed to stop. More quakes were confirmed in Russia, across the American continent and throughout Asia. *The whole god-damned world is coming apart.*

Usually, watching the news didn't affect Ed much. It was all too far away, concerning only people he didn't know. But now he couldn't help but think about his family. He thought about

Australia. He thought about Brock. The immense sadness that so many families would experience after the losses they suffered today filled his heart with empathy for countless strangers and the sorrow he shared with them. Random lives were being ruined today, again, and it pained him to think about it.

He turned off the TV and absorbed the silence in the room for a few minutes before he went to make himself a cup of coffee. Too many things were happening that all felt unnatural – impossible even – beginning with his own excursions into an alternative reality. Somehow, Ed felt, these things must be connected. There must be an explanation for all of this. On his next visit, he should focus on getting some answers from the scientist. With everything that he had shown her, he reckoned she should at least be curious now.

Chapter Twenty

ONE OF THE SECURITY GUARDS opened the lab door and called Lora's name. "There's a man at the door who insists he needs to speak with you," the guard said, when she came over.

Even though there were only two security guards in the building, their faces were different every day, and Lora had no idea who this one was. *They must rotate through forty of them.* She followed the guard into the foyer, where she saw Visitor waiting outside.

"Do you know if Ian is in today?" she asked the guard.

"Haven't seen him yet. I think he is supposed to be over at B-Site again, but that might have been yesterday."

Good. "You can let him in."

"You need to sign him in. I think you forgot that last time as well." The guard handed her a clipboard and a pen.

"He's um…" Lora said, thinking how she could get away with not knowing the name of her guest. "He's an anonymous sponsor, so I can't put specifics. In fact, I think he'd prefer if I didn't sign him in at all." She handed back the clipboard.

The guard scratched his head and looked outside at the man in the red suit. "I have to put something," he said. He shrugged and wrote, "visitor". "Let him in," he said to the other guard.

Lora quickly led Visitor to the same desk in the quantum lab as before. She took an office chair and directed her guest to another. As before, he didn't take the seat.

"I seem to have misplaced my phone yesterday," Visitor said.

"Oh, yes! Let me go get it, I left it with Jarod."

Just then, Gary walked by, carrying a stack of papers.

"Gary!" Lora said, exaggerating her excitement to see him. "Could you spare a few minutes to entertain this man for me, while I go find Jarod? He's a visitor." She didn't give Gary time to respond and quickly walked away, toward the electronics lab.

"Gary. Gary Sutherland. How are you doing?" said Gary, extending his hand to Visitor, who did not immediately reciprocate the gesture. "Suit yourself," Gary mumbled as he retracted from the handshake attempt and sat down in Lora's seat.

He looked the stranger over. He found him looking out of place, and oddly dressed. The man in red had grabbed on to the back of a chair, as if he needed to support himself, and appeared sickly to Gary. Very pale.

"So, to what do we owe the pleasure of your visit?" Gary asked, wondering if this man was even capable of speech.

Visitor, very quietly, said, "My dad…" He suddenly breathed in loudly and then tried again to speak, but still managed no more than a whisper. "My father was also…"

Gary now had a concerned look on his face. To him, it sounded like his present company was about to break down crying. The sunglasses made it hard to be certain. "Are you feeling alright? Do you need a drink of water or something?"

Visitor nodded and whispered, "Yes, water, thank you." He watched as Gary got up and left to fetch him something to drink. He had to sit down.

Since he first set foot in this place, Visitor had gone through an entire spectrum of feelings, most of which he had anticipated, and could largely be ascribed to nostalgia and grief. But now there was a whole new, unexpectedly intense rush of emotions when he just saw his long dead father alive and well, standing right in front of him, offering his hand. The man, who was now getting him a cup of water, looked, and talked exactly as he remembered him. Just older. Gary Sutherland was his father. But here, in this strange world, he apparently was not. Gary didn't seem to recognize him even a little.

Gary returned and sat back down, rolling his chair closer and handing Visitor his drink.

"What is your name, son?" Gary asked.

The man in the red jacket suddenly lost control and broke down. He *was* crying! Gary shook his head and wished he were somewhere else. This wasn't his thing. The visitor removed his sunglasses and placed them in his lap. Eyes closed and tears streaming, he covered his face with his free hand. His shoulders shook irregularly, causing him to spill some of the water from his cup. Gary got up from his seat and looked around for help, but there was no one close by. What sort of a mess had Lora left him with now? He debated internally if he could leave the man by himself, or if he had to find some way of comforting him. He gently patted the man on one of his shoulders, not knowing what to say. Could he say something traditional, like "there, there now"?

Thankfully, after another minute of this awkwardness, the visitor replaced his sunglasses, got up from his seat, and said with a broken voice, "Excuse me, I… I need to see a restroom."

Gary took the water cup from him and was relieved to see him go. He made a mental note never to babysit any guests of Lora's again.

Moments later, Lora was back and asked, "Where did he go? Is he still here?"

"He's using the bathroom," Gary said, collecting his papers. "Who is that anyway? What's he doing here? He doesn't seem to belong here."

Lora just said, "He's a visitor. Thank you, Gary."

Gary took his leave. He had no time for this.

It took some time for Visitor to return and rejoin Lora at the desk. "The bathrooms turned out nice," he said.

Lora was confused. He looked different, she thought. "Is everything okay?"

The only response was a nod. Visitor seemed a little out of it, but Lora didn't want to pursue it further. "Jarod has your phone," she said, "but I couldn't find him. I left him a message for when he returns."

Another nod and some more silence followed. Finally, Visitor asked "Gary… has he been here long?"

"Yeah, you could say that. He's the only veteran among us. He worked with Dr. Shim almost from the very start of his project. Together they were the driving forces behind the development of The Shim."

"Hmm. I thought they all left after Dr. Shim retired."

Lora nodded. "That's right, but Gary came back right away, probably at the request of Dr. Shim. He was old enough to retire along with the doctor, but I guess he just can't get enough of this place."

"He seems nice."

"Yeah, he is one of the good guys, once you get used to him," Lora said, with a smirk. "He and Dr. Shim are close friends. Together, they helped me get this project on the road. Gary helped me a lot in getting the expansions designed and built, and the doctor with battling for funding and acquiring custom made parts. So, in effect, I had two old guys watching over me all this time." Meanwhile Lora had moved to one of the consoles and was poring over its screens.

"And um… That tennis ball under the purple beam right now, that's Gary's?" Visitor asked.

Lora looked up at him with raised eyebrows. "Did Gary tell you about that? That's not normally something he tells strangers."

There was another long pause, as Visitor tried to decide what answer was closest to the truth. He clearly remembered Gary – his father – telling him a long time ago how he had placed the tennis ball on the plateau. It had been very funny to him. But today, Gary – not his father – hadn't said a word about it. To answer Lora, Visitor settled on another question. "Why did he put it there?"

"Ah. So, you don't know *that*, do you?" Lora seemed pleased with that. "Okay. I don't know if any of this is true," she said, "but the story is, that there was once a meeting near the beginning of the project, long before my time here. Gary was there, and Dr. Shim and a bunch of other people, most of whom I've never met. At that stage, when a lot of the work was predominantly theoretical, they had mathematicians on the team. Quite a few of them in fact, all present at the meeting. One of them, allegedly, joked that, ideally, a target object should be selected that was perfectly spherical, because otherwise the physicists in the room couldn't do the math." Lora rolled her eyes as she said this. "The next day,

Gary brought that tennis ball to the lab. To everyone's amusement, he placed it, with great ceremony, on the plateau that was already built then, years in advance of the arrival of the machine."

Visitor grinned slightly. He remembered his father telling him about the importance of spheres in physics calculations, although he failed to understand the joke that was undoubtedly in there.

"From then on," Lora continued, "the ball became a symbol. Everyone involved in the project was aware that the tennis ball was set to become the first ever object to be teleported with this machine. Moving it in any other way prior to that moment would bring bad luck. Throughout construction, it remained on the plateau precisely where Gary put it that first day. Even when workers were standing on the plateau, installing parts of the machine, they took care never to touch the ball. One contractor went as far as to mount a metal box over the ball to protect it. It all started out in good fun, but when The Shim finally became operational, a great deal of superstition surrounded that thing, still sitting under the box. It remained untouched, never used in any experiment, all through Dr. Shim's project, and even throughout two-thirds of mine. We used it for the first time at the beginning of Phase-C, which is the current and final phase of my project, and the last to be run on this setup."

Visitor seemed to have regained some of his normal color and was more alert now.

Lora's eyes scanned the screens on the console one more time. Everything looked normal. A smile appeared on her face as an amusing idea occurred to her. "Isn't it interesting, that you can leave your phone behind but not stay here yourself?" She sounded pleased, as if she had just uncovered a hole in his story. "It also makes you wonder what else you could put in those pockets to bring home to your world."

"Yeah, I tried that. I can't take anything home. Not even pictures on my phone. Just the phone and the glasses."

"And that jacket," Lora added.

"Oh, yeah. But not really. I have never owned a jacket like this. It only exists here." Visitor looked around, as if to make sure no one else was listening, and then said, "So, I overheard something in the bathroom earlier. It was about your project."

Lora laughed. "This is very much the only thing anyone talks about around here. Who was it?"

"Not sure. One Jim, who seemed familiar to me, and one Ian, who I really don't know."

"Ian is in the building now? Interesting. He wasn't here when you arrived, according to the guards anyway. Basically, he's the boss in this building. If he sees you in here, he'll throw a tantrum and have me escort you out. Lately, I don't see him around here much. He's always over at B-Site overseeing preparations for the relocation of The Shim. Oh, and Jim is probably Jim Ferguson, the investor who is funding my project. My guess is they are meeting about that," said Lora.

"Relocation? I heard them mention that, actually."

"Yeah. When we wrap up this project, they're moving The Shim from this lab back to B-Site."

At this point Jarod joined them, carrying a cup and a phone. "Hey man," he said to the stranger in the red suit, who nodded. He turned to Lora. "Sorry to interrupt. I heard you were looking for me. I was already coming to see you, but I went to Delaney's first, because I couldn't show up without… your tea, boss." He handed over the cup with an exaggerated gesture of courtesy. Lora smiled and thanked him. Jarod continued. "So, I looked at that phone of yours."

Visitor stuck out his hand to take it. "That's my phone."

Jarod said, "Hold on a sec."

Visitor was impatient, but Lora, sipping calmly on her tea, said, "Go on."

"It was interesting. This was the quietest phone I've ever seen," he said. Lora nodded. "So, I opened her up and—"

"You what?" Visitor interrupted him sharply.

"Dude! Calm down, man. I got this," Jarod said, putting his hands up in a defensive position. He took a theatrical breath and started again. "As I was saying, I took a peek inside this thing and couldn't really find anything wrong with it. Luckily, we have a bunch of phones laying around the lab for parts and experimenting, and I found another one of these, so I just swapped out the antenna hardware. Just to see what would happen, you know?"

Visitor looked stressed, but Jarod didn't let him speak.

"Long story short, it works fine now. Don't ask me why. It looks like a normal phone from where I stand. I couldn't really test much, because it's locked, but it has signal." He handed the phone to Visitor and added, "You're welcome."

Lora said, "Thank you, Jarod. But just in case… do you still have the original parts?"

"Sure. You want them?"

"Yeah. Just bag them up and let me know where to find them."

Jarod confirmed and left Lora and Visitor alone again.

"I have a few bars. Can I call your number to see if it works?" Visitor asked.

Lora opened a drawer underneath the console table. She put her tea down and rummaged through the drawer until she found a menu for a pizza place. She handed it to Visitor, who smirked in response.

Apparently, this was not a good way to get someone's number in this universe, he thought. He dialed the number and hung up as soon as he heard a voice. "That works, but I hope it didn't interfere with the mind control thing." Visitor stared hard at Lora's teacup sitting on the console edge. Instantly, it shimmered out of existence and reappeared, without the tea, on the floor below the desk.

He sighed with relief and said, "Thank god, it still works," while Lora, ejecting herself out of her seat in a panic, yelled, "Jesus Christ!" The hot tea splashed all over one side of the console, just missing her legs. Some of the lights under the console buttons dimmed, flickered, and then turned off entirely. There was a faint burning smell coming from the panel, and error messages began to appear on the screens. "Jesus!" she yelled again.

Lora ran to the emergency stop button on the other console. When she slammed it, the purple glow of the beam disappeared from the room instantly. Along with it, Visitor also vanished, and this time she saw it happen. Her knees wobbled. She had to grab on to one of the office chairs to steady herself. She sat down. What did she just witness? *Visitor is only here while The Shim is running!* He had disappeared instantly, without any transition. *Nothing like a ninja.*

Chapter Twenty-One

NEIL WAS RINSING GLASSES after a few bar regulars had just left the restaurant. Delaney's relied on regulars, and on university students and workers. Tourists, even during the busy season, didn't venture into the university district as much as they did downtown, so they could not be counted on. He stared out the window across the street and noticed Dart, the local superhero, walk the sidewalk by the apartment buildings. Neil smiled, because even though Dart was no longer welcome at Delaney's for a variety of reasons, he appreciated what the strange green man had done for the people in this city. When he saw what happened next though, he almost dropped his glass.

Dart wasn't having a great day. A few minutes ago, he passed a toy store. In the window was another one of those cursed Dartman branded action figures. Maybe, at one point it had been funny that people called him Dartman, but the joke had worn very thin and at some point, it was time that people learnt that. It's not as if the name Dart was harder to remember than Dartman, was it? When he went into the store to ask them to remove the toy, he didn't find there to be a lot of understanding for his plight. The salesperson explained to him that they wouldn't normally sell them at all, because demand was surprisingly low. Someone had bought this specimen in one of their larger stores downtown.

"But the kid," the toy store worker said, "didn't want it. They returned it here and got one of *these* instead." She picked up a box and handed it to Dart.

"Fortnite Legendary Series Brawlers Meowscles," he read out loud, making a face as if he was trying to read a foreign language. "What even is that?" He handed it back. The enthusiasm of the store worker grew visibly. "Don't answer that," Dart said just in time to stop her from starting a long monologue about the character and the features of the toy. Or so he thought.

"Did you know," the girl offered, "that Calico cats in real life are almost never male? It has to do with their genes." She was right. In fact, the Tri-Color appearance of these cats, on which the character is based, relies heavily on the presence of female chromosomes. "Yet Meowscles is male, and so is his son, Kit." That last bit is significant, because even though a rare genetic mutation might produce the odd male Calico cat, it would inevitably be infertile. It makes the existence of Kit a bit of a mystery. But this was exactly the kind of information that Dart was not looking for.

"The Dartman toy cannot be sold in stores," Dart said.

"Tell me about it! I personally haven't had any luck with them. I never even sold a single one, to be perfectly honest with you."

Dart was getting tired and angry. He asked, "How much is it?"

"Excellent choice mister, you will not be disappointed! That'll be sixty-three dollars, altogether."

Dart raised his eyebrows. "Are you kidding me?"

"It's a bit of a collector's item nowadays. Officially you can't even get these anymore."

Dart left the store with the toy, feeling robbed, and as soon as he was outside, he took the ridiculously muscular green action figure out of its offending packaging and threw the box in the nearest garbage can. He walked briskly, wanting to get away from the store.

As he neared the university district, he slowed down and regained some of his composure.

"Oh, crap! It's Dartman!" said a man who seemed to be in a big hurry, running straight at him.

Dart wasn't even going to try with this guy. He made a fist and swung it at the man's face as he passed him. The man made a half turn and went straight to the ground. Dart looked at his action figure and nodded at it. "The name is Dart," he said as he stepped over the man and started walking again.

Neil emerged from Delaney's and came running across the street. Others were rushing in from all directions. At first Dart thought that they were coming to the rescue of the man on the ground, but most of them were headed for him instead.

Someone shouted, "Well done!"

There was some cheering.

A woman reached him first and, half out of breath, said, "You got him! Thank you! I thought for sure he was gone."

Dart had no idea what she was talking about, but he wasn't one to dismiss gratitude. He felt there was often a shortage of that. "It's what I do," he said.

As the woman seemed to think this over, others were now joining her around him. Neil was there too. He was one of the few who witnessed the incident from across the street.

"Dart, my good man, I think you just prevented a thief from getting away with his ill-gotten gains," he said, laughing. He pointed behind him at the man on the ground, who now also had a few people gathered around him. They were extracting some small items from his pockets.

Another man joined the group around Dart, and this one he recognized as well, although he couldn't remember his name.

"Hey Dart," the man said. It was the owner of Pawn Pros, a pawn shop just around the corner from here. Dart knew this because that was where he had purchased his costume, many years ago. "When he came into the store, he said he was just looking around, but I caught him pocketing a few things. He made a run for it, and I went after him, and so did she," the pawn pro said, pointing at the woman who had talked to Dart first, "but he was too fast for both of us."

"Dartman! That was awesome!" a young fellow shouted at him from behind where the thief was still laying on the sidewalk. "He's out cold!"

Dart flinched and whipped around. "Dart!" he shouted. He knew he shouldn't be doing this. This was not a good time or place, with so many good people around.

"Dartman!" The young man shouted back. Apparently, he thought he was being funny.

Dart catapulted forward and grabbed him, probably a student from one of the apartments, by his throat.

"Try that again," he said, hissing at his face.

"Dartman?"

Dart pushed the boy away and screamed, stomping his feet in anger. He had to get out of here before he made a fool of himself. He ran across the street, barely avoiding a passing car, and quickly disappeared into Delaney's restaurant.

Neil called after him. "Dart! No, please!"

Seconds later, sounds of shattering glass, accompanied by more of Dart's frustrated screams, emanated from the building.

"Not again!" exclaimed Neil, now running across the street.

Chapter Twenty-Two

Lora put her phone, and then her elbows, down on her desk and rubbed her temples with both hands. She just came off the phone with Jarod, who was leading the repair efforts on The Shim in the lab. The incident with the tea had done damage to the console, and the resulting malfunctions had propagated all the way into the coherence pods. Jarod assured her everything was on schedule to get her back up and running in just a few days. She worried nevertheless, because the longer the break in experiments, the bigger the risk she could lose her chance at finishing them.

When he found out about the tea spill, Ian was fuming. "It is beyond me why you thought it was alright to have a hot drink sitting on a console table. You do realize we have rules for a reason, I hope? As the lab leader, it is your responsibility to enforce them, not break them!" He warned her that things like this made it difficult for him to defend her position at the lab to the investors.

Lora thought her project had ended then and there. But surprisingly, without even having to defend herself beyond an apology, Ian then quickly turned around, saying that she was vital to the success of the project and that he needed her to continue the otherwise excellent job she was doing. Somehow, Lora got away scot-free, and with what could be mistaken for a compliment. Of course, she never told Ian about Visitor's role in all this. As far as she could tell, Ian was not aware that Visitor was ever in the lab, or that he even existed. On her way out of his office, Ian had told her that she would need to make up for the delay caused by the repairs, because the project deadline could not be changed.

Ian had always been clear about the deadline he set for her. After the upcoming convention, the machine was set to be dismantled and then moved to another location. She had argued that moving the machine might make the current success of Phase-C unreproducible, as it depended on the position and nature of the target object. But she knew that her specific interests weren't shared by those who decided on this matter. They weren't concerned with what happened in other universes. They were instead preoccupied with where their money went in this one.

When Dr. Shim proposed his first machine, the university, with the help of investors, had acquired an off-campus manufacturing hall for the sole purpose of building equipment for the NMU labs. The machine was built at B-Site, as the otherwise unnamed location was most often referred to, but never made it into the quantum physics lab. Initial tests at B-Site had failed, and when Dr. Shim abruptly moved on to his next idea, the machine was simply abandoned, serving only as source of inspiration while building The Shim.

The first part of The Shim to be built there was the plateau. It was designed to be permanent. It was firmly attached, stable and solid. To move it would be bordering on the impossible. For that reason, while the machine was in development, a duplicate of the plateau was constructed in NMU's quantum physics lab. When initial tests at B-Site began to show promising results, The Shim was moved to the lab to sit over this second plateau.

Even though B-Site had been around for such a long time, all activity there predated Lora's career. As a result, she had only seen it a few times, with nothing going on there. While Dr. Shim was running his experiment at the lab, B-Site had fallen into disuse. No significant equipment was being developed for the lab anymore. Over the years, much of the building's inventory, primarily consisting of specialized machines and manufacturing tools, had been sold off. The doctor's first machine, and the original plateau remained behind, almost like museum pieces, in an otherwise practically empty hall. At the start of Lora's project, B-Site was just about to be revived as the future location for the officially selected follow-up project. Her expansions, for that reason, had been built entirely at the NMU location.

Soon, The Shim was going to be returned to B-Site, where it would sit over its original plateau. A whole new lab was going to be built up around it. There, the follow-up project, run with an all-new team, would focus entirely on performance improvements. The goal was to increase the machine's speed, reduce its energy consumption and, if possible, take a first step toward miniaturization of the technology. Most likely, by the end of it, the machine, or its design, would be sold. It was a decidedly nonscientific endeavor, in Lora's opinion. Her intention was to be involved in no more than an advisory capacity.

Lora's thoughts shifted to Visitor. Nothing about him made sense. Since she met Dr. Shim, thinking about the concept of the multiverse as a convenient way to understand his theories and the mechanism by which The Shim operated, had become second nature to her. But there was never any substance to those other worlds, or a need to treat them as more than a visualization aid.

Visitor didn't start showing up until Phase-C started, which was when The Slicer was first introduced. If Visitor really was a traveler from another universe, literally, brought here by some side-effect of The Shim, The Slicer must be targeting a slice so narrow, it was effectively just a single other universe. During tests, no one had succeeded in programming The Slicer to a narrow enough slice to even confirm that it worked as expected. And now, Lora had achieved this incredibly perfect result, based on only her simulations, that was beyond the specification of the machine? Even if it was possible through some unlikely stroke of luck, it shouldn't be repeatable like it had been. What if all her results were an effect of an unknown malfunction in the device? Was she relying on some unexplained phenomenon, essentially magic, for her research? Was it all just a fluke?

Visitor's universe contained the Everett building, she knew that much. *It's impossible to know that, but he showed me!* The accident that ruined the building there, occurred during construction on the building itself, which happened mostly after the plateau was already built. And Visitor had mentioned the tennis ball, so that existed there too. What if the target object existed on that unfinished plateau, the same as it did here? Maybe that environment was somehow found by the beam. But where did Visitor himself fit into all of this? How did The Shim open a portal just for him? And why *him*, and not someone else? Regardless, Lora was convinced Visitor's days of traveling to this world were numbered. When the machine was relocated, or more specifically, the target object was moved or switched out, she realized, she would never see him again.

E D SPENT HIS TIME alternating between frustrated and angry. His carelessness on his last visit had clearly damaged the machine that allowed him to walk, and he was furious with himself. The first couple of days he spent most of his time lying in bed, sulking. They were long days, interrupted only twice by the doorbell ringing and the subsequent difficulties in answering it.

Emily, his foster mother, dropped by because, she complained, she couldn't get him on the phone. She was bringing him more bad news about his family. His original family this time. One of his natural aunts, who had moved to Europe a long time ago, years before the accident in the lab, had died as a result of a building collapse caused by one of the smaller earthquakes over there. Ed didn't really know her, but it was strange to hear about another family member who died as a direct consequence of these incredibly strange phenomena of late.

Hearing about his aunt, and his recent encounter with his father's counterpart in Lora's world, brought Ed to thinking about his family. Not long before the accident, his father, Gary, who Ed suspected might have been a tad tipsy that evening, had told him that he figured Ed had saved his mother's life by merely existing. At first, Ed didn't know what that meant. Later he found out that, about a year before Ed was born, his mother had attempted suicide by taking pills. His father had found her, and she was rushed to the hospital. It took several days before she recovered from her coma. The doctors had told his father that she was very lucky to have survived. If she had taken any more of those pills, they claimed, she would have surely succeeded in her attempt to end it all.

"I flushed two of those damned pills down the toilet the night before," his father told him. "She survived. And because of that, we now have you. When you came along, something happened to your mom. She changed in the best way possible. If it wasn't for you, son, she would have tried it again, I am sure of it." Ed was too young to fully grasp what he was hearing, but even after all these years, he remembered the conversation word-for-word.

Soon after Emily's visit, one of Ed's neighbors came to check on him. The news he brought wasn't any better. Two people in the neighborhood had been confirmed dead in Australia, and a third, who Ed knew as the guy with the spray tan and the overly whitened teeth, was still missing. His guest knew that the death toll in Australia had almost doubled from what Ed had last heard, as more bodies were found in, and recovered from, more remote locations away from the city. A similar pattern was true for the earthquakes. The combined number of confirmed deaths was now in the thousands, while many more were still missing.

Ed spent a lot of time, mostly in his bed, leafing through his notes and thinking about everything that had happened so far. One of the things he couldn't let go, was what he had learned when he went to the bathroom after meeting Gary in Lora's lab. He had intended to quickly clean himself up and go back to talk to the man who didn't know he had a son in an alternate reality. But when he got in there and found himself alone, he broke down again and had difficulties getting his sobbing under control. It wasn't long though, before he heard voices and footsteps approaching. In order not to be seen in the state he was in, he had to hide himself in one of the stalls.

Two men entered the room and took their positions at the urinals. He didn't recognize their voices, although one of them sounded vaguely familiar.

"I'm just saying… that woman is phenomenal. Shim did you a real solid with that one. I mean, I was optimistic from the start, don't get me wrong, but we've already got three good ones on runs sixteen, nineteen and twenty-one. I mean… holy shit, Ian! I thought we would need fifty or more before we even got it working, but now we only need two more! Two more and we are done! Whatever she did with that machine, it is unbelievable. It's accurate to a tee," said the somewhat familiar voice.

Ian responded in a more tempered manner. "I know, I underestimated her, but luckily Dr. Shim was persuasive. She'll get the job done well before the convention, with plenty enough runs for us."

"It's perfect! She's going to make us a fortune."

"I still think we could cut her in," replied Ian. "She deserves to be a part of this. I mean, she created this."

"No! She's just not the type. She won't understand. Same as Shim, he will throw a fit!"

"How do you figure that? I think most people would be quite susceptible to this kind of opportunity."

Both men seemed to magically finish the voiding of their bladders simultaneously, zipped up and moved to the wash bins.

"We stick to the plan, Ian. We keep it limited to five runs and just you and me. If something like this comes along again, we'll reconsider the ethics. Buy her flowers if it makes you feel better."

Ian laughed. "This will never happen again. Not in a billion years, I think. Whether she's a genius or just lucky, I think we can all agree this will be inimitable. Too many things must be just perfect, and we don't even know what all those things are. When we relocate The Shim, it's all over. And I for one, think that's not a bad thing. There will not be a trace left behind of what we're doing. I think, the sooner we get this over with, the better."

The men each took some paper towels from a dispenser, while Ian continued. "The other investors are breathing down my neck, pushing me to kill this project and move on with the relocation. Preparations at B-Site are well on their way. At *their* expense, I might add. It's been quite challenging to explain to them how this project is being funded when none of them are doing it. Though I wouldn't be surprised if some of them suspect it is you."

"What are you worried about other investors for?" Jim asked. "I am funding this until it is over, and then you'll never need to set foot in this place again. There is nothing for you to worry about. You just keep your girl doing her job and it's a smooth ride into retirement."

"Unlike you, Jim, I care a lot about this place. If I am going to abandon it, I want to leave it in the best state it can be in. I want it to continue to thrive. I do that by pleasing the investors. This lab needs to move on from The Shim and pick up something new."

As they walked out the door, Jim said, laughing, "If you love this place so much, maybe you can just buy it. Buy it all."

Replaying the conversation in his head, Ed thought about the connection between Lora's experiment and his transitions into the other world. These two men were apparently in control of how long she would be allowed to run it. Jim Ferguson and Ian, whose last name Ed didn't know, had suggested that he might have as little as two visits left. There could be more, but there was no way of knowing on what circumstance it depended. Two walks before going back to permanent disability. The thought was unbearable.

Runs sixteen, nineteen and twenty-one. Ed looked through his journal again. There were twenty-one entries for as many visits so far. He looked at the date for his sixteenth visit, but he already knew what he would find. That was the day of the dragons. The pattern emerged immediately. Whatever Ian and Jim were doing, it was causing chaos in Ed's world. Australia on run nineteen and permanent earthquakes on run twenty-one. Why were they doing this? Were they out to destroy his universe? Whatever the reason was, they were doing something behind Lora's back, and it was jeopardizing both the continuation of her project and the sanity of Ed's world. It was killing a lot of people, not the least of whom were his foster father and now his aunt and two neighbors.

Jim Ferguson turned out to be easy to find online and when Ed found a photo of the man, he recognized the face, but he still couldn't remember exactly where he had seen him before. It must have been a long time ago. Apparently, Jim was one of the first investors attracted by the partially privatized quantum lab at NMU, predating The Shim by a few years. There were few details about the nature of these investments, but there was contact information, so Ed sent off an email. Maybe the version of Jim Ferguson that lived in his universe might answer some questions to help understand what might be going on between Jim and Ian in Lora's world.

Dear Mr. Ferguson,

My name is Ed Sutherland. I believe you to be familiar with my father, Gary Sutherland. He and Dr. David Shim were involved with the development of a machine for the quantum lab at NMU when the unfortunate construction accident ended both of their lives. My mother didn't live long past this incident, so I grew up

without either of my parents. Recently I have found myself looking into my own roots and I was hoping that you might speak to
me about my father.

As a result of the aforementioned accident, I am confined to a
wheelchair. Traveling is inconvenient for me, so I am proposing a
video call instead of an in-person meeting.

Awaiting your reply,
Best Regards,

Ed Sutherland.

Before sending the message, Ed attached an invitation with a
link for a video call. He had to omit including his phone number,
because, after his foster mother had pointed it out to him that he
couldn't be reached, he found that the phone no longer worked to
make phone calls. Whatever it was doing was certainly interesting,
if not frightening, but Jarod's modifications were not letting Ed
use the phone in any normal sense.

Next, Ed searched online for Ian's name in relation to the physics department of NMU. It didn't yield him any results. It was of
no help that he didn't know Ian's last name. Hopefully, Jim would
be able to clear that up for him.

Chapter Twenty-Three

"Ed? Is that really you? You're Gary's boy?" Jim had accepted
the invitation for the video call and was now talking to Ed
from the screen of his laptop.

"In the flesh," Ed replied.

"Man! I always wondered what became of you. I mean… Gary
and I didn't get along, but what happened to him… to all of them,
I have no words. My god. And your mom! What a terrible shame!
And you, in a wheelchair, I can't even imagine…"

Ed acknowledged that it was all terrible but didn't want to
spend much time talking about himself or the accident. He came
straight to the point. "As I've alluded to in my email, I have been
looking around for information about my father. I ended up in
another city, and whatever my parents left behind was lost to me.
For example, I don't know much about what my father was doing
at NMU before the accident."

"Ah. Well, you came to the right person. What everyone seems to have forgotten, is that the documentation for David Shim's projects, including anything Gary contributed, is still archived at B-Site. The printed material at least. I am not sure what happened to all the digital stuff, as most of that was located at the university."

Ed recognized the name, B-Site. Apparently, it existed in both universes. "At the risk of sounding ignorant, what's B-Site?"

"Yeah, that was before your time, I suppose. NMU bought this manufacturing plant, on the industrial park off highway six, with some help of external investors, for the purpose of building stuff for the lab. This was early on, in the history of the lab. It's where they built and tested Project E, and then later wasted their time on trying to build that damned teleportation contraption that David had concocted."

Jim obviously overestimated how much Ed already knew. "I was only eleven when the accident happened, so I'm not up to speed. I think, now that you mention it, I do remember dad sometimes going to this other place. Didn't know what it was called."

"Technically, it wasn't called anything. That's why we're still calling it B-Site." Jim paused for a second. "You know, Ed, I was at your house a few times when you were still a little boy. I can imagine you might not have the most pleasant memories of those visits. I apologize."

"I do not remember that. But maybe that's how you came to look familiar to me. What happened?"

"Gary and I didn't see eye-to-eye. He was in cahoots with David Shim. Ugh… where do I start? Do you know anything about what Shim was doing?"

"I know he was building a teleportation machine, as you mentioned. I think it was named The Shim."

Jim laughed loudly. "Not officially, it wasn't! I knew it mostly as Project T, but yeah, some people had started calling it The Shim. I'm sure David got off on that. So, you don't know about Project E, then?"

Ed confirmed that he didn't.

"David Shim had two ideas in his life. A good one, which was Project E and a boring one, which was Project T, or The Shim if you prefer. Mind you, for David it was all about science at first. He talked about the multiverse and superpositions and who knows what else. Back then I didn't understand most of it, I was just interested in the results. This man had an idea so grand, that I was willing to invest into its realization at scale. I worked with Shim and the university to round up a few others. We had no problem there because what he proposed to build was very easy to sell. He was pretty good at selling it himself."

Ed interrupted him. "So, now you're talking about Project E, not The Shim?"

"Yeah. I wanted nothing to do with The Shim when it came up. I'm not saying The Shim was all bad. It was a teleportation device after all. I mean, come on, people want to see that happen. But to abandon Project E in favor of The Shim, was the dumbest thing I've ever seen." Jim looked behind him, suddenly got up from his chair and walked out of view. Ed had to wait a few minutes before he returned, which gave him time to catch up with his notes. When he came back, Jim said, "Sorry, Ed, someone was at the door."

Ed was relieved to see him back in his chair. "So… what was Project E?"

Jim grinned. "I don't get to talk about this stuff much anymore. It's like the whole world has forgotten about it. People always think I'm making shit up when I mention it. Project E was a machine that could teleport objects, not just on a fancy table, like The Shim, but from anywhere. Anywhere! The machine consisted of a chamber, about the size of a decent fridge, but shaped somewhat like a jet engine. You program it to find specific objects and bring them into that chamber. It's more complicated than that, but that's the gist of it. It finds them, as David Shim put it, in the multiverse, however you want to interpret that. He liked to say, and I'm paraphrasing, that if it's possible for something to exist in that chamber, somewhere in the multiverse it will already be there. Project E would find it and teleport it into our universe. But the better way to sell it, without all the mumbo-jumbo, is to describe the practical effect. It's an anything-synthesizer! A make-a-wish machine! You tell the thing to get you a chair, and it produces a chair. Any chair. Want a pair of unmatched shoes or a chocolate bar? You got it! Anything you can think of."

Ed sat back and thought about this. "Hang on, isn't that asking for an economic disaster? I mean, how would you sell chairs if you could just wish one into existence? Why would you make any chairs anymore? Or anything else?"

Jim nodded enthusiastically. "Right you are. But, think about it, Ed! If everyone has access to one of these machines, then what does it matter? It levels the playing field. Everyone can just have everything they need. And more! A lot of labor becomes unnecessary. Environmental impact from production is eliminated. Even money itself would become pointless if it worked well enough. If that doesn't make the world a better place, I don't know what does!"

"But where does all that stuff come from? Surely, you can't just make something out of nothing, can you?"

"You're right, Ed, you can't. It's more of an exchange, really. The machine consumes whatever you put in the chamber to begin with. But that can just be air, so no big deal. And it uses a lot of energy."

"Are you serious? Is that even possible?"

"David sure thought it was! And I believed him! I believed *in* him. Like I said, Project E was built, at B-Site. But when they started testing, it was a mess. Honestly, it just didn't work. The most we ever saw in that chamber were clouds of disassociated molecules, which Shim assured me were coming from all over the multiverse. There never was a solid object. Nothing even recognizable as whatever we programmed the target object to be. So, is it possible? Maybe not. But they gave up on it way too early. I am convinced that higher powers were pushing back on it as well, using that economic argument you just brought up. There was a lot going on over our heads."

Ed was amazed. "They built and ran Project E? I don't remember my father ever mentioning anything like it. He only talked about teleportation, with a tennis ball."

"That's right. Your father wasn't involved in Project E at all, that was just Shim and a bunch of other scientists. Gary came in when Project E was already failing, and Shim was already giving up on it. At that point Shim began to have the idea for the teleportation device. Gary came in to help him develop that idea."

"So, my father and Dr. Shim invented The Shim together?"

"Ha-ha, no. Shim had the idea, Gary was brought in to help him realize it. Due to the lack of results on Project E, some investors were getting cold feet. Shim didn't help the situation by openly doubting his own work in front of them. I assume he was being pressured into doing so. Then, when he and Gary presented their proposal for The Shim, it was much better argued than Project E ever was. They showed experimental results and a crapload of math, that suggested that the machine had a real chance of success from the get-go. Not to mention the commercial opportunities it promised. Shim had no issues selling it, just like he had done with Project E. Soon enough, the majority of the remaining investors, including new ones waiting to get in on the action, started pushing the university to abandon Project E and switch over to Project T. When they did, activity for Project E came to a grinding halt. Before I knew it, every scientist and every engineer who worked on it vanished into thin air. An entirely new team appeared that was allocated exclusively to The Shim. I was the only one left who cared about Project E. I still can't wrap my mind around it. I fought for Project E all the way until the accident in the lab. That ended everything." Jim looked away from the camera and his mood seemed to have gone down. "God-damned scientists," he said. "They were given a chance to make a real difference in the world."

Ed was taking notes and needed a moment to catch up. He looked for a lighter question to ask. "You mentioned you didn't get along with my father…"

"Yeah. Gary was completely on Shim's side. When he came in, he wasn't interested in Project E. He didn't seem to think that it could ever work. Sometimes I thought he was almost scared of it. That's when I came to his house – *your* house – a couple of times to see if I could change his mind. Him and his tennis ball. Pissed me right off."

Ed smiled. "The tennis ball is one of the few things I can clearly remember," he said. "I suppose it is possible that the ball is still on that plateau to this day."

Jim raised his eyebrows. "Yeah. I never even thought about that. But the NMU ruins are inaccessible. Dangerous too, I imagine. Especially with that weird earthquake going on there." He paused briefly, looking around at something, or someone, in the room. "Listen, Ed, I will have to go soon. But if you are interested, I can get you into B-Site, no problem. That place was all but forgotten after the university closed, except by me. Project E was abandoned but never dismantled. Some parts of The Shim are still there as well. And of course, your father's files. I spent an unreasonable amount of time there, reading through his, and Shim's. As sad and pointless as it is, I think I'm now the leading expert on Project E. And Project T for that matter."

Ed accepted the offer and thanked Jim for his call. "Oh, wait! One last question," he said. "Was there someone named Ian involved with Project E or The Shim?"

"Ian, you say? I don't think so. Ian who? It doesn't ring a bell."

"Never mind. I thought I heard that somewhere."

Chapter Twenty-Four

Jarod and his team had put in long days with the result that The Shim was ready to work again after only four days of total downtime. Lora had a poor night's sleep, something she wasn't used to, even if it happened more frequently lately, causing her to arrive at the lab later than she would have liked. Fortunately, there was Randy, who had already started the process of realignment and calibration, so that by the time she joined him, they were almost ready to restart the experiment. Lora was set on running two today, to make up for some of the delay. Just when she was over at the levers to start the experiment, she noticed Ian and Jim approaching them from the direction of Ian's office.

"This can't be good," she said in a low voice to Randy.

When they arrived at The Shim, she offered them seats, but they went straight to business.

"Jim wanted to speak to you personally," said Ian.

Lora swallowed. "Mr. Ferguson, I am so sorry about what happened. I promise it won't happen—"

"It won't," said Jim, sounding very final in his assertion. "I think you are well aware that I am financing this whole project of yours by myself. I don't want it squandered. Let's not have any more delays, shall we?"

Ian nodded in agreement. "So, how are we doing today?"

Lora looked around and said, "We're about ready to start her up again. The hope is that we can do two runs a day from now on. Even if we manage one a day, every day, we can still get enough data for the convention. It just gets very tight on the data analysis."

Jim stood a little too close to Lora for her comfort. He looked directly at her. "Tell me something," he said. "At what time do you normally start this experiment?"

"We don't really have set times," Lora said, feeling uneasy and trying to take a little more distance. "Whenever we get it ready."

"I thought this was a science lab, not some high school project. Do you not keep some type of schedule?"

Lora knew this man was always like this, even when he was in a good mood. "We don't even know how long each run will be. Honestly, I don't think the starting times of the experiment matter at all. If we get enough completed runs, we're good."

Jim looked unsatisfied and, as a result, so did Ian.

"Right now," Lora said, irritated, "we're standing here talking instead of running The Shim."

Randy laughed, but quickly realized that was inappropriate.

"Careful, young lady. I hope you realize who you're talking to," Jim said, looking more amused than annoyed now, as he rubbed his thumb and index finger together to indicate where the money was coming from.

Ian shot Lora a disturbing look, which she ignored. "Jim, I think we should leave these people to do their work. We will go do ours," Ian said. He turned to Lora. "In the future, I expect you to show some respect to those who are paying for your mistakes."

Lora suppressed the urge to roll her eyes at him. She said nothing, waiting for Ian to leave.

As he did, he said, "I am off to B-Site for the rest of the day."

Jim gave both Lora and Randy a nod and as he walked away, said, "Run this thing for the second time at two sharp this afternoon, and I will be impressed with you again, young lady."

Randy and Lora both shrugged and didn't respond. Before Ian and Jim had exited the room, the purple glow of the beam once again lit the area around The Shim.

VISITOR FOUND HIMSELF in an alley he hadn't seen before. As soon as he walked out onto the sidewalk, he quickly got his bearings. He was coming out of the last alley that was still across from the park. This was probably the furthest from the university he'd ever arrived, except for that one time he was somewhere else entirely.

After a few days of not being on his feet, this was another one of those moments where just the sensation of standing up filled him with joy. What he wanted to do most, was just to walk.

But it was different now. Whenever he spent time in this world, his own world was in danger. He owed it to so many people who had lost their lives or their loved ones in the disasters that Ian and Jim had caused, to find out how to stop anything like that from happening again. In addition, there was the knowledge that every walk could be his last, depending on whether Lora and her team would continue to run their experiment. Even without the threat of Ian and Jim cutting the project short, it wasn't a realistic expectation that a whole team of scientists could be persuaded to continue to perform an expensive experiment indefinitely, just so one Visitor from another world could keep his legs. Meanwhile, the physicist was still not pulling her resources to facilitate a permanent residency for him in her world.

He checked his phone and saw the full five bars. Apparently, it was working just fine here, but over the past days he had discovered that his phone became a different thing entirely when he tried to use it in his own world. It had been sitting on his desk, being charged, when he first touched it and received what he perceived to be an electric shock. There were visible sparks jumping from the phone to his hands. Whatever it was, was so powerful that at first, he thought he had gone blind. But it wasn't blindness any more than it was an electric shock. It was something else, a sudden change in his vision. It was as if the world had changed color to become an unpleasant shade of purple. Of course, he let go of the phone immediately, and to his relief everything went back to normal with no ill effects. He decided it might not be a good idea to handle it with bare hands anymore. But then, subsequent attempts to operate it with protected hands, using oven mittens, gloves or just the fabric of a T-shirt, were unsuccessful. He didn't get the shock, or whatever it might be, and he wasn't blinded, but the phone just wouldn't respond.

Later, now two days ago, he had tried to touch it again, just with his index finger, to see if he could get something to appear on the screen. Instantly, the purple vision was back. The shock wasn't painful, it was just so very strange. He left his finger on the screen for as long as he dared.

Looking around the room felt odd. It was all there, in a different color, but it somehow didn't feel important. It was all just a background image to something more relevant that he couldn't see. It was disturbing and uncomfortable for a moment. Then, suddenly his sensation changed to being in a kitchen. He still saw his purple room, but he felt like he was not there anymore, instead now finding himself in a much more comfortable place. It was pleasant, but it was so strange, and it felt so irreversible, that he pulled his finger off the phone, just to make sure it would go away. *That is the weirdest thing I've ever experienced.* Coming from him, that meant something. What he was left with was the feeling of having narrowly escaped something extremely dangerous and as a result, for the moment at least, he had no interest in trying it again.

Now he was walking toward the university campus, hoping that he would see Lora again. When he reached the gate, he saw two men coming out of the Everett building, one of which he immediately recognized as Jim Ferguson. The other, he could assume, was the infamous Ian. This is where he wished he didn't stand out so much with his suit and sunglasses. There was no point in trying to hide, so he just walked onto the campus as if he belonged there. The two men weren't interested in him in the least. As they walked past, at a reasonable pace and ignoring him completely, Visitor could overhear some of their conversation.

"You didn't have to be such an ass to her," the man he assumed was Ian said.

"She's got spunk. I like her," Jim said. "She can handle it. It's disappointing she can't tell us more exact times though. If we know in advance when it starts, we have a much better shot. In fact, I think the timing is critical. We'll still get it done. I'm going to work on the assumption she'll get one started at two sharp today."

Someone had snuck up on Visitor and asked, "Are you lost?"

For a second, he wondered if he should go after Jim and Ian. But he saw them split up and each walk to their separate cars as soon as they left campus through the gate. He turned around and felt his heart skip a beat when he saw who had asked him the question. "Oh! Hello mister Doctor! I mean Shim! Doctor Shim, I mean." Visitor felt like an idiot.

"Mister Doctor. I don't dislike it," Dr. Shim said, looking Visitor up and down.

The doctor was shorter than Visitor remembered, but the last time he had seen him, he was only eleven. "I'm sorry, I wasn't expecting to see you here."

"That's alright. I might say the same of you. So, are you? Lost, I mean? You don't strike me as a student."

"No, not lost. I am visiting Lora at the quantum lab."

Dr. Shim looked at him with suspicion. "As am I. But I don't remember her mentioning you. You know you can't just go in there, right?"

"I'm just an old friend, visiting."

"Tell you what, old friend, I'll give her a call and then she can come to let you in if she so desires."

Visitor wasn't at ease. Meeting the famous doctor was probably a good thing for him to do, but he wasn't making a very good first impression. He thought of something. "Ian and Jim are headed to B-Site today? I thought Jim wasn't involved with The Shim. Wasn't he more interested in Project E?"

Dr. Shim's bushy eyebrows went up much higher than they should. "Project E?" he asked, incredulously. "Where did you dig up that nugget? Even Jim has come to his senses on that one." He held up his finger as apparently someone talked to him on his

phone. "Lora? I'm outside and I've got your old friend with me."
He took his phone away from his ear and said to Visitor, "I didn't
catch your name."

"Visitor."

The doctor started walking away from him, shaking his head
now, going toward the lab and talking into his phone again. "I will
relay that message to him. He's not to come in."

Visitor followed the doctor and, when he caught up, asked,
"Can I talk to her? Please?"

"He wishes to speak with you… Are you sure?" Dr. Shim
handed the phone to Visitor and said, "Make it quick," before
turning around as if to give him some privacy.

"Visitor?" Lora asked. "I'm very sorry, but I really cannot let
you inside the lab anymore. It was already a bad idea from the start.
Now, I nearly lost my job over this incident."

This was alarming news to Visitor. "Can you come outside
then?" he asked.

"Not today, no. I have to talk to Dr. Shim about something.
I'm sure I'll see you another time."

"I saw Ian and Jim again. They're up to something, at B-Site."

"They were just in here, giving me a hard time about the incident with the tea. And Ian mentioned he was on his way to B-Site.
He is there a lot lately. I really have to go now. I'll see you later."

"Maybe this afternoon then? At two sharp?"

There was a long pause, but Lora didn't take the bait. "Maybe,"
she said. "It depends, I'm quite busy today."

Visitor handed the phone back to the doctor and thanked him.
Even if they let him inside, Lora wouldn't have time for him. Instead, he thought, he would see if there was a way to get to B-Site
and check it out. As he walked back to the road, he took out his

phone and searched online for a taxi. It was refreshing to see it just work. Bringing up a map, he found that he could now use navigation as well. *Not bad, Jarod.* He couldn't exactly determine the correct location for B-Site. It obviously was not named that way on the map. But he remembered that Jim mentioned an industrial park off highway six, so when the taxi arrived not five minutes later, he told the driver that's where he wanted to go.

The drive was quiet and comfortable. When the driver pulled onto the industrial park, just over half an hour later, he asked him to just keep driving around the park, because he didn't know exactly where the company he was visiting was located. Once he saw it though, there was no doubt. It was a large boxy building, in the middle of a fenced area. There were cars, vans and trucks parked inside the fence, close to the building. Most were near the entrance doors, a few were parked off to the other side of the building. Among them, he recognized Jim's car right away. He noticed a single door in an otherwise blind wall on that side, and fencing separating the side from the front of the building. *You guys have your own secret entrance, do you?* He got out of the taxi and asked the driver to wait, as he would not be long. There was no need to wait however, because when Visitor took two steps away from the car, he saw the dreaded flash inside his head. It was over, for now.

CHAPTER TWENTY-FIVE

EVEN THOUGH SHE HAD PROMISED herself that she wouldn't use Randy as her personal servant, Lora had asked him to go over to Delaney's and get coffee and tea, while she retreated into a meeting room with Dr. Shim.

"He said he was an old friend of yours. But then he started babbling about Project E. That's not a common topic I hear about from perfect strangers. Did he get that from you?" asked Dr. Shim.

Lora was dying to share the full story of Visitor with someone, just to get it off her chest, and to have someone to talk about it with. But where would she start? "The old friend thing is not true. I only met him a couple of weeks ago. It's precisely because he seems to know things that he shouldn't that I became interested in him. He knew about the target object. He…" Her eyes were staring into the distance. *He showed me pictures of this very place, ruined, in another universe.* "He isn't from here."

"Regardless, you really shouldn't let him in here. He might be a reporter, or worse. He doesn't belong here."

Lora smiled and assured him he was not a reporter. "And what could be worse than a reporter?" she asked, joking of course.

"Alright Lora. I'll trust your judgement."

"I just find it fascinating that he knows so much about this place. I admit that I did let him in here, and I agree that I shouldn't have."

The doctor nodded and then changed the subject. "Ian and Jim are up to something at B-Site. That's what your friend told you on the phone, right? What is that supposed to mean?"

Lora shrugged. "He overheard them in the bathroom the other day, talking about me. I told him that's not uncommon around here."

"What were they saying?"

Lora smiled, amused at Dr. Shims uncharacteristic interest in gossip. "I don't know, he didn't really say much about it."

After a few more minutes, Randy came back with the drinks.

"I promise I'll get it myself next time," Lora said. "What's Neil been up to?"

Randy made a face and said, "No idea. Didn't ask."

It was time to get to business. Lora was the only one who remained standing. She opened a laptop computer and brought up some data from previous runs of The Shim. "We have been running with The Slicer unmodified from the start. Even after the initial failed run, only two minutes, we didn't change anything about The Slicer. But after sixteen runs, I suddenly had to go in and make changes to the settings. Here, let me show you." She brought another data table onto the screen and shifted the laptop over to Dr. Shim.

"That's a rather particular modification, isn't it?" he asked.

"Yes. It's as if suddenly my target had shifted, but only slightly."

"Oh, I wouldn't say slightly. Something in the multiverse changed. Either here, in our little neck of the woods, or over in some other universe. This machine is sadly not going to tell us what it was that changed, but I'm sure it would be noticeable for those who live there. Wouldn't that be nice if we could just ask them?" the doctor mused.

Lora thought about Visitor, but she still couldn't say it. Especially with Randy here. "The slice is extremely narrow, David. Much narrower than we ever thought possible. We're effectively targeting only a single other universe." Dr. Shim was ready to protest that statement, but she didn't let him. "It happened again on runs nineteen and twenty-one. Here," she said, scrolling through more data on the screen. "There doesn't seem to be anything special about those runs. I can't find any kind of pattern to link them. I just want to make sure I'm not making a mistake here. If my changes to The Slicer are incorrect or uncalled for, then I'm jeopardizing the whole project. The data isn't going to be useful if I make weird unexplained changes to the programming at seemingly random runs."

Randy asked, "Can't we just filter out those runs?"

Both Lora and Dr. Shim answered in unison, "No."

Dr. Shim elaborated. "Unfortunately, you can't. Once you change the program, it remains changed, so everything after that is using the new settings. I can't see a basis on which to filter out individual runs without discarding the prior ones."

Dr. Shim and Lora moved to a whiteboard and started a discussion that went a little over Randy's head. Lora had asked him to be a lab worker and he felt that was still all he was to her. He hoped that she would sit him down and explain in detail some of the theory behind the project. Sure, she had given him a few documents, and pointed him to where he could find more, but that hadn't helped. There was so much to go through, it was hard to just find a starting point. Sometimes it was hard to tell if she liked him or not. The board was quickly filling up with math that he could understand for the most part, but its relationship to the problem at hand was more of a mystery.

Lora's phone, which she had left on the table, vibrated. She ignored it at first, but then apologized to the doctor and picked it up. She looked at the screen and made a face that indicated she had no idea who this was.

Lora opened with "Hello?" Shortly after, she followed with, "Yes, that would be me." After that, she remained quiet for a while, listening to whoever it was. Eventually she asked, "You want me to do that *today*, do you?" It stayed quiet again for a long time. "Why are you coming to me with this now? A little short notice, don't you think?" Another silence followed. "Fine. But I can't leave here until the current experiment is finished. So, after lunch. Will that work?" She hung up and apologized. "That," she said, "was a building supervisor at B-Site. They want someone who uses The Shim on site, to go over some issues regarding the new location for the machine."

"That would be you," Randy said. "Can I come with you? I've never been."

Lora thought for a moment. This would mean that there wouldn't be an afternoon run, and certainly not one at two o'clock sharp. "Sure," she said, as she went back to the board with Dr. Shim. After some time watching them, he wasn't sure if they even knew he was still in the room, so Randy decided to leave them alone and go look for something else to do.

When he walked into the lab, he was noticed first by Alice, the chief analyst on the team who had apparently just arrived. Her desk was the closest to the door that separated the lab from the foyer. She waved Randy over.

"Come see what I found!" she said, sounding excited.

Randy thought maybe she had noticed something interesting in the data of a previous run, so he went over straight away. Instead of showing him data, Alice pulled out a small item from a shopping bag and proudly presented him with it.

Randy took it and turned it over in his hand. "A snow globe?"

"Yeah, but look at it though!"

Inside the snow globe, with the word "Science" inscribed on its base, was a small scene, crudely depicting a scientist in a white lab coat standing at a table and peering into a microscope.

"Isn't it cute?" Alice said, with a big smile. "I thought it was cute, so I had to have it."

Randy had a hard time sharing her excitement. "Why would it be snowing in a science lab?" he said, with a smirk. The cheaply made plastic toy was too small for the figurine inside to have any details. "What will you do with it?"

Alice took the snow globe from him and placed it on her desk. "I'm putting it right here. A little knick-knack for my boring un-decorated workspace." That was a stab at Ian's infamous clean-desk policy that no one cared about.

"You better start doing the paperwork then. I'm sure Ian has forms for bringing decorative foreign objects into the lab," Randy said, feigning a serious look.

"Yeah, well. It's not going to kill anyone if I have a little snow globe sitting on my desk, is it?"

"I won't tell a soul," Randy said.

Alice glanced over to the meeting room Randy had just come from. "You really like her, don't you?"

Randy's face went bright red in an instant. "Um... I... I don't know... I mean... what?"

"Ha-ha, don't worry, your secret is safe with me. Word of advice though. I have known Lora for a long time, and she is... Well... it's complicated. Just don't get your hopes up, that's all."

"Oh no, a complicated woman?" Randy joked nervously.

Alice laughed. "Touché."

Chapter Twenty-Six

L ORA PULLED UP at the B-Site fence around one-thirty, after she had taken Randy to Delaney's for lunch. She got out of the car and opened the gate. It was a large manual gate that was locked with padlocks during the night, but normally remained unlocked when people were present. It required some effort to drag it open. After she drove through, she asked Randy to close it behind them before she pulled up to a parking spot near the entrance. There were a lot of construction company vans and trucks, and a few cars. Randy held the door open for her, a favor which she then returned by holding open the inner doors. Inside was a small reception area, but there was no one at the counter, as the building wasn't in use. They found a door marked with a note, in Sharpie scribble, that seemed to have been there for as long as the door had. It read "factory floor". Behind the door was the large hall where the new lab was being built. The concrete floor was smooth and painted white, but not very clean with construction still in progress. There were a few people working in various places throughout the hall. The plateau for The Shim stood out as one of the more organized areas, so that's where they headed. Lora looked up toward the very high ceilings.

"We'll put in floating ceilings over the machine, so it doesn't look like you're in a three-story hangar," a man said loudly from nearby the plateau. His voice reverberated through the hall. "Don't worry, when we're done, it will look like a proper lab and hopefully not sound like a church in here anymore."

"It sure doesn't look like a church," Randy said.

Lora had been here only twice before. The first time, just after the decision was made to move The Shim back here, Ian had shown her around. Back then, she couldn't visualize this space as a lab. It was a big mess, as they were still in the process of removing machines that hadn't been sold yet and cleaning up the clutter left behind from disassembling those that had. Not much about that first impression had changed the second time around, when she was there with Dr. Shim and Ian. That time, she had asked Dr. Shim about Project E, which was sitting unused at the other end of the hall, but he had dismissed it as a failure. It wasn't clear to her why they brought her there that day. They were in heated debate among themselves, ignoring her most of the time. Her third visit, today, still left her with the impression that this room wasn't a laboratory, although the nice white floor and partially finished construction helped a little to see where it was going.

"I assume you are the scientist I spoke to on the phone before?" the man asked. When Lora confirmed, he introduced himself. "Hi, Mitchell Hayward with Concrete Lab Industries. I'm the supervisor for the construction surrounding The Shim."

Lora introduced herself and Randy and said, "I'm a little surprised by the invitation. Not sure what it is I could do for you."

"Oh, no worries. As you may know, our company also took care of putting together the machine in the university lab. Afterwards, we got some feedback from Dr. Shim, who was running that lab at the time. It was mostly about practical things that could have been designed better with hindsight. We've been trying to get into contact with your office from the start, but it's been a bit of a struggle to get answers. Yesterday I was suddenly told to contact you directly. Never heard your name before. I apologize if I should have."

"My office?" Lora said with a giggle. "You must be talking about Ian. Ian Byrne?"

"That sounds about right. One of the things they had issues with back then, was the placement of the consoles in relation to the machine itself, as well as the location of the control computers and some of the manual control elements. It's all about ergonomics. We are about to do some significant damage to this floor when we put in the consoles, so we would like to know where you prefer to have them."

Lora looked over at Randy. "Isn't that all decided and drawn up already?"

"Sure, it is," said Mitchell. "But at this stage, as you can see, we can pretty much put those things anywhere. If you have good reasons to want them somewhere else, we can accommodate. Really, the only thing we can't do is move the plateau."

A very deep hum suddenly sounded through the hall, while all lights in the room slightly dimmed. The sound was so low, Lora could barely hear it, but it was loud enough that she could feel it in her stomach. It lasted only a few seconds and then faded away, as the lights came back to full brightness.

"What was that?" Lora and Randy asked in tandem.

"You tell me. It happens once or twice every day. Sometimes more. I assume it comes from over there." Mitchell pointed to the other end of the hall, which was nothing more than a gigantic black wall that terminated the entire building on that side.

"I don't remember ever seeing that. Weren't there windows on that side? That's where Dr. Shim set up his old project."

"I am not sure madam. That area is strictly off limits to us."

"Oh! So, there is an area behind that wall?"

"I'm pretty sure there is. In our business it's not uncommon for there to be access restrictions. It's none of my business, I guess. But those power surges are no good to us. That's just another thing I've been trying to get addressed with your office."

Lora looked at her phone and saw it was almost two already. She was still hoping to get back to the lab and start a second run today. "I can put in a word for you," she said. "Let's go have a look at the plateau. But I'm not sure you should just change your plans based on my opinion. I don't even expect I will be working here much."

Once Mitchell got Lora talking about the practical aspects of using The Shim in its current configuration, the ideas started flowing quickly. Mitchell turned out to be very helpful with suggestions and recommendations from previous experiences building other labs. Before they knew it, they had spent several hours slowly converging on the ideal placement for consoles, computers, levers, and controls, all while sharing mostly work-related stories. Lora quite enjoyed the idea that she could have this much influence on the construction of a new lab. When they finished, Mitchell said, "Madam, this has been very helpful. I apologize once again for the intrusion, but I was left with very little choice in the matter."

Lora replied, "It was my pleasure. This was fun."

"Alright. When you leave, just drop the hard hats in the reception area, I'll find them. I'll go and update my office on our findings." Mitchell started to walk away, but Lora called him back.

"Do you know if Ian is still around here somewhere?"

Mitchell scratched his hard hat. "I don't think I've ever seen him in here. Maybe once or twice in the beginning. I spoke with him on the phone and met him at our offices a few times, that's all. You're free to look around though. Just be careful and watch your step."

"Oh. Okay, thanks," Lora said, pretending not to be surprised by what she heard. She hadn't seen Ian at the lab a lot lately, and every time he had said he would be at B-Site, today included. She led Randy through the hall toward the big black wall. There were no windows, just a few inconspicuous doors to the very left and right of the hall. In the center was what looked like an oversized garage door, or a loading bay door, but it was well integrated into the wall and barely noticeable from a distance. She made her way to the leftmost door and tried it. It was locked. The next door was a short distance to its right and was also locked. Lora knocked on the door, but nothing happened. To get to the doors on the other side, she had to walk back into the hall and around some workers who had set up a table saw and other equipment by the garage door. They were building a series of smaller rooms along the outer wall that ran the length of the hall. Lora guessed these would be meeting rooms or offices. When they reached the two doors on the right, they found them locked as well. Randy knocked on one door, while Lora was doing the same on the other, but there was no answer. Finally, Lora pulled out her phone and called Ian.

"Lora? What's going on, why didn't the experiment run at two?" he asked as soon as he picked up.

"We were called away. I was looking for you."

"I'm not in the lab, I'm still over at B-Site."

"Yeah, so am I. But I don't see you."

It remained quiet for a while. She could hear some muffled sounds and assumed Ian must be talking to someone else while covering his phone. When he came back on, he just said, "I'm outside," and hung up.

Randy led the way through the hall this time, on the way to the exit. They dropped their hard hats off and found Ian standing outside, just casually extinguishing a cigarette with his foot.

"What in the hell are you two doing all the way out here?" was how he greeted them.

"Mitchell called me over to discuss The Shim. What's your excuse? How did you know we didn't run at two? Where were you hiding all this time? What's behind the black wall?"

Ian was visibly irritated. "Nothing. We just wanted the room smaller."

"What is going on here, Ian? Are you hiding something in there?"

"Nothing is going on. Did you finish your business with Mitchell? Are you still doing another run today?"

Lora, annoyed at Ian's evasiveness, answered, "Maybe. Maybe not, Ian. It's probably too late to start another one today. We still have to recalibrate."

"Right. Well, you better get to it then." Ian turned around and walked to his car, parked just beside Lora's. She was quite sure that it hadn't been there when she arrived.

She watched him drive away and then said to Randy, "Well, that was rude. Let's have a look around, shall we?"

They walked immediately in the direction where the hall had terminated into a black wall. On the outside of the building, it was hard to tell where the wall divided the building. Nearer the end of the building, there were signs slapped onto the wall with varying messages ranging from "No Trespassing" and "Keep Out" to "Authorized Personnel Only". When they reached the end of the building and turned around the corner, fences blocked the way. Apparently, it wasn't allowed to walk around the building. She saw one parked car behind the fence, even though she couldn't see how it would have got there. Besides a few covered windows, there was only one small door in the shorter wall of the building, but the fencing made it unapproachable.

"Oh, this looks serious," she said to Randy. She considered herself authorized personnel, so wasn't too worried.

Lora squeezed herself in between the start of the fence and the building wall, bringing her inside the fenced off area. Randy followed suit and they started on their way to the door. They didn't get very far before the door swung open and two security guards came rushing toward them. From the looks of their outfits, they must be working for the same security firm that provided the guards for the lab.

"This is a restricted area! You can't be in here," one of the guards barked at them, skipping any pleasantries.

"Restricted to whom exactly?" Lora asked, with a friendly smile.

Both guards took their batons out of their holsters in response. "Madam, just turn around and leave. There is nothing for you on this side," the second guard said, sounding slightly more reasonable than the first, despite the weapon he was holding.

Lora kept smiling and said, "We're just going for a walk around the building. Just stretching our legs."

"Not on this side, you're not," the barking guard replied.

"I see. What's inside then?" she said, pointing at the door.

The guard picked a walkie-talkie out of a holster on his belt and said to Lora, "I wouldn't tell you if I knew. Now, leave." He brought the walkie-talkie up and said, "Code 4," before replacing it where it came from. The other guard disappeared, rushing back into the door.

Lora was confident that if she kept insisting, she would end up being escorted off the property and half considered it would be worth it. Randy beat her to it, surprising her by just walking around and past the guard to make his way to the door. As might be expected, he didn't get very far again. The second guard came back out the door and sprinted toward Randy. He tried to grab his arm. Randy elegantly evaded the move and kept going, but then the guard roughly shoved him. Randy fell. The guard put his knee to Randy's back, bent his arms behind his back and proceeded to put handcuffs on. Not so reasonable after all. Lora watched in horror at how quickly this was escalating. Randy was brought up on his feet and shoved back toward Lora. For a moment, another man peeked out the door, but as soon as he saw what was happening, turned around and went back inside. Neither Lora nor Randy got a good look at him.

Immediately after, the walkie-talkies loudly projected a voice. "Let them go! Get them out of here!"

One guard grabbed Lora's arm and started pushing her back in the direction of the parking lot.

"Hey! Take your hands off her!" Randy yelled at him.

It was a firm grip Lora thought might leave her arm bruised. The reasonable guard pulled the same move on Randy's arm.

"Don't touch her!" Randy said, trying to wriggle his own arm free. "Let her go, or I swear…"

The guards escorted them outside the fenced area, squeezing through, the same way they came in.

"Where's your car parked?" the first guard barked.

Lora pointed, with her hand shaking, to her car. She thought the voice on the walkie-talkie might have been familiar, but it was so loud and distorted she couldn't figure out who it was.

The other guard removed the handcuffs and said, "Go to your car and leave at once."

They had no choice but to comply. During the drive back to the lab, Lora and Randy sat quietly processing what had happened to them. It worried Lora that Ian was keeping her in the dark about something. More so because of the way he was doing it. She had found out little secrets of his before, mostly related to project funding, but he had never responded in this odd way.

When they got close to the university, Lora said, "I couldn't believe how you just pushed past that guard. You've got some nerve. I was impressed!" She smiled and gave him a little pat on his shoulder.

Randy blushed, and he knew it, wanting desperately for it to stop. He talked. "It just seemed so ridiculous to have two guards at a door in the middle of a big building, you know? For no good reason. And fences everywhere! And just a whole bunch of signs, right? I sure didn't expect them to carry handcuffs, did you? Is that legal? I didn't expect that." He stopped, realizing he was rambling.

Lora laughed a nervous laugh. "There's an experience you'll never forget. Neither will I." She pulled up by the campus gates and looked at the clock. "What do you think? Should we go in and get it ready for tomorrow?" she asked, nodding in the direction of the Everett building. "We really need two runs tomorrow. I'll order in pizza."

"I'm not turning down free pizza," Randy said, getting out of the car. Lora was happy because she didn't want to go home and be by herself just yet, even though she also wanted to work on her convention presentation a little tonight.

When Lora finally did get home, it was already almost nine. She sat down at her desk and stared at the screen for a long time without even opening the presentation. *What the hell, Ian?* It took her a lot of willpower to finally do some work for the convention.

And then, the evening got weirder. Enough so, that she gave up and went to bed, at first unable to fall asleep.

CHAPTER TWENTY-SEVEN

LORA OPENED HER EYES but didn't expect to see anything. She was just going to glance at her phone to see what time it was, maybe take a sip of water, and then turn around and go back to sleep. It was the middle of the night, and it should be nearly pitch black in her bedroom. It wasn't. Disappointingly, bright light poured in from behind her curtains. Her phone was not there. *I left it on my desk.* She felt like she had barely slept at all. It had taken her a long time to get to sleep with everything that happened the previous day going through her mind. She needed a few moments to adjust to the idea that it was probably time to get up now. Thoughts and memories began pouring into her head. Today she was supposed to be at the lab early.

Where was that sound coming from? The phone was ringing. She sat up and concentrated to make sure that's what it was. *I'm late.* She sprang into action, performing a complicated dance of getting up, getting dressed and running to her study all at the same time. When she picked up the phone, with her arm still trying to find its way into the second sleeve of her shirt, it had stopped ringing, but it reported three missed calls from the lab. She called back immediately, while thinking she should have answered nature's call first.

"Ian, I'm sorry, I'm running a little behind schedule. It's just that I had so much to do for the convention and last night I—"

"Lora! Enough! Just get here, now!" Ian hung up.

I have to stop pissing him off like that! She made a face at her phone and said, "Whatever."

She called Randy. "Randy, are you at the lab?" Of course, he was. "Can you and Gary do me a favor and start up the experiment right now?" With everything already calibrated and aligned last night, that shouldn't be a problem. "I will be there as soon as I can, but I have one stop to make on the way, to drop something off at a printshop."

Randy told her that he was already on it, with Gary, and that the experiment would be up and running within the next few minutes. Lora stuffed the phone in her purse and started to put her shoes on when she realized the bathroom really could not wait any longer.

Breathe.

Gary and Randy would get the experiment going, so that gave her at least an extra half hour to get there before it ended. She walked into her home office again and saw her physics themed keychain, a corny gift from Dr. Shim whose impressive set of talents did not include buying gifts, sitting on her desk. Maybe his present wasn't as tacky as the snow globe Alice was trying to convince everyone in the lab was the greatest find in shopping history, but it was in the same ballpark. Regardless, the keychain wasn't supposed to be on her desk. Ever since she first brought it home, it had been sitting on one of her bookshelves. Last night, while she was working on her presentation, that had changed, which was one of the reasons she couldn't fall asleep. *That really happened.*

There was no time to dwell on it now. Ten minutes later she was out of her house, walking to her car while tying up her hair. To her left, coming from around the corner of the house, she barely noticed a curious blue glow. As soon as she saw it, it disappeared and a moment later Visitor walked around the corner. He recognized her immediately but didn't do the same for his surroundings.

"Lora! What is this place?"

"Visitor? What are you doing at my house?"

"Your house?" Visitor walked up to her and asked where she was going. When she mentioned the lab, he invited himself along for the ride.

"This really isn't a good time. I am in no mood," Lora replied.

"It's just a ride. Please?"

"Fine, whatever. Get in. I'm late." Lora got in the driver's seat, started the car, and began driving immediately.

"How far is it?" Visitor asked.

Lora glanced at him briefly. "If you don't know that already, how did you get to my house?"

"I didn't. And I didn't know this was your house. This is the second time this has happened to me, that I have come into this world away from the university." He thought this over for a moment. "I've assumed until now that I enter somewhere near the university because that's where the machine is running. Maybe instead, I visit you, not the machine." He sounded excessively cheerful now.

Lora laughed but didn't find it funny. "You're saying, you always appear near me, regardless of where I am when the experiment is started."

"Yeah. I have found no way to control where I go. It just happens. It occurs to me now, that in some way, the universe is putting us together."

They were now stopped at a traffic light and Lora turned to face him. "Do you know how stupid all of this sounds? I have to present my results at the Physics Advances convention soon. I can't even mention any of this without sounding like an idiot! I will talk about moving Gary's tennis ball around on a plateau and try to make the case that I am doing the same in another universe. But I can't say anything about the fact that I know exactly which universe, and that I have been in direct contact with someone who lives there and who showed me pictures of it." She was looking at him, her eyes moving rapidly, as if she was looking for something in her mind. "I bet, that if you were to go into that destroyed Everett building, you'd find Gary's ball there, sitting on the plateau, moving around every time I run The Shim. Gary must have put that ball there, just like he did here. Even just saying that makes me sound like—" A car horn sounded behind her.

"You're green," said Visitor, pointing out the window. He waited for Lora to pull away from the light and then, out of nowhere, added, "Gary Sutherland was my father. He died in the accident." *Identity revealed.* "And yes, he did put that ball there."

Lora's car swerved, and another car's horn sounded behind her. "Jesus Christ!" she yelled as she steadied the vehicle. Both she and Visitor sat quietly while she took the next exit and stopped the car at a gas station. "Gary is your dad?" she finally asked. "Gary?"

"He was, where I come from. Here, where he is alive, it seems he has no idea who I am."

"He doesn't even *have* children. Gary's wife died soon after he married her. I think it was a disease, but it could be an accident, I am not sure. He never talks about it. Oh my god, you are Gary's son?"

Visitor nodded and stayed quiet.

"Did you tell him this, when you were in my lab?" she asked.

"I couldn't. It was obvious he didn't know me, and… I mean… What was I supposed to tell him? How do I talk to my long dead father who never even had a son?" He sat quietly for a little longer. Lora also didn't know what to say. She started the car again and began to drive.

Once they were on the road again, Lora asked, "What is so special about me, that makes the universe put you near me when you appear?"

"Oh, well, you are definitely special to me! I sit in my wheelchair every day, waiting for you to bring me here, so I can walk. You're nearly a god in my life right now."

Lora's eyes narrowed. Her hands were squeezing the steering wheel. "I have nothing to do with that. All I do is run my experiment! You cannot put that on me. I move a ball, and that is all I do."

Visitor was frustrated. This scientist seemed to care almost exclusively about herself. He took a moment. There was no use in making her angry, he wanted to keep her talking to him. "You're special in another way," he said. "I have found that everyone who exists in my world, also exists in yours. Well, for the small sample that I have checked. Some people are dead in one world, like my father, but they always shared at least some time in both worlds.

That pattern broke only when I tried to find you. I think you were never born in my world. Your parents existed, but both died overseas not long after they met, and probably before you were born. Over here, I think they live down south, right?"

"Yeah. Well, when they're not travelling, they do. How do you know about them?"

Visitor ignored the question and continued. "You just told me that, in this universe, my mother died before I could be born. It seems we share a strange fate."

"I don't exist in your world, and you don't exist in mine. Is that what you're saying?" Lora asked.

"Maybe," Visitor said, "that's how we are connected. I go where you go, because in a way we are alternatives to each other. We each fulfil a similar purpose in our own universe."

Lora didn't say anything and was thoughtlessly increasing her speed. The large amount of unexplained information coming her way frustrated her. "I am slowly going crazy," she finally said. "This experiment is driving me crazy, and it is about time that we wrap it up."

Visitor turned to look at her. "Wrap it up? When?"

"I have funding until the convention and every intention on getting all planned runs finished before then. After that, this experiment is officially over. After the convention, the machine is going to be moved to a new location, where it will be used by a new team. I will probably not be involved much anymore, and with the way things are going, I might not want to be."

"What does that mean? Is this new team still going to be running the experiment?"

Lora snickered. "No. They are not interested in other universes. They want to commercialize teleportation. What I am doing, with

The Slicer, isn't marketable. With what I know now, it's a bit of a mystery how I was funded, to be honest. But even if they were running experiments with The Slicer, moving the machine, and with it the target object, will cause a different slice. It's impossible to target your specific universe ever again. It was pretty much impossible to begin with."

"What is a slicer?"

"Before The Slicer, we could not say anything about which universes participated in our experiment. With The Slicer we can narrow that down. At present, it appears we've somehow narrowed it down to mostly just yours. Once the ball is moved in any other way by someone in either universe, it's over. Everything I have done becomes permanently unreproducible." Lora took a deep breath. *So much for non-disclosure.*

"So, you're just going to stop bringing me here, forever?"

Lora thought about this for a second. "Essentially, yes."

"You can't just stop! I will never walk again! Do you realize what that means? What kind of person does that?"

Lora glanced at him, then returned her eyes to the road. "I cannot make you walk any more than I can make decisions about the future of this project. It was already a longshot from the beginning that this experiment would even be possible. If it wasn't for Dr. Shim's support, and his influence with Ian, I don't think any of this would ever have happened. No one would have paid for this based solely on my proposals. Not at NMU."

"You're condemning me to a wheelchair for the rest of my life, after first getting me out of it! That's tantamount to torture!" Visitor was raising his voice now.

"I am not in charge of what projects run in the lab. I just lead the lab for this project. And this project is slowly driving me insane!" Now *she* was raising her voice. She took a moment to compose herself. "Last night I was working in my office, at home. Suddenly, and for no reason that I can think of, a keepsake keychain, that I had laying around, moved. I mean, it was sitting on a shelf a good distance from my desk, and suddenly it was sitting right in front of me on my desk. The Shim wasn't even fully operational at that time, but I was seeing things shimmying around in my own house! To me, this feels like the pictures on your phone. Or your mind trick. I know what I saw, but I don't accept it."

Visitor just said, "I am real. Everything I showed you, and everything I told you, is real…" He suddenly changed his tone. "Wait! That was in your house?"

"Yeah. My home office. What do you mean?"

"I had no idea it was your place! The phone!"

Lora was pulling into the parking lot of a small strip mall. "What are you talking about?"

"I swear, I didn't know. The first few days after your machine broke, I spent a lot of time in bed. I was exhausted from not sleeping. When I finally got around to checking my phone, I found that thing is completely off-the-charts weird now." He took out his phone and showed it to her. It looked perfectly normal. "In this place it still works. See? Five bars. Back home when I picked it up, it was like the thing was zapping me with electricity! As soon as I touched it, everything around me changed. The colors were all mixed up, and everything looked like it had an ugly purple haze around it. Distasteful, really. The first few times I dropped it immediately. It scared me, to be honest. But yesterday, when I held it longer, I felt as if I was somewhere else. In a room with shelves all around, and books. There was a desk and a lazy chair and a little table."

"That's my study. My home office. Are you telling me you were in my office?"

"No. Well, not exactly. Not at all, really. It was more like a feeling. It felt like I was in that room, but I wasn't physically present. I didn't see it, I sensed it. I explored the whole room, starting from the desk. It was almost like an out of body experience. I was floating around." Lora tried to grab the phone from his hands, but he pulled it back and continued. "I somehow just knew where everything was in that room, without actually seeing it."

He was having a hard time describing the sensation of being in two places at once. The area around the desk had felt comfortable and very detailed, with the positions of all objects clearly defined. It was warm, welcoming, and bright if that was possible without seeing. At the same time, he was just as aware of the room he was physically in. It presented itself with a purple glow, but it was all very clear. He could see his own hands, one of them holding the phone. The TV, the wheelchair, it was all present while he was experiencing a completely different room in his mind. He found that he could make himself drift away from the desk, without physically moving, but the further he got, the more undefined everything became. It was harder to precisely sense where things were, and it felt somehow darker, colder, and less comfortable. His sense of his real environment became equally muddy, as if the purple haze thickened around him. It felt as if the color itself was gaining weight, pushing down on him and squeezing him. He could still somewhat make out his own hands, but they felt strangely absent, not unlike how his legs always felt. Trying to move them, felt like he was dragging them through molasses. Trying to float back toward the desk in the other room was equally difficult. It seemed to cost him considerable energy to make it happen, but the more he moved toward it, the easier it became.

"When I found the teacup on the side table, it made me think of what happened in your lab, and I wanted to stay clear of it. I sensed the keychain on the shelf and wondered if I could touch it. That didn't work. I had nothing to touch anything with. No fingers, or hands, or anything really."

It had felt as if it was impossible to approach anything closely. All he could do was float, disembodied, around the things in the room.

"It made sense then, to try the same thing I do when I am here. I focused on the keychain in my mind, imagined where it should go, and it just went! It wasn't that much harder than when I do it here. It shimmied into thin air, or whatever you call that, and then appeared where I wanted it, on your desk. It was extremely satisfying."

By that time, he had felt worn out and had to let go of the phone. All the sensations and visions instantly disappeared, and he was left slumped in his wheelchair, once again exhausted. He fell asleep and slept for hours, in his chair, which was very unusual for him.

"I was mentally preparing myself to try it again this morning, but I was taken here before I got to it." He could see Lora was not amused. *Of course, it just had to be her house I was floating around in!*

Lora took a moment and then laughed. It was a loud, hysterical, and insincere laugh. She was not having fun. "Let me get this straight," she said. "You were spying on me, from another universe, using your modified cellphone." She rubbed her forehead with one of her hands. "I am losing it. I'm officially insane." She sounded much closer to crying than laughing now.

Visitor put his hand on her shoulder. A gesture no more sincere than her laugh. "I am sorry," he said, "I wasn't spying on anyone. I didn't even know it was your room, or anyone else's. There was no one there, from what I could tell." As he said this, he started to realize that Lora must have been sitting at the desk. Somehow, he had made contact with her and was able to explore her immediate surroundings independent of her. He could in fact alter her environment using his strange mind-over-matter trick remotely. Stray away too far though, and he became lost, losing control over both her world and his own.

Lora got out of the car and shut the door. She paced back and forth beside the car a few times before opening the door again. She grabbed a flash drive from the center console area and said, "I'm going to take this to the printers, and when I get back, you're going to give me that phone so I can have it restored." She wiped a tear or two from her cheek and pulled a few tissues out of a box. "I don't need you haunting my house like some poltergeist."

Visitor watched her walk away and thought about everything he had just learned. *A ghost!* This newfound ability seemed danger-ous but interesting. It was certainly not something he wanted to give up without first exploring it further. *If I'm going to have super-powers, why not give me something simple and useful, like flight?*

When Lora came back a few minutes later, she got into her seat and said nothing.

"Jim and Ian," Visitor said, "are planning to cut your project short. At least, that's what I think I heard them say in the bathroom."

"I don't care," Lora said. It was a lie, but she was done talking to him. She drove fast.

"Jim and Ian," Visitor tried again, "are destroying my world." He held up the phone and showed a picture of dragons flying around a castle tower. "Whatever they are doing, it is causing very strange things to happen. It started after my sixteenth visit." He changed the picture to a gruesome image of deformed bodies piled up in what looked like a department store. "Run nineteen. People are dying because of this. Thousands of people are dead because of them."

Tears started rolling down Lora's cheeks. It took her a minute to answer. "I can't take this anymore, Visitor. You need to leave me alone." She stopped the car by the city park and stared quietly out the side window.

"Lora, I understand that it isn't easy. But please, just please, think about a way to keep me on my feet a little longer. I need to find a way to fix this." His finger tapped on the screen of his phone, where Lora, glancing at it quickly, could see some European looking city with damaged buildings. "Run twenty-one. Earthquakes everywhere. I'm begging you. This place, this glorious universe of yours, is the best thing that has ever happened to me. I wish I could stay here forever. But first, I need your help to save what is left of my world. Maybe, together, we can still save some of these people." That was a stretch. A flat-out lie even. Was he really going down that road now? But nothing else had worked to get her to help him. He doubled down. "Hundreds, if not thousands, of people have gone missing, and I think I can bring them back. I just need the experiment to continue."

Lora sniffled and kept staring outside. The numbers, sixteen, nineteen and twenty-one, were ringing through her head. Those were the runs she had to adjust The Slicer configuration for. Was she somehow responsible for the gruesome events Visitor just showed her? Finally, she said, as if she hadn't been listening to him at all, "As I said before, I can't let you in the lab anymore. Give me the phone, so I can have it fixed."

Visitor was angry now. He opened the door and said, "They killed my family, Lora!" as he got out of her car. She gave no response. He slammed the door closed and watched Lora drive the short distance toward the university gate. He cursed loudly. How could she be so insensitive? Even if she didn't care about his looming disability, was she impervious to the fate of an entire world? It was as if she still didn't believe any of it existed. His fists were clenched so tightly he could feel his nails driving into his skin. Up the street, past the university, was the restaurant with the nice bar. Maybe, the limited time he had left on this walk, would be best spent with a drink or two.

Chapter Twenty-Eight

"WELCOME BACK, sir," Neil greeted Visitor as he walked into Delaney's restaurant. Neil remembered how the man in the red suit didn't have money on him during his previous visit.

"Bartender, I know it's a little early, but you need to hook me up with one of these," Visitor said, pointing both his index fingers at one of the taps while he took a seat on a bar stool near the middle of the bar.

"Certainly," Neil said, picking up an empty glass from a rack behind him. "That will be seven dollars, please." He could sense irritation in his guest, who pretended to sound cheerful but was speaking through clenched teeth.

Visitor looked around as if he was looking for a friend, but there was no one else here. "I'm good for it," he said. Of course, he knew that wouldn't work. He was in no mood for this.

"I'm sorry sir, I do need to take payment before I can serve you."

"Look," Visitor said. A glass disappeared from where Neil had just picked one up. It immediately reappeared in mid-air, directly in front of Neil's face. It fell to the ground and shattered at his feet. A second glass followed the example set by the first. "I am a wizard of sorts. Right now, this wizard is having a particularly bad day." Another glass appeared and dropped. "So," he continued, "unless you wish to see me do a few more tricks like that, I suggest you pour me my drink."

Neil thought that he might have to consider introducing a dress code for this restaurant. People dressed in brightly colored costumes were costing him a fortune in glassware lately. "Very well," he said and proceeded to tap the beer. He placed it on a coaster in front of Visitor and smiled. "On the house," he said. He turned around and proceeded to clean up the broken glass, while Visitor impatiently gulped down half of his drink.

Visitor made a satisfied sound and said, "You are a good man."

Neil walked to the far end of the bar, where two mostly empty glasses were sitting, left behind by previous customers. He picked them up and placed them by a sink, used for dishwashing. Visitor observed him carefully. When he saw Neil picking up his phone he said, "You know… I'm not crazy about people using their phone in the company of others." He was worried that Neil was contacting someone, maybe the authorities, about his suspicion that his current customer might cause trouble once he finished his complimentary beverage. "Just put that away, please."

"Right away, sir," Neil said. He didn't actually do what he said though, and his thumb was still moving around on the screen.

Visitor considered his options. His wizarding skills would not allow him to take the phone from Neil. That ability to move things was limited to stationary objects. A new idea occurred to him. *So simple.* Another empty glass disappeared from the rack with an ever so slight sparkle of light and reappeared mid-air in approximately the same place as where Neil was holding his phone. The effect was astounding. The glass intersected the phone as well as some of Neil's thumb. Neil screamed in pain as the glass separated almost half of his thumb from his hand. The phone and the glass broke apart, almost exploded, in Neil's hand, sending pieces including the partial thumb flying in all directions. Neil held up his hand and observed in horror how blood poured out from where the top of his thumb was now missing.

He yelled for help. "Help! Someone, help me!"

Visitor looked around but still saw no one. He got up from his barstool and started toward the end of the bar where Neil had backed himself into a corner. "Shut up!"

Neil was wrapping a kitchen towel around his bleeding hand. He didn't shut up at all, instead calling for help even louder than before. Feeling threatened by Visitor's approach, he picked up one of the dirty glasses and held it out in front of him as if it was a weapon, pointing it at Visitor. "Help! Help, please!"

"Shut up, you fool!" Visitor yelled. *What a mess.* "Why couldn't you just put the god-damned phone down when I told you to?"

As Visitor came nearer, Neil moved in the opposite direction, first toward Visitor and then passing him. The two men effectively switched places. Neil now behind the center of the bar where he had served Visitor his drink, and Visitor in front of the end of the bar, near the dishwashing station.

"I wasn't trying to hurt your hand. It was just an accident. I am still learning how to control this," Visitor said. "Calm down already!"

Neil persisted in his calls for help. If this continued, someone outside might hear him.

"Shut the hell up!"

Neil suddenly dropped the glass and reached under the bar. When his hand came back up, it was holding a gun. A small revolver that clicked in his hand before he pointed it, shaking, more or less at Visitor's face. Everything was different now. Visitor backed away and held up his hands in front of him, as if to shield himself. Both men were in uncharted territory here. Neil had held this gun in his hands at times but had never pointed it at a human being, let alone fired it at someone. He never wanted a gun. The only reason he had a loaded weapon hidden under his bar, was because a friend and fellow bar tender had urged him to, after narrowly surviving a shooting at a bar where he worked. Visitor in turn had never seen a gun pointed at him, or at anyone else for that matter.

"Okay, alright, let's think this through," Visitor said.

"Get out. Get out of my restaurant!" Neil, who was holding his weapon in the wrong hand because of his missing thumb, used it to gesture toward the door.

"Man, I really didn't mean to hurt your hand, you have to believe me! They can probably sew that back on." Visitor had backed up too far and no longer had a direct line of sight to the empty glasses on the rack behind the bar. He thought he could use one to disable the gun in the same way he had disabled the phone.

Neil could see Visitor's eyes search for something to use. It was clear to him what would happen if he found something. His voice now a high-pitched squeal, he yelled at the top of his lungs, "Get out of my restaurant or, I swear, I will shoot!" His outburst came with a flash and a bang.

Visitor stumbled backwards and grabbed the left side of his own neck with his right hand. He felt a sharp, burning pain and warm blood forcefully pumping out of a wound there. His hand was doing very little to stop it.

Neil screamed and dropped the gun. "Oh god! Oh god!" he yelled. He had pulled the trigger unintentionally.

Visitor lunged forward and grabbed on to the bar with his free hand. He tried to speak, but all he produced was an ugly gurgling sound. Blood oozed out of his mouth whenever he opened it. It was all he could taste. He struggled to breathe, as if he was drowning, and he couldn't seem to swallow anymore. Neil slowly backed away from the bar, holding his injured hand in his other. Visitor understood that he had only seconds left standing. If he was going to do anything else, it had to be now. A nearly empty whiskey bottle disappeared, shimmering, from the liquor display behind Neil. The bottle, leaving its remaining contents behind, reappeared inches above where Neil was standing and fell, bouncing off the top of his head, and shattered on the floor. Neil reached for his head with his uninjured hand, rubbing where the bottle had hit him. *Missed!* Visitor's grip on the bar weakened and he started to slide, his knees no longer supporting him. Another bottle disappeared, the liquor spilling, splashing down the display and dripping on the floor. The empty bottle reappeared exactly where Neil's head was.

Visitor collapsed to the floor, the stream of blood from the wound in his neck already slowing. Blood pooled on the floor around his head. *Lights out.*

Neil stood silent for a few seconds, the empty bottle grotesquely protruding from the top of his skull. Blood was seeping from his eyes and ears. He collapsed and dropped to the floor, his head strangely breaking apart in chunks delimited by the intersecting bottle. Another pool of blood formed.

CHAPTER TWENTY-NINE

DART'S UNCANNY ABILITY to randomly find people in distress had led him to the large Hemingway square in the city center. It was a tranquil spot that was popular with all sorts of people. Recently there had been some protesters who wanted the city to change the name, because of some controversy that Dart was not familiar with, but they weren't here today, adding to the generally positive atmosphere.

The square featured a fountain in its center. Dart had once saved a young child from drowning there. To this day he felt he handled that job poorly. When he pulled the kid out of the water, there had been no one to witness him do it. Unfortunately, the child, along with its parents, had subsequently kept the incident quiet, so Dart had not enjoyed any positive publicity for his heroic act. He should have waited just a little longer for at least a car to drive by.

Directly on the square was only one building, the city's largest and oldest public library. This attracted a crowd all its own. All other sides of the square were framed with roads, with buildings across the street from the square. Two sides were lined with trees, and there were benches placed in several places near the trees and near the fountain. There were skate boarders, people reading library books and people walking and talking, or just hanging out with the pigeons. Today there was even a street musician, an accordion player. Quite unnecessary if you asked Dart. Most people had seen Dart around enough that he didn't provoke much of a reaction anymore. Tourists would sometimes poke fun at his unusual appearance. If they ever needed him to save them, Dart was sure they wouldn't be all that worried about his outfit.

A child's voice suddenly called out, "Mommy! Mommy!"

Dart looked over and saw a young boy, maybe nine years old, standing by the fountain next to his mother, pulling on her coat, and pointing at him.

"It's him!" the boy exclaimed.

The mother was focused on her phone and didn't even look up.

The boy tried again. "Mommy, look!"

Dart felt that tingle of his. Where was the danger here?

The woman looked annoyed and said, "What is it?" She looked where the boy was pointing. "Oh, him," she said, sounding slightly disappointed. "Go say hi if you must." She promptly returned her attention to her phone.

Dart started toward them but had to pause for a skateboarder zipping by in front of him. He shook his head at the speed demon before introducing himself to the child. "Hello, I am Dart!"

The boy jumped up and down in excitement a few times and said, "Mom! It's Dartman!" He looked up at Dart. "I have a

Dartman action figure. It's lame because his arm keeps coming off. It also doesn't have any accessories, which is lame."

Dart said, "Actually, my name—"

The mother interrupted him, without looking up from the phone, and said, "I'm sorry. He talks a lot. His name is Daniel. He's a handful." Her thumbs never stopped drumming on the screen of her device.

Daniel continued. "I got it from a yard sale. I guess they didn't like their Dartman stuff anymore, because they had all kinds, and it was super cheap!"

Dart tried again and said, "My name is Dart. Not Dartman. You should know this." Dart tried to smile but managed no more than a crooked grin.

With his head cocked to one side, Daniel looked up at him, squinting. "Actually, it came in the original box, unopened, and on the box, it says…" Daniel said, tracing out an arc with one hand, "Dartman to the rescue!" He waited for Dart to say something, but nothing came. Undeterred, the boy kept talking. "Okay, so, do you have a sidekick? Because I think Dartman should have a sidekick. Arrowhead or Benjamin or something. Where are your darts? I think if you call yourself Dartman, you should—"

Dart was getting angry now and interrupted the boy. "No! Stop!" he yelled, "It's Dart, you moron. Get it right!"

The mother finally looked up from her phone and said, "Excuse me?" but her son didn't care and trudged on.

"You should have darts. Where do you hide them? Maybe you can shoot darts out of your—"

His mother interrupted him this time. "That's enough Daniel. I think Mr. Dart has other places to go." She quickly glanced at her phone, and then back at Dart. "Right now."

Daniel, being the handful that he was, still wanted his questions answered. "Mom, can you ask Dartman if he has darts?"

Dart hissed back at him and said, "Next time you say Dartman, I'll drown you in the fountain."

The mother raised her voice now. "That's it! Get out of here, you weirdo!"

Dart looked around and realized this looked bad. There was nothing to do but to make a quick exit. As he walked away, Daniel looked up at his mother, who was already focused back on her screen, and said, "Mom, we should have a yard sale soon."

A skateboarder zoomed by Dart so fast, he could feel the air move. His tingle intensified and he turned around, but he knew immediately that it was too late. He should have listened to his sixth sense the first time it tried to warn him.

Screams sounded across the square from nearby the fountain. The relentless accordion music finally stopped. The skateboarder had crashed into Daniel's mother at full speed and the collision sent him flying. He landed hard on the ground, sliding forward, his face grinding on the pavers. The teenager stayed down and didn't move, his skateboard rolling away at a distance. Daniel's mother was knocked over to one side, and her head hit the marble edge of the fountain. Her skull was cracked open like an egg, spilling some of its contents on the pavers. Her phone was swallowed by the fountain. Some people started running toward the scene, but they would be of no help to her, or to the skateboarder. Daniel's screams pierced the air. Dart dropped his shoulders, realizing he had failed this job. Daniel had distracted him from his tingling sensation, and now his mother was dead. Dart didn't care much for Daniel.

CHAPTER THIRTY

THE AFTERLIFE, Ed learned, was the same as ordinary life. It was for him at least, because he found himself in his wheelchair, facing the TV, feeling no different than before. But not really. Receiving a gunshot to the neck and then futilely fighting for his life, desperately trying to keep the blood inside his body, had changed his perspective a little. The only consolation was that the horrendous experience ended soon after it began, once and for all, in death. But here he was, remembering every dreadful second of it. No one should have memories like that. No matter how you die, you shouldn't have to deal with it afterwards. The scenario played back in his mind in a loop and each time it repeated it was more vivid and more gruesome.

How could he have let this situation spin so far out of control? And how was he still here? His special ability to move objects with his mind had until now seemed benign, like a harmless party trick.

Today it proved not to be so innocent. He had seriously hurt, and probably even killed a man. A man who, almost certainly, did not have another world to retreat to after death. It was something Ed could never undo, and it was bound to get him in trouble in what, he now no longer doubted, was his favorite of the two worlds he lived in. If the authorities there were looking for him, which was entirely possible if someone had seen him enter the restaurant, or if there were security cameras around, he would have a difficult time during his future visits. Little consolation could be found in that today was proof there was nothing lasting they could ever do to him. If they captured him, he would disappear from whatever confined space they kept him in when the experiment finished. And if they killed him? Would he now have immortality to rely on? *As superpowers go, that's not a bad one!*

It was still early enough that Ed had to be prepared to go again today. This time he was planning on making a video recording of his exit from the room. If it was true that no one ever saw him arrive in the other world, he wondered what it would look like when he left this one.

Before he broke the machine, there had been only one transition a day for some time. Those had all been later in the day. Now that Lora had lost almost a week due to repairs, he expected she would try to get more runs in a day. That sounded good, but it also meant she would reach her target sooner. Or Ian and Jim's target, whatever it was. And then, what? Back to normal?

THE SOUND OF CARS further behind him and the familiar feeling of soft grass under his feet. Visitor preferred entries into the park over those in alleys. One time he had found himself in the middle of the road just a little past Delaney's restaurant, but somehow, he had always ended up somewhere outside, and never was he in any immediate danger the moment of entry. There were a few people dispersed throughout the park, but nobody showed any particular interest in him. The first order of business would be to find out what the situation was at the restaurant. What happened this morning worried him. He didn't have to walk far. By the time he reached the campus gates he could see police lights further up the street. The street was closed. He could see an ambulance among several other emergency vehicles. It was obvious that what happened this morning had not worked out well for the bartender.

A few people were grouped around a bench on campus, near the Everett building, and he recognized all of them. Sitting on the bench was Lora, and she did not look happy. Randy was seated right beside her, with his arm around her shoulder and a box of tissues in his lap. The rest were standing around them. They were Jarod, Gary, and the elusive Ian. Ahead of Visitor, a police officer was walking toward him from the direction of Delaney's. The officer was looking directly at him, as most people tended to do when their eyes caught his conspicuous attire, but he didn't appear to be in a hurry to approach. So far, it didn't seem like anyone was looking for him specifically. He looked over at the group by the bench and at Ian in particular. There was no way of knowing how many more times he would have a chance to talk to Ian. It wasn't ideal that he had so many people with him, but this opportunity should not be wasted. When Visitor approached, he saw that Lora was in tears, again. The woman was a nervous wreck, largely on account of him. The others were there, trying to offer her some comfort.

"Hey. Look who it is," Visitor said to the group, making clear he was referring to himself by pointing at his own face.

"Dude, this is not a good time," Jarod said, looking at Lora and then back at him.

"I sympathize. What's bugging her?"

Gary, who was standing a little off to the side, said, "She lost a friend today. We all did."

"That is terrible." Visitor felt a sudden need to express a lack of compassion. For the people in this world, but especially for Ian. "I've lost a few people myself lately. A few thousand by now," Visitor said. "Ian, why don't you explain to me, and all your friends, what the hell you and your buddy Jim think you are doing over at B-Site?"

"Hey, just leave us alone man," Jarod said. "We've got enough problems here."

"Yeah," Randy said, handing Lora a tissue.

Visitor pulled out his phone and pushed it in Ian's face. "That is your doing. On run sixteen you killed over 130 people, runs nineteen and twenty-one killed over two thousand more. What for? Why are you doing this to us?"

Jarod stepped toward Visitor and gave him a light push. "Yo, bro! That's enough of you!"

"I wasn't talking to you," Visitor said, straightening his jacket and turning back to Ian. "What about it, Ian? Let's hear it."

"Look, I don't know who you are, but you need—" Ian started, but Lora interrupted him.

"That is Visitor. And like him, I am quite curious what you are hiding at B-Site." She handed the soaked tissue back to Randy, who wasn't sure why he took it from her, or where to put it next. Lora rubbed her upper arm. "Your security outright molested Randy yesterday, and they weren't too soft on me either." She sounded like her normal self but still looked a mess with puffy red eyes and wet cheeks.

"You are out of line. There is nothing at B-Site that concerns you, other than what you came to see yesterday."

"Why do you have your own fenced off backdoor into that place?" Visitor asked.

Lora raised her eyebrows at Visitor. *How does he always know about stuff like that?*

Ian looked uncomfortable. "Who are you?"

"I'm Visitor, just like she said."

Gary, Jarod and Randy all looked perplexed. They had no idea what was happening now. Lora got up from her seat.

Staring hard at Ian, she said to Visitor, "Show him the pictures of the lab." Then, to Ian, she said, raising her voice, "He's telling the truth. You're killing people!"

Even if he was focused on getting information from Ian, it hadn't escaped Visitor that he finally seemed to be getting through to Lora as well. He did what she asked.

Ian half looked at the screen but wasn't interested. "I really have no idea what you are talking about. But if you raise your voice at me again, you can look for a new job."

"Keep the threats to yourself, Ian," Visitor recommended. "If you do anything more to jeopardize Lora's experiment, or my world, you will regret it." He paused and then added, "Yes, that is a threat."

Ian turned to Lora again, "Who is this guy? Do you know him?"

Lora looked around the group, making eye contact with all her friends in turn. She said, "You guys, please trust me." Then she faced Ian again and took a deep breath. "Visitor is an as yet unexplained side-effect of my experiment. He exists when the machine is running and disappears when it is not. When he isn't here, he lives in a universe that we are targeting with The Slicer."

"Have you completely lost your mind?" Ian wanted to know.

Lora thought she might have, but she didn't answer. It was as if a great weight was lifted off her shoulders. This was probably the dumbest sounding thing she had ever said among colleagues, but to get it out was a huge relief.

"It's about time you stop asking questions and start answering some of ours," said Visitor.

Jarod grabbed Lora's shoulders, almost as if he was about to shake her, and looked into her eyes. "Are you alright in there?"

She calmly looked back at him. "It's alright, I promise. I know how it sounds, but it is true."

Gary, still keeping his distance, just shook his head.

Visitor raised his voice once again. "One of the people you killed happened to be my father," he said. He briefly looked at Gary, then over to Lora. "My foster father," he clarified. "I take that very personally." He grabbed Ian and planted him hard on the bench. "Sit down!" When he looked up, he found that not only the group, but also several bystanders were now looking at him. Lora noticed the same.

"Why don't we continue this conversation inside, in Ian's office," she said. "Hopefully we can make some sense of all this."

Visitor pulled Ian off the bench and shoved him ahead.

The guards in the foyer let the group in, without stopping them, which might be considered a security risk, but it was what usually happened if Ian was part of the group.

Ian's office had two doors, so that it could be reached from the quantum lab, and from a hallway outside the lab. Lora led the group into the office through the hallway door. There was a window with a view of the lab, although most of the view was obstructed with nearby equipment and shelving. The Shim, at the other end of the lab, was barely visible, but the purple glow in the background left no mistake that it was there. Inside the office was a desk with a computer and a few filing cabinets. There was also a couch with a coffee table. On the wall were pictures, including one of Dr. Shim shaking Ian's hand, and some framed certificates. And a dart board without any darts.

"Now, sit," Visitor said as he dropped Ian in the desk chair.

One by one, the items sitting on the desk disappeared, each with a little twinkle of light, only to reappear in mid-air beside the desk and then dropping to the floor. A pen, a wireless computer mouse, a stapler. More pens. Pieces of paper. Gasps were coming from those in the room who had never witnessed this trick before. Visitor methodically cleared the desk of everything that was small enough to move with his mind, seemingly without having to make much of an effort.

"That should give you some indication that I am not just a regular visitor," Visitor said. He bent down, picked up a pen and placed it back on the desk, adjusting it a few times to make it clear he was doing this for a purpose. "So, Ian, what are you, and your pal Jim, doing at B-Site?"

"Are you being serious right now? Who do you think you are?" Ian looked at Lora. "Where did you find this clown?"

"Just answer the question," Visitor said.

"Do you know who I am? I'm calling the police."

Visitor snatched the phone from Ian's hand the moment it cleared his pocket and casually dropped it in a waste basket under the desk. "What did I tell you about asking questions? What is going on at B-Site?"

"Nothing! Okay? B-Site is where The Shim will be relocated to. The site is currently being prepared to receive it."

Lora wasn't sure of what was happening now. How did she end up in a room with Visitor interrogating Ian? With two men threatening one another? And why was Ian still lying to them?

A loud scream briefly filled the room. Ian gasped for breath and almost jumped out of his chair. Visitor pushed him back down. The pen was no longer on the desk, and instead was half embedded into Ian's stomach. Ian yanked it out of himself with another shriek. There was a hole, but surprisingly little blood spilled from it, just enough to stain his shirt.

Everyone in the room recoiled, with shocked looks on their faces, except Visitor, who continued his interrogation with a remarkably calm voice. He had come this far, and now it was hard to back off. "Ian," he said, as he bent down, picked up the stapler and placed it on the desk where the pen had been earlier, carefully adjusting it to be parallel to the edges of the desk. "I think you can imagine how this is going to get a lot worse. What are you and Jim doing at B-Site?"

Lora, with a tremble in her voice, said, "Visitor, what are you doing? Please stop this."

"You stabbed me, you maniac! You're insane!" Ian yelled, spittle spraying in Visitors face. He pointed the bloody pen at Lora, and then the rest of the group. "And you're all just going to stand there?"

Lora was scared now. She understood exactly how Visitor's new variant of his trick with the pen could become very dangerous moving forward.

Gary had moved himself close to the door to the lab and looked like he was about to make a run for it. Visitor was already keeping an eye on him.

"Everyone, please stay calm," Lora said. "Visitor, please don't hurt him any further," she said. "Please don't hurt anyone else."

She looked around the room. "Gary, it's okay. Jarod. Please, just hold on."

Visitor, hearing Lora's nervous pleas, thought he might have gone a little too far. But the path he was on now had no way back, and so, he doubled down on the threat. "Is it worth the pain, Ian?"

Ian's face had changed. Visitor had him. Words started spilling. "It's Project E! Alright?"

Visitor did a double take. "Project E? You're running Project E, at B-Site?"

"Yes! No, Jim is!"

"To what end? Shim assured me that even Jim came to his senses about that one. It was a failure."

Gary suddenly spoke up. "Project E was a disaster. A waste of time and money. Why would you revive that nonsense?"

Even now, Visitor still wasn't used to hearing his father's voice. He continued. "Jim, in my world, explained Project E to me. In my world, Jim isn't an asshole," Visitor said. He looked over at Gary and said, "I don't think Jim believes Project E is a failure." Turning Ian's chair so he could face him directly, he asked "What are you doing with Project E?"

"It's true," Ian said, "Jim has discovered that when Lora configured The Slicer the way she did, we can run Project E successfully when we run it in parallel with The Shim. Somehow, The Slicer is enabling Project E. We don't understand why, but it works."

Lora was sitting on the couch now, next to Jarod. "Seems to me, this whole project is turning into one big mystery. So, why the secrecy?" she asked. "Wouldn't that be something we should be investigating here, in the lab?"

"Yes, sure. But I don't think Jim cares much for the science anymore. He was quite invested in Project E. The abandoning of it cost him greatly. The subsequent success of The Shim project, which he didn't support, has put him off. But it was Jim who first realized that Project E and The Slicer were complementing each other, and he had different plans with it. Hence his interest in supporting Lora's project." Ian took a few labored breaths before he continued. "He wanted to use Project E to covertly bring a modest amount of material from the multiverse into ours. He said he could do it by himself, but he needed my support to gain access to the Project E hardware at B-Site. I refused at first, but he made me an offer that was impossible to resist. No one would resist that. He took care of everything, paid for it all. I just had to hand him the keys. Jim was the one who put up the wall in B-Site to separate Project E from the rest of the building."

Lora still thought this didn't make sense. "But why keep it a secret? If Project E is working, it would be revolutionary. It should be known, especially to us as facilitators."

"Jim is convinced it will only work with The Shim in its current state. He says it is impossible we'll ever get it to work again once you finish your project. When we relocate The Shim or when we reconfigure The Slicer, it is over. You struck gold on your first try, Lora. Literally. The tennis ball, the current location, the configuration, all of it combined turned out to create perfect conditions." Ian looked tired now, and he seemed a little out of breath from talking.

Visitor shook the chair Ian was sitting in. "Answer the damned question already! Why was it a secret? Were you aware of the damage you were causing to my world? The people you were killing. What are you stealing, anyway?"

"It was supposed to go unnoticed. In all worlds involved. That was the point. Jim wanted to extract five small batches of gemstones, preferably diamonds. If successful, we'd be looking at about fifty to a hundred million dollars' worth. It was going to be a relatively low-key inter-universal heist. The first of its kind, and almost certainly the last. When this project ends, there won't be a shred of evidence left behind. It will be impossible to know where the diamonds came from or how they got here." Avoiding the glaring stares of his astonished audience, Ian took a deep breath. "And to answer your other question, we never anticipated that the exchange would affect the multiverse in any other way than to remove goods and add energy somewhere. We swap energy for diamonds."

Lora got up and picked up a pen from the floor. She flung it hard at Ian. "Are you serious?" she yelled at him. "Money? That's what this is all about? You are using the world's most advanced physics experiment to steal diamonds? What the hell is wrong with you?"

"And they were using you to do it, Lora. Your project enabled theirs," Visitor said, adding fuel to the fire.

"Damn you, Ian! All our data could be worthless now. It *is* worthless now!" Lora yelled. "Who knows how Project E interacted with The Slicer? Or what kind of interference it caused. What is the point of all this now?" She pointed through the window at the purple glow. "Have I been doing this just to facilitate your scam?" Her emotions getting the better of her once again, her voice cracked. This was turning into the worst day of her life. "What do you have to say for yourself?"

Ian sat there quietly, not even looking at her.

"This is my life we're talking about!" she yelled.

Visitor mumbled, "Now you know what that feels like…"

"Get out of my way," Lora snapped at Gary. She left the room to go into the lab, slamming the door behind her.

Ian suddenly slumped in his chair, almost sliding off. Visitor stepped back and held his hands up to indicate that he didn't do anything. The stapler still sat neatly on the edge of the desk.

"We need to get him to a hospital," Gary said. "I think he's bleeding internally."

Visitor was skeptical. "Just from that little pen in—", but then, he was suddenly gone. And so was the purple glow in the lab.

Gary went on his phone to call an ambulance while the rest of the group came to see Lora at The Shim. She was standing by one of the consoles, her hand still resting on the emergency stop button and tears streaming down her cheeks.

"I'll be putting a man in a wheelchair," she whispered, acknowledging this for the first time. "I've killed a thousand people."

Randy took her in his arms, and this time she let it all out.

CHAPTER THIRTY-ONE

S EEING AS PEOPLE were now sharing their secrets, Ed shared one of his own with Jim, by sending him a video of himself disappearing from his wheelchair in a blue ball of light, along with another invitation for a video call. He had watched the recording himself a dozen times already. It was surreal to see himself begin to levitate above his chair, with blue light emanating from below him. He saw himself slowly tilting backward as the blue light engulfed him and lifted him higher. By the time the sphere surrounded him, which took only a few seconds, and masked him from view completely, the ball collapsed into a point and disappeared. A few of those electric arcs fizzled out around the area and then there was just the empty chair.

Ed's last foray into Lora's world had not gone as well as it could have. He now had information about the scheme Ian and their version of Jim were running, but the way he handled it might have put a premature stop to Lora's project. *Talk about shooting yourself in the foot.* His intention had never been to hurt Ian beyond just getting him to talk.

Jim accepted the invitation the next day. This time, Ed wasn't holding back.

"What if I told you, and I know this for a fact, that there is another universe out there, not unlike this one, where my father did not park his car across the road on the day of the accident? He didn't have me with him in the car because I didn't exist there. In that world, the cement truck swerved for the pedestrian, but didn't have to swerve a second time to avoid the parked car. The driver regained control, and no one ever even heard about this near incident."

"Well sure. If that scenario is possible, I'm sure, somewhere it will exist. Ed, what are you talking about?"

"Over there, my father is alive, and The Shim was built. Dr. Shim became nothing short of a legend."

Jim made a face. "Oh god. And rich too, I imagine. He'd have transformed the transport industry by now."

"No, no. The experiment was successful, but it's still just an area of active research. The Shim exists only in the NMU lab. It has limitations. I don't know the details. For one, it is kind of slow and hungry for energy."

Jim laughed. "Your father always said you had a vivid imagination. But where are you going with this?"

"I'm not making this up, Jim. In the video you can see what has been happening to me once or twice a day over the past weeks. I pop out of this universe and into theirs. They call it a side-effect of their experiment."

It took Ed most of the afternoon to tell the whole story. Everything from his cellphone related mind-control to the weirdness that occurred after his phone was modified by Jarod. From the young physicist who was leading the current project, down to the scam that Ian and Jim's alter ego were running.

"Ian and Jim are running Project E, in parallel to Lora's project. When they are successful, it causes major disruptions in our reality. The dragons, Australia, the earthquakes, it all happened precisely on the dates they ran Project E successfully alongside The Shim."

By the end of the call, Jim was quiet, as if numbed by information overload. Ed felt confident that he had convinced Jim he was telling the truth. He ended by pointing out that it was possible his days of walking in the other universe had ended when he confronted Ian. A point driven home by another day without a transition.

The next day, Jim sent a message inviting Ed for an in-person meeting at B-Site, with a renewed abundance of enthusiasm. He said he would be happy to make any arrangements needed to accommodate Ed and his wheelchair. Before long, after a few back-and-forth messages, Ed was booked into the same hotel he had used during the convention. He packed his bag, throwing in a few clothes and his weird phone, using a shirt to pick it up with. He traveled at night, just in case another transition would occur, which of course it didn't.

Very early the next morning, Jim came to pick Ed up at the hotel, with a wheelchair accessible van he had rented for the purpose. Ed had requested they would travel only outside of the normal hours where transitions could occur, and Jim had been happy to oblige. Before seven in the morning, Jim pulled up at B-Site. Ed recognized it immediately, even if the surrounding area looked a little different here, with fewer buildings. Jim got out of the van and walked to the gate in the fence, digging out a key from his pocket. He opened the padlock and the gate, then drove the van through, leaving the gate open. Jim had more keys, some of which he used to open the door to the building.

"I'm not sure if anyone else even has keys to this place anymore," he said. He took position behind Ed's wheelchair and started pushing. "Why don't you get one of those electric wheelchairs?"

Ed grunted. "I had one. Then I made a mistake filling in some forms. Now I don't. Can't afford to buy one right now."

"Don't you work in insurance?"

Ed ignored the question. He was quite sure he didn't tell Jim that, but Jim had clearly done his homework. They entered the reception area. It was dark inside.

"Just give me one second," Jim said. He left Ed behind and went through a door to the left of the reception area. A few moments later the lights came on. Jim came back and said, "I turn the power off when I'm not here, I don't want to attract squatters or have it burn down. I pretend all of this is mine, as nobody else seems to care. I have tried a few times to buy the building but, not knowing exactly who is selling, that didn't go anywhere."

On the other side of the reception desk was a door with a handwritten note on it, that read "factory floor". As soon as he entered, Ed could hardly believe what he was seeing. The hall was in pristine condition. A little bit of dust, but other than that it looked as if it was still being used. He saw The Shim, partially built, with cables running from it in all directions, toward what looked like folding tables stacked with old computers and other equipment. Those would become the future consoles, he assumed. He saw a paper cup sitting on one of the tables and smirked. It was surreal to see an incomplete version of The Shim after already seeing the final version in operation in Lora's lab.

He had never seen it in this form before, as his father had never taken him to B-Site.

Jim kept pushing him through the hall. Most of it was filled with large machines that Ed could not identify. All the way near the end of the hall, where they found real, fully finished console tables, Jim stopped. The consoles were set up around a predominantly black machine with a shape and size that resembled a jet engine. A large white letter E was painted on the side, making it clear that this was the infamous Project E.

Jim positioned Ed at one of the consoles and left him there. He walked toward the machine and turned to face Ed. "This machine," he said, "if they had pursued it, could have improved the quality of life of everyone on this planet. It would have provided basic needs and luxury alike. I am convinced that it would have saved countless lives by now. It could have made the world an objectively better place, for everyone. Not developing it, leaving it here unused and unattended is wrong in so many ways. To me, the inaction of Shim and his team back then, is nothing short of passive genocide! It is an attrition!"

Ed sat in silence as he thought about how to respond. "If you're trying to sell this thing to me, Jim, I must disappoint you. I can't afford it. And it doesn't work, does it? Not without The Shim and The Slicer."

Jim pointed a finger at Ed and said, "Exactly!"

"You don't have either of those."

"Ed. If I understand you correctly about what The Slicer is—"

"I don't even know what it is. Not in detail."

"Well, let me ask you this question. Do you think it matters on which side The Slicer is doing its job when Project E is active?"

"I don't understand."

"I think," Jim said, pointing back at Project E, "that we can run Project E, here, if they are running The Slicer there. In fact, I am certain of it."

"Oh." Ed's eyes suddenly opened wide. "Oh! One problem though. For the past few days, they haven't been running it."

Jim walked back over to Ed. "You have told me their project isn't finished. So, why would they stop now? You don't think they will resume at some point?"

"I have been on a mission to try and get it prolonged, but everything I did has had the opposite effect. When I extracted the information from Ian about his scheme, I may have gone too far. I may have seriously hurt him. I'm not sure if the project isn't already dead." Ed stopped to think. "You know I killed a man there? One of Lora's friends. She doesn't know it was me."

Jim shrugged. "So, what? You got one person killed in some other universe! Do you know how many they killed in ours? You haven't killed anyone, Ed. No one in our reality was harmed by what you did. Why should you care what happened in that other universe? It's not as if they care about us, is it?"

"It seems that way, yes," Ed said.

"Besides, when their machine isn't running, then whatever happens, or happened in their universe is of no consequence to us. Nothing they can do has any effect whatsoever on anyone alive over here. Even if they blow up their universe, all of humanity, along with all the aliens in our universe, will be just fine. We won't even know it happened."

Ed sat in silence.

"I mean, come on Ed, I know you can see it! We can make a difference here. Here! In *this* world. The world where everyone who matters lives. Their world is none of our business, except that we need them to run their experiment. One more time! If they do that, we have a shot at a near-utopian future. Paradise, Ed! This thing has the potential to make everyone happy. It's a happiness machine."

"I suppose," Ed said. "Can you even run this machine after all this time?"

"With some help, I can get this thing up and running in just a few days. I know how to operate it, but I will need a few technical people around who can help me get started or fix stuff if something doesn't work. But that isn't a problem, Ed, I can get people."

Ed thought of something. "I overheard their Jim say that Project E works better if they know in advance when The Shim is started. Apparently, that was already difficult for Ian and Jim in their universe, because they were operating behind Lora's back, but it will be even harder for us. Besides, when they run their machine, I won't be here. I will be *there*, with them."

"I thought about that already. It seems to me that we should be starting Project E just prior to, or at the same time as, when they start The Slicer."

"Why can't we just leave it running?"

"Because of the energy requirements, for one. The generators won't sustain it for more than a few minutes at a time in startup mode. Once we've synced up with The Slicer in their world, we can run for as long as they let us. We can do many runs in a row during one run of The Shim."

Another thought popped into Ed's head. "What will happen to their universe if we run this thing successfully? Are they going to have the same problems as us. Will there be dragons, too?"

"I'm not sure what is going on with all that. I wish I did. Seeing as dragons didn't naturally occur in this world, and I suspect they don't in their world either, they must be coming from somewhere else. Somehow this Slicer thing is leaking, or Project E is interfering with it, causing it to leak. My guess is they will get all the same shit that we got, but worse."

"Why worse?"

"A lot worse! We cannot count on them running this project in perpetuity. If weird stuff starts to happen, they'll pull the plug on it. So, I think, realistically, we have only one shot at this. And during that one shot, we need to take everything we can. The biggest heist in the history of the multiverse! I think we can assume that the more we take, the more weirdness they'll have to contend with."

Ed was impressed. "It's been what? Two days, since I told you about their world? And you figured all this out already?"

Jim laughed. "I have spent years studying Project E since it was canceled and even after the accident put an end to The Shim. I was always convinced there's a way to run this thing. Here we are, and I am not going to miss it!"

For Ed there was not much left to say, except, "They're not running the project anymore. What if they already pulled the plug?"

Jim put his hand by his face, shaped as if he was making a phone call. "Can't you just call them on that fancy phone you told me about?"

Ed thought for a second. *How did I not think of that?* "It's not that simple, Jim. Even if I can send them a message, I am not sure what it should be if it is to compel them to do what we want."

"Tell them," Jim said with enough confidence to show he had thought about this detail as well, "that thousands of lives are at stake. Hell, millions of lives! Tell them that you can save them all with just one more run of their machine. You know, make up some crazy shit. Make them feel much obliged to help us. Lies have no consequences if you tell them only in another universe."

This line of thinking was well out of Ed's comfort zone, but he could see the point. He nodded slowly, looking down at his hands.

"Great!" Jim said, "I am going to put together a small crew. We'll have this thing ready to go in no time. You can tell them an exact date and time, so we can be ready on the first try."

The look on Ed's face still didn't give Jim the impression he was fully on board with the plan.

"What is it, Ed?"

"It's just… I don't like the idea of cutting off all my access to their world. I can walk there, Jim! If we go through with this, I'll never get out of this chair again."

Jim waved his hand. "If this works out, you'll have everything you need to buy yourself a pair of legs. I'm sure there are some medical solutions for your problems. Or technological ones. It is my experience that a lot of problems can be solved by throwing money at them."

"Maybe," Ed admitted.

"You don't seriously think a bunch of scientists in another universe are going to voluntarily run their experiment forever, just because you like marching around in their world, do you?"

Ed seriously didn't think that, but he still felt reluctant about giving up on being Visitor.

"Are we in business, or what?" Jim wanted to know.

"We are."

Chapter Thirty-Two

IT HAD BEEN FIVE DAYS since Lora came home on that dreadful day when first she found out Neil had died, and then Ian was hospitalized. Until now, Ian had undergone two surgeries, but still had not regained consciousness. Doctors told Lora that almost any outcome was presently possible, ranging from recovery to permanent coma or death, but that the longer it took for him to come to, the worse his outlook would be. As the Everett building also accommodated a few smaller physics labs that were used extensively and exclusively by students, the university had decided that the building would remain open despite Ian's absence. Nevertheless, the quantum lab was closed pending news of his recovery. Once Ian was back, *if* he came back, Lora knew she would not return. Her project would be canceled, and The Shim dismantled for relocation.

The police were investigating, and Lora had received detectives at her house a few times. Her story, which matched those of the other witnesses perfectly, was as close to the truth as possible without going into details about Visitor's origins. An unknown individual wearing a red suit, who had visited the lab twice before, posing as a potential new investor, had gained access to the lab and stabbed Ian with one of his own pens, demanding money. When Ian lost consciousness, the stranger disappeared in the ensuing commotion. The group had agreed on this story immediately after the incident. They all agreed that if Ian was to wake up, he would probably not just tell the truth, because that would expose him and Jim. What they were doing at B-Site, one way or another, had to be illegal. If Ian did decide to talk and tell the truth, his story would be rather hard to believe, even for the most open-minded detective, if he remained the only person to tell it that way.

Lora had spent most of her time at home, with a lot of it spent going over everything that happened and worrying about what lay ahead. Jarod and Gary had visited her twice. By now she had told them everything that happened in the past weeks.

Alice, her chief data analyst, had shown up at her doorstep asking her to sign a get-well card for Ian. She did, and even donated money to get him a present.

Randy came by every day and spent a lot of time talking with Lora. He too, now knew everything she knew about Visitor and his powers. Randy especially had been very supportive and turned out to be a good listener for when she needed to vent. Occasionally he made her laugh, which was not an easy thing to do the last few days. When one day he brought a box of chocolates for her, they ended up eating all of it together before he left.

Dr. Shim had called her a few times, but she was still reluctant to tell him the story. There was no need to feel that way because, as it turned out, he had already found out most of the details from

Gary. All these people were her friends, and they were all being very nice to her. She felt grateful for, and undeserving of, their kindness. If she hadn't talked to Visitor, all of this might have been prevented. She felt guilty for bringing the project to a premature end for her crew, as well as for what happened to Ian. She would have gladly seen him lose his job over what he and Jim had done, but he didn't have to get hurt.

At present, Randy had just left after only a short visit this time. Now that the lab was closed, he had found new motivation to do his schoolwork and he was making somewhat of a comeback in that area. Lora was in her home office, nestled in the comfortable chair, with a fragrant cup of tea and a book. Reading was always one of her favorite things to do, and she often wished she had more time for it. If she could get well enough into one of these stories, it was a great way to escape the far stranger reality she had been a part of. Today it wasn't to be.

Lora made it about an hour into her book when a loud, unexpected but strangely familiar sound yanked her out of it. When she looked over at her side table, she felt the blood drain from her face. The teacup, her favorite, was in pieces, the fragments now on the floor in the middle of the room. The tea was dripping from the table, while some of it was soaking into another book she had left there to read later. Was there someone in the house? There were no other sounds, and she saw no movement. *What now?* She half expected the power to go out, and then to hear footsteps or voices in the basement. *What basement? Get a grip!* Then she remembered what happened with the keychain.

"Oh no... Visitor?" she whispered. "Oh god, please no."

She dropped her book and got up from the chair. One of the books on the shelf across the room disappeared in a subtle twinkle of light, and then fell from the ceiling above her head. She moved just in time, and the book only just hit her shoulder on its way to the ground. "What do you want?" she asked. There was no one else in the room. She was a little afraid to move.

Another book disappeared from the shelf, and Lora tried to shield herself with her hands, but this time the book reappeared only just above the ground, by the remnants of the teacup and dropped on the ground as if placed there purposely by an invisible hand. Another book followed and landed beside the first. More books followed at an increasing tempo. "Stop it, please! Leave me alone!" Her voice sounded unnecessarily loud in the quiet room. The moving books were making hardly any noise.

When another book dropped, it neatly completed a circle on the floor. O.

It stayed quiet.

Lora took a step away from the chair, hoping to get to the door, but immediately another book dropped from the ceiling, this time hitting her on the back of her head. It was painful. She rubbed her head and looked at the book on the floor. A heavy, imitation leatherbound edition of *Frankenstein*. This was going to be another reason she preferred paperback books over hardcovers, she thought. "Okay, okay. I'm not moving." *I thought you said you can't see me.* Besides afraid, she now felt mostly annoyed. "Are you putting them back for me as well?"

A few books from one end of the circle on the floor disappeared and moved elsewhere in the room, as if discarded. Another pause followed, leaving an open circle. U.

Is he sending a message?

More books were discarded, and others adjusted, to make a straight line. I.

"All vowels," she whispered. *What is the point of this?*

The pattern broke with the next letter. A few were added back from the discarded pile, adding a hook to the straight line. J.

The next letter took longer to form, as all books were brought back into play. A.

Nothing more happened.

Lora sequenced all the letters she had seen so far in her mind. "Ouija," she said. She waited a little longer without moving, but no more books followed. A nervous laugh escaped her. *Is he seriously proposing a séance?*

As a rational scientist, Lora had an irrational attitude toward ghosts. It wasn't that she believed in them, of course not, but more that she didn't want to do anything that might accidentally bring one about. A Ouija board wasn't something she ever wanted in her house. But this was no ordinary ghost. First, this one was real, which wasn't a property she usually attributed to other ghosts. Second, this wasn't so much a haunting as it was a home invasion. This ghost did not belong to someone who was dead. Then again, it didn't belong to anyone alive in the universe either.

When she was finally satisfied that no more books would attack her, she moved to the desk and went online to find a printable copy of a Ouija board. *Why not? Maybe that way, I can tell him to get lost.* She printed it across two sheets. From a drawer she pulled a well-used roll of sticky tape and used it to tape the two halves of the board onto the surface of her desk. Her disembodied tormenter would need something to point out letters on the board with, so she placed the almost empty roll of tape on the board, covering the letter A. She waited.

She waited about fifteen minutes, but nothing happened. It appeared that Visitor had left her alone. For now.

After rummaging around in the drawer once more, she picked out a travel-sized foldable makeup mirror and flipped it open. She looked at herself, gazing deep into her own eyes. Thirty seconds went by. *Have I lost it? How crazy am I?* She imagined Visitor, or whoever the son of Gary Sutherland was in his universe, watching her in her own house. He had told her that he couldn't see her when he did this last time, but what would that look like? Could he see her in the mirror, like she could? Was he still watching, or did he leave for real? When would he be back?

Lora's thoughts were interrupted when her phone rang. It was an unknown number, but she felt a chill, as if she knew what was coming. She picked up and listened, covering her mouth with one hand. Ian was dead.

E D WOKE UP IN HIS WHEELCHAIR, in the hotel room. He was at the back of the hotel on the ground floor, in a wheelchair accessible room this time, which was considerate of them, but it also meant that his view was now that of a beverage dispenser and an ice machine, located directly across from his window. He would have much preferred the view of the campus ruins he had last time. His phone was on the floor beside him, and he reached for it. Nothing happened when he touched it. It was dead and needed to be recharged. He plugged it in, careful not to touch it with his skin when he did and looked at the time. It was the middle of the night. *How did I sleep through half a day?* Using his power to manipulate Lora's world by phone, it seemed, was an exceedingly taxing experience. After he had dropped the last book, the phone had slipped out of his hand, simply because he was too exhausted to hold it. He fell asleep moments later, just after he had regained his normal color vision.

Ed's approach to making contact was a plan forged largely while learning about some of the limitations of the inter-universal phone by engaging in a series of exploratory missions into Lora's home. He found out quickly that if Lora moved, so did the area in which he could roam. There was a decent amount of space around her that he could explore in detail, but when he strayed too far, or if she moved away from him, soon he would find himself restricted in both her world and his.

The first time it happened he didn't understand what was going on. While he was exploring Lora's kitchen, which was open to a dining area, which in turn was open to a living area, she must have suddenly walked out, possibly out of the house, leaving him behind far enough that he lost all sense of location in her kitchen, along with his view of the room he was in. The purple fog thickened rapidly, soon a nearly opaque, viscous goo, through which even his fingers, which he could no longer see, wouldn't move. How would he let go of his phone now? Simultaneously, his ability to discern details in Lora's kitchen waned until there was nothing but a disorienting mélange of inane shapes, drifting aimlessly through an undefined space. Deprived of meaningful sensory input from both worlds, Ed found it impossible to imagine how to facilitate an escape from this empty and dreary environment, or to gauge how much time he had spent in it.

When Lora finally returned to the kitchen, she brought with her the warm and comfortable, detailed world she lived in, as well as his own purple background environment. He realized he had been in real danger just now, but her return was so gratifying that his concerns on that matter quickly made way for elation and a resulting powerful desire to stay with her. What if he was left behind somewhere Lora wasn't coming back to? When she moved, he realized, he would have to follow her, floating, or he might be stuck, possibly forever in that desolate no man's land between two worlds. Luckily, that turned out to be easy enough, now that he knew what to expect. The focused, crisply detailed area that surrounded her, noticeably shifted in the direction of her travel whenever she started moving. He just had to make sure to pay attention to it and stay inside that area.

Ed only made it into the living room of Lora's home once when she happened to have two visitors. Here he learned that his inability to sense Lora did not entirely preclude him from determining where she was. Inside the focused area, he found that sometimes there were specific spots that were hard to discern, even if everything else was crystal clear. In this instance, he had a clear sense of a chair, but somehow the seat, and part of the backrest were not really there, obscured by a darkness. *A shadow, maybe?* In front of the chair, he noticed a similar problem with a small area on the floor. It had to be where she was sitting. He couldn't correctly perceive things that she was touching. Despite these strange limitations in his ability to sense Lora directly, he had no such problems with other people near her. He could tell where they were, what they were wearing and even the color of their eyes if he got close enough, even if all he could really see was the violaceous view of his room. In this case, he also knew immediately who they were. Gary, on the left, and Jarod. Both had placed their phones on the coffee table in front of them, and Ed was very much tempted to make the devices move to scare the living daylights out of these guys, but he didn't want to upset Lora. Not yet anyway.

On his last exploratory excursion into Lora's home, she had been sitting in her comfortable chair, in her office, reading a book.

On the little side table was a cup of tea. The book was barely and only partially there, just enough for him to know where it was and how it moved. The cup sometimes disappeared, or nearly so, as Lora presumably picked it up to take sips. He observed the chair, mesmerized by the movements of these inanimate objects, while occasionally roaming the room, thinking about how he could communicate with Lora. Soon enough, he found that spilling the tea was going to be the easiest way to announce himself in a way she would recognize. But how would he tell her what he needed from her? He couldn't move things along a path, he could only make them disappear in one location and reappear somewhere else, so writing with a pen, or pressing keys on a keyboard, or pointing out letters in a book, was not easily achievable.

His thoughts were interrupted when he unexpectedly returned to the real world. He was exhausted, as he had been every time he came back, but he didn't come back of his own volition this time. The mystery soon unraveled when he realized that his phone had died. After some consideration, this came as a relief to him. If he made sure to use the phone only when it was not connected to a charger, never to touch it unless it was untethered, he had an insurance policy, an escape clause, in case he ever found himself trapped in the dreadful purple goo again.

It was the middle of the night. Lora would be asleep, so he would wait until the next day before he tested his idea of using a Ouija board. Ed was sore from sleeping in his wheelchair, so he worked himself into the comfortable hotel bed and tried to get some more sleep.

In the morning he ordered breakfast in his room and then called Jim to confirm that Project E would be ready to go on Friday, at two in the afternoon.

Even though he knew from his observations that Lora was most likely to spend late afternoons in her study, sometimes well into the evenings, Ed didn't want to wait that long. Instead, he found her in the dining room, most likely sitting at the table, judging from his initial position and the lack of detail in one of the chairs. He sensed her phone on the table. Once in a while, it briefly disappeared. There was a plate of nachos as well. A chip would occasionally disappear off the plate, never to return. Ed probed around for something that Lora wasn't going to touch. All he needed was to draw her attention, not to scare her or, worse, inadvertently hurt her. He had taken enough of a risk throwing books at her, without having a way to gauge weights and having only her shadows to estimate where exactly she was. There was an empty napkin holder at the far end of the table. He willed it a little closer to her. Her chair moved away from the table. *She's getting up.* A moment later it moved back to where it came from, and the nachos resumed their vanishing act. *Is she ignoring me now?* It was interesting to feel how much energy he had used just to move one small object, compared to the relaxing, almost hypnotic effect of merely observing his invisible target. He would have to be as efficient as possible in his communication with Lora, so he opted to wait until she finished eating.

The chair moved and the focused area started to shift. Ed floated with it. There was such a big difference between being close to her, which felt like such a warm and happy place, and taking even half a room distance from her, where it quickly got cold and dreary, and that obnoxious purple color seemed to seep through into her world.

He was led directly to the desk in the study. Immediately he noticed the Ouija board. *It worked!* He felt a jolt of excitement. It was a standard board, with all letters of the alphabet, the numbers zero through nine and the words, "Yes", "No" and "Goodbye", along with four other symbols. The first message he sent, by moving the roll of tape first to H and then to I on the board, was just to test if he could be sufficiently accurate. Besides the energy he had to exert to make each move, it wasn't difficult at all. He could be just as precise as he would be using his hands. It felt natural. *How will she reply?* The roll of tape moved again, this time without Ed's influence, sliding across the board until it stopped by the bottom edge, on "Goodbye". Ed chuckled. *She's talking back using the board.* Ed sent his next message. He was going to come directly to the point before trying to have any more fun, because he didn't know how many moves he would be able to make before exhausting himself. He sent, "1 RUN FRI AT 2".

Nothing happened for a while. "One run, Friday at two, please," Ed said out loud. "Easy enough." He waited.

Finally, the roll of tape moved, this time to the top right corner of the board, where it read, "No". Ed moved it to the top left, to say, "Yes". He waited again but there was no further activity on the board. *What is she doing? I am the ghost here; I should not be the one waiting for answers!* It was an amusing thought to be on the wrong side of this strange game. He shifted his attention away from the board and immediately noticed the computer monitor. She was typing a message, using some large font, on the screen. He could read it perfectly, despite the strange way in which he was perceiving it.

Lora wrote, "Lab closed. No access. Go away."

Ed was already beginning to feel the effects of sending just two messages. He thought about the best way to respond and ultimately settled on "WHY". He wanted to add a question mark, but there wasn't one on the board. *Are ghosts not allowed to ask questions?*

Regardless, a reply materialized on Lora's screen, and it sent chills down Ed's spine. "Ian passed away yesterday."

Just like that, in only four words, Ed was now aware that he had, in a single day, killed not one, but two men. Three, if he considered that he got himself killed as well. It took him a moment to process the news. How did he, a disabled former insurance worker, turn into a murderer – a *serial* killer – overnight? Considering the limitations of the current communication channel, and the intended goal for today, he decided not to dwell on the topic of Ian, other than to send, "SRY". *I am sorry. The bar tender didn't have to die. But Ian was a prick.* Then he reiterated his earlier request. "FRI 2PM SHARP", following up with "NOT EARLY", and finally adding, "LAST 1".

Lora simply moved the tape roll back to, "No".

Now, Ed was about to repeat a lie. It had been sitting dormant in the back of his mind ever since his ride in Lora's car. Despite the situation he was now in, he didn't feel comfortable lying to her. Jim had tried to convince him of the insignificance of those who lived in other universes, and maybe he had a point. But Lora was special. She gave him something that no one in his own universe could ever have given him. Jim was right about some things though. For one, Ed's actions paled in comparison to the devastation that Ian and other Jim had caused. And for another, Ed's walking days in Lora's world were numbered, one way or another. With the news of Ian's passing, it was even possible that the last one had already come and gone. To walk again, he would have to convince Lora to run the machine. If Jim's plan with Project E was successful, maybe that would compensate for some of the misery that Ian and other Jim had caused. The way forward was clear. It had to happen.

Ed sighed. He started to move the tape roll. He sent, "SAVE MANY LIVES IN 1 WALK". After a moment he added another lie, "I KNOW HOW".

There was a long pause before Lora replied. It was not what Ed hoped for. "Impossible. Lab is closed. Leave me alone."

Ed, now exhausted, responded slowly with, "FIND A WAX". The tape roll ended up on the letter X, but he meant to say Y. There was barely enough energy left in him to make the correction, but somehow, he found a way. *Find a way.* He dropped the phone and watched the purple dissolve as his eyes adjusted. For now, he needed to rest.

L ORA SAT AT HER DESK staring at the Ouija board. She typed "Hello?" to the screen, but there was no response. Her phone was on the desk, and she picked it up to call Dr. Shim. She needed someone to talk to who was physically present in her universe. Someone not a ghost.

"Visitor asked for just this one run of The Shim, on Friday, at exactly two in the afternoon," Lora said.

"That's impossible. For what purpose, might I ask?"

"Well, he said he found a way to save the lives of people affected by the disasters in his world caused by Project E."

The doctor groaned. He had spent some time thinking about how Lora's experiment was enabling Project E, but he was completely in the dark. He and Jim hadn't been on speaking terms since the abandonment of Project E, but why had Jim not informed him of this most remarkable discovery? In the same way, he couldn't understand how Project E was doing so much damage to the slice carved by The Slicer. The extractions should be completely clean. Ian and Jim's scheme should have worked flawlessly if Project E was indeed working correctly in combination with The Shim. He asked Lora to say more about the nature of the disasters, but other than to shock him, it didn't do anything to give him further insights into the mechanism by which they were caused.

"The lab is closed, and Visitor is giving us only two days. He urged me to find a way," said Lora. "There is no chance NMU will reopen the lab so soon. I don't even know if I still have a project."

The doctor agreed. "Without Jim, there is no financial backing and without Ian there really isn't anyone to defend your experiment anymore. Other than me, of course. I'm sorry, Lora. I really wanted you to have this." After a short pause, he asked, "Do you know why Mr. Visitor is asking for such a specific time?"

"No, I don't," Lora said, "but he said he knows how to save those people. Maybe the time is a critical aspect of that."

"Well, I suppose if all he wanted was to walk again, then the exact time would be of no importance to him."

"Right. And I assume he would have asked for more than one."

"Then the question that remains is, do you, Lora, want to help him on his quest to save these people?"

"Is it strange to want to save lives in a different universe? And can I really bring back the man who killed Ian?"

"They are people. No different from you and me, or Ian. Surely if we have bestowed such suffering on them, we can be morally obliged to offer a helping hand."

"The lab took his father and his legs from him," Lora said. "My project gave him his legs back, and in some sense his father as well. And now it is taking all of it away again. Then it also enabled Ian and Jim to run their selfish scam and cause a series of disasters that caused a lot of suffering and killed so many people including his foster father. But then he goes and kills Ian! Even if, maybe, that wasn't his intention."

It remained quiet on the line.

"If all it takes to fix it," Lora continued, "is one more run of The Shim, then maybe I should allow it. But how?"

"If that's what you want, I may have an idea. Let's set up a meeting with the others. We will need their help."

Lora wished she could see the doctor's face, because there was a giddiness in his voice now, that made her doubt if he was being serious. Regardless, she moved the tape roll to "Yes" on the Ouija board, convinced that somehow Visitor would get the message.

Chapter Thirty-Three

T HE EVERETT BUILDING was mostly deserted. The quantum lab was still closed. With the Physics Advances convention starting in town, virtually everyone who worked in the labs was not here today. They were either attending the convention or depending on someone who was. The guards in the foyer were not made aware of this circumstance and found themselves wondering why they hadn't seen anyone come through the door since they started their shift this morning.

"This is just typical, Rupinder. I asked for the afternoon off today, but they wouldn't let me because it was too last minute. 'Fridays are usually busy,' they said. And here we are. It's quieter than a library on a Monday morning."

Rupinder looked up at Doug from his book, after taking time to finish reading to the end of the paragraph and blinked a few times before speaking. "It was pretty quiet until just now."

Doug could never tell if Rupinder was joking or not. He had worked with him maybe a dozen times now, and those days were not the ones he cherished.

Today, luckily, Rupinder cracked a smile and continued by asking, "You had plans for the afternoon then, Doug?"

"Yeah. I was supposed to help out a buddy of mine with some work he's doing in his basement. They had a flood after a pipe burst. Total mess. And it has to be fixed and cleaned up today, because tomorrow he's leaving to visit family over in Europe for two weeks. So, I was thinking we could get it done this afternoon, because tonight my daughter has a band concert at school that I promised I would come see. Whichever one of those two things I skip out on, I bet it's not going to work out great for me."

Rupinder sighed just a little too hard. He put his book down on the desk and took his feet off it. In the same laborious fashion, he brought out his phone, so that Doug would understand that he could have easily done this himself, instead of interrupting Rupinder's book. Of course, Doug could argue that reading a book on the job like that wasn't allowed. As guards they were supposed to always pay close attention without distractions. To be honest though, guarding this building was not an adventurous job. In total, over the years, only a handful of people had been denied access to this building by a guard. Only two people, on a single occasion, had to be physically removed and escorted off campus. The presence of security guards in the foyer was enough of a deterrent to stop almost anyone from trying to gain unauthorized access.

Rupinder put away his phone and said, "They told me there is no one here today because of some convention in town."

"Busy on Friday, my ass," Doug replied.

"I'll tell you what, Doug. I can probably cover for you a few hours this afternoon if that helps. Just go home early and I'll sign you out when I leave. At this point it's unlikely anyone will even know we were here at all today."

"Oh man, that would be… Hold on now. What the hell is that?"

Rupinder jumped up from his chair and joined Doug in staring outside. Five figures were slowly approaching the building, walking in a sort of V-formation, much wider than the path. Five people dressed in white hazmat suits, wearing full-face gas masks, approached the entrance. The person in front waved a key card by the sensor, attempting to open the door. There was a beep, but nothing happened. Doug and Rupinder knew why. All keycards, except the ones for the cleaners, had been blocked since the quantum lab was closed. And these people did not look like regular cleaners. The man outside gestured at the door with one hand. In the other hand he carried a large white, semi-transparent cylindrical container that appeared to contain some sort of blue liquid. On top of it was a manual pumping mechanism and a hose terminating in a sprayer nozzle.

Doug recognized it as a garden sprayer, similar to the ones his father liked to use to water his house plants or spray herbicides around the yard. "Do we let them in?" he asked.

Rupinder slowly shook his head. "No, Doug, I think we should call to confirm first."

All five figures outside were now waving at them, pointing urgently toward the closed quantum lab. All of them appeared distressed. One of them made an O-shape with their arms and then expanded it overhead, a depiction of an explosion, maybe. Or a growth. Or maybe it was a tree. There was some muffled sound of them yelling, to accompany the pantomime.

"Do you know what they're saying?" Rupinder asked.

Doug shook his head. The gas masks and the glass of the windows and doors made the message undecipherable. The person in front pointed a finger straight at the guards, then placed a hand under his own chin and made a slicing motion. This time there wasn't a lot of room for interpretation.

"Are they going to kill us, Doug?" Rupinder now asked, with an increased level of urgency in his voice.

"Either that, or they're trying to warn us about something." Doug grabbed his baton and went toward the door. "Open it up Rupinder. I'll go talk to them. And if they try anything funny, you call it in."

The moment the door opened five voices started yelling at the guards. A loud cacophony of warnings, questions, and instructions was bellowed at them while the intimidating characters slowly made their way inside. Doug was backing up in front of them, unsure how to act.

"Do not step outside! You must remain quarantined until we get this contained!"

"How long have you been exposed? Do you feel lightheaded, or nauseated, or dizzy?"

"Remove your clothes and put these on!" one of them yelled as he shoved a briefcase in Doug's hands.

"Do you have any signs of skin burns?"

"You didn't drink the water, did you? Did you have any green vegetables to eat today?"

One of the characters in white suits, carrying another briefcase made his way over to Rupinder. Placing the case on the desk and opening it, he said, "This is a radiation suit. Take off your uniform and put it on. Now."

"What's going on? Why?" Rupinder asked.

"It's going to be alright, son, but it is imperative that you act quickly! We're here to help you."

Doug was already taking off his clothes, down to his underwear. The man with the garden sprayer sprayed him with a cold, slightly blue colored, odorless liquid, after which another one of the white suits handed him a towel. Rupinder followed Doug's example and received the same treatment.

"Can you please tell us what is happening?" Doug asked.

"We have a possibly catastrophic problem in the quantum lab. It should never have been left unattended for this long. You may have been exposed. But don't worry, we'll get it cleaned up. No time to lose, suit up!"

After both guards finished toweling off, someone slid over a garbage bin with their foot and, pointing at the towels and then the bin, said, "In there." They deposited their presumably contaminated towels in the bin and proceeded to don their suits. They were the same as the suits worn by their uninvited guests, one of whom now handed them each a gas mask.

"Put the mask on. Is there a closed off room in this building? Something without windows? Somewhere where you could hide or seek shelter?"

The guards looked at each other but still didn't seem to act in a way befitting the severity of their predicament.

Another one of the intruders said, "Come on guys! We need to get moving. We need to get into that lab and stop this… this thing that's happening!"

"Storage room, yes sure," Rupinder said, pointing to a door at the end of the foyer. "Outside that door, to the right is a room we use for cleaning supplies."

All the white suited invaders looked over at the one carrying the sprayer, who, after a brief pause then gave a slight nod.

"Right! Let's go!" said the one who had given Rupinder his suit. He set off in the direction of the door, expecting the two guards to follow. "Hurry!"

"Wait, we need keys," Doug said. He hurried over to the desk and grabbed them from a drawer, then followed Rupinder and the white suit out of the foyer. The rest of the suits went directly into the lab.

"THAT," JAROD SAID, "was absolutely legendary!"

Lora managed to laugh, even if she didn't entirely agree with his assessment of what they had just done. Like Jarod, she took off the gas mask and took a deep breath. "Where did you even get these things, David?"

Dr. Shim had also removed his mask and was getting out of his suit. "Those are the real deal," he said. "Back when I was working on Project E, over at B-Site, I was overly cautious and had these ordered in. They were left unused and eventually ended up in my garage at home. I honestly didn't think I would ever use them until the next world war, but here we are."

"It was awesome!" Jarod said. He laughed and then asked, "Who asked them if they ate any green vegetables?"

"Me," Randy said, with a smirk on his face.

Jarod high fived him. "Man, I almost pissed myself!"

Gary walked in the door now to join them. He was still fully suited up and started to take his mask off. "The Guards are in the supply room. I found them a deck of playing cards to keep them busy. I locked them in there and told them we'll keep them posted on the progress. We really scared the crap out of those poor bastards."

Lora slowly shook her head but couldn't completely hide she too had enjoyed the look on the guard's faces when no one other than the famed Dr. Shim was hosing them down with colored water. "Let's get to it then," she said. "The Shim has been left unattended longer than ever before. I'm sure we'll run into alignment and calibration issues."

Jarod replied, "Before you touch anything, let me go check the panels. I expect they manually tripped the breakers to prevent any unexpected damage while we weren't here." He walked past The Shim to the far wall, where the electrical panel for the machine was located.

"We have to get it running at exactly two," Lora said, looking at her phone. "That gives us only an hour and fifteen minutes. Randy, with me please."

When Jarod returned, he said, "Looks like we're good to go," pointing at the consoles that were now booting up.

Lora and Randy took their familiar positions at the consoles. Gary, meanwhile, retreated to one of the data analysis stations.

"Make sure you get me a good live feed," Gary said to Randy. "If we do this right, we might get some useful data out of it. With some luck we may have enough to publish after all."

Lora laughed to herself. *Who cares about the research anymore?*

Chapter Thirty-Four

AT PRECISELY TWO o'clock, after completing the preparatory work without encountering any unexpected issues, Lora pulled down the levers for the two expansions in rapid succession and then, after getting a thumbs-up from Randy over at the console, the third lever, to activate the beam. Familiar purple light illuminated the room and Gary's tennis ball was officially starting its last journey across the plateau, on the way to pod two.

Only a few minutes passed before Jarod, who was furthest from The Shim and closest to the exit at the time, noticed loud noises coming from the foyer. When he went to check it out, he found Visitor banging on the glass doors. Instead of letting him in, he went to see Lora about it.

"He's here," he said. "He wants to come in."

"Why? What does he need in here?"

Jarod shrugged.

"I will see him outside."

"Then I'll come with you," Jarod said. "Or you won't be able to get back in. The guards seem to be on a break." He grinned, but Lora didn't think it was funny. "And, you know, the key cards don't work. There's that."

Lora knew from previous observations how to open the doors from the security desk. As soon as she did, Visitor pushed through the doors. He was slightly out of breath, as if he had been running.

"Lora, Jarod. It is good to see you," he said, not actually looking at either of them.

"What are you doing here? What do you need?" Lora asked.

"Let's go inside and I will explain." Visitor checked his phone for the time and looked outside, as if to see if no one had followed him here. "Quickly."

The three of them joined the others near The Shim. Gary remained at his desk and Randy at his console. The rest stood by the plateau, near the beam.

Visitor checked the time again. "Eight minutes."

"Eight minutes to what?" Lora asked.

"Until we start saving lives."

"And how exactly do you hope to achieve that?" Dr. Shim wanted to know.

"All we need is for the machine to run for forty-five minutes. After that—"

Lora interrupted him. "You know as well as I do, that we cannot control how long The Shim will run. At least thirty minutes is the best I can do." She thought Visitor appeared different than before. He seemed nervous. He wasn't looking at her, instead fixing his sunglasses-covered eyes on the floor more than anything else.

"I am aware, but it doesn't have to be much of a problem. If it runs too short, I will need you to run it again, that's all."

Lora shook her head. "We agreed to one final run. It will be however long it is. We're not supposed to be in here, so there is a chance that we will not even be allowed to finish one full run."

"I am trying to save the world. It takes forty-five minutes. You'll find a way, I'm sure of it."

Yes, there was definitely something different about him, Lora thought. Maybe this was just because it was his final visit. She had an uneasy feeling. *He doesn't belong here.*

Dr. Shim reiterated his question. "Mr. Visitor, how exactly are you going to save the people you spoke of? By what mechanism is our running the machine one more time helping you to realize that most noble goal?" When Visitor remained quiet, Dr. Shim sought a way to incentivize him. "It occurs to me that, seeing as we are all risking our careers to help you today, maybe you can at least give us some insight into what we are working toward."

Visitor had to improvise a little. "It is not really any of your concern. But the short of it is that we're going to be reversing some of the damage done by Ian and Jim. I am working with a scientist in my world, who has ensured me that with forty-five minutes of close contact between our two universes, through The Slicer, much of what they did can be undone."

The doctor was rubbing his chin with a thumb and index finger, pacing back and forth in front of Visitor.

Lora had a puzzled look on her face. "A scientist? That's the first I heard of that. What scientist?" Visitor seemed increasingly uncomfortable to her.

"I only met him recently, after you stopped the experiment," he said, without much conviction.

"You're the one who stopped the experiment when you killed Ian!" Gary said from behind his desk.

Dr. Shim stopped pacing and stood next to Lora again. "Undo what, exactly?" he asked. "I imagine you are not suggesting your new scientist found a way to bring back the dead, did he? The adverse effects that you have described do not appear to me to be reversible at all."

Visitor looked at the time. Only just about a minute until Jim would begin the Project E extractions. He was beginning to feel that coming to the lab may have been a mistake. When he entered Lora's world, in the park this time, it seemed obvious to him that he would come here, both to make sure that Lora and her crew would keep their end of the deal, and for the simple selfish reason that he wanted to see her one last time. Jim was right when he said that no matter what happens, after today he would never see her again. But that was easy for Jim to say. After all, she meant nothing to him. Tomorrow it would be as if she didn't exist. Whether she even lived to see the end of the day, Visitor would never know. She didn't deserve what was coming. He wished he could save her.

"Well?" the doctor asked.

"We're not bringing back the dead, I don't think. But we will bring back the missing. We can stop the permanent earthquakes. We can bring back the light in Australia. Surely, we can do those things."

"Mr. Visitor, please. If—"

"It's time," Visitor said, interrupting the doctor. "All we need to do now is wait, and keep this machine going long enough, no matter what."

For a moment everyone seemed to be holding their breath, but nothing noticeable happened.

Gary got up from behind his desk and joined the group by the beam now. Randy remained at the console, seemingly more interested in what it was showing him on its screens than what Visitor was saying. "So far, everything looks normal," he said, more to himself than anyone else.

"Mr. Visitor!" Dr. Shim called out. It wasn't often that he raised his voice like that, and it was made more dramatic by what sounded like thunder coming from outside. The weather must have taken a rather dramatic turn for the worse, on what was forecast to be a very nice day, especially this late in the year. "If you and your scientist know how to reverse what Ian and Jim have done, then you must also have some idea of how Project E was able to cause so much damage in the first place. If such is the case, I would be very interested to know more. We will want to prevent disruptions of this magnitude in the future, as you can no doubt appreciate."

"Actually," Visitor said, relieved to finally get asked a question that didn't force him to come up with another vague and evasive non-answer, "the problem is with The Shim and its expansions, and not so much with Project E itself. We think that The Slicer isn't working exactly the way you expect. Or rather, maybe, not as well as you think it does. Somehow, The Slicer seems to be leaking, letting some things seep into the targeted universe from elsewhere. Jim says that it is likely a problem caused by interference from Project E, when it is running in parallel to The Shim, but the exact mechanism isn't clear. But we know we can reverse it."

Visitor hoped that his work here was done now. He wanted to make up some excuse for why he would have to leave. He wanted to walk. Even if the weather was not great, there was nothing he would rather do with his final moments in this world, than walk, possibly for the last time in his life.

The doctor was rubbing his chin again. "Hm," he said. "And why would Jim say that to you, and not to me?"

Lora was wondering the same. "Jim talked to you about this?"

Visitor didn't answer, but he knew his mistake. The silence, if you could call it that with the sound of thunder filling it, felt long, even though Gary broke it soon enough. "He's talking about Jim in his own universe," he said.

"Is *that* your scientist?" Lora asked, trying to look at Visitor, who still seemed to be avoiding eye-contact.

"God help us all," Dr. Shim mumbled.

"Alright, alright!" Visitor said. "I'll tell you how it works. I don't know the details since I'm no scientist. And then I will leave and enjoy my last walk, if that is alright with you."

"Please," the doctor said impatiently.

"Jim has discovered a way to reverse what Project E has done, basically by running it backwards. He—"

"Yes, yes, you already said as much. Let me stop you there and tell you what I think," the doctor said. "I think you and Jim's alter ego have access to a second instance of Project E in your own universe, which is possible, because it predates The Shim. You are not reversing what Project E has done, you are merely reversing Ian's scheme. We are here, running The Shim, because you don't have one. And Jim is over in your universe running Project E." The doctor peered at Visitor with raised eyebrows.

Visitor sighed. He looked at the time. Barely five minutes in.

"Well, how am I doing, Mr. Visitor?" Dr. Shim asked.

"Right. You're right. We're running Project E in reverse to undo the damage. That way we can bring back what was lost and hopefully get rid of most of what we were dealt." Visitor knew it was a weak story now, but he had nothing else.

Gary said, "But that's not what you are doing. You are doing exactly what Ian and Jim were doing, just in the other direction."

Visitor halfheartedly tried to produce a smirk. "Isn't that what reversing means?"

"So, you're stealing from us now? I thought we were here to save lives! All those people. You lied to me!?" Lora said.

Dr. Shim shook his head. "He's not technically stealing, and certainly not from us. Project E simply finds…"

Randy suddenly got up and took his phone out of his pocket. "Hey, I really can't talk right now." Everyone was looking at him. In the silence, the storm outside sounded like near constant thunder. "I'm sorry, okay? I won't be that long." For a moment he took the phone away from his ear and looked at its screen. "I haven't been ignoring your texts, I was just busy." It was quiet for another second. "Come on, that's not fair!" He glanced over at Lora, then turned his back to her and the rest of the group and continued in a lower voice. "I am not alone with her, the whole team is here, okay? Look, I really have to… hello?" Randy shrugged and turned back to look at the group.

"It's a good thing Ian isn't here… I mean…," Jarod said before thinking it through.

"Yeah, I'm sorry about that. Seems I got cut off anyway," said Randy, as he put the phone down on the console table and sat back down as if nothing had happened.

Lora wanted to say something to him, but Randy had already resumed staring at the console screens. Instead, she returned her attention to Visitor. "You lied to me."

He had. Visitor wasn't enjoying it. He had betrayed her. Not just by lying to her about the purpose of this last visit. Not telling her about what he did to her bartender friend may technically not be a lie, but if she found out, the effect would be the same. It seemed that it was finally time to give up on Lora. He had already lost her. Even if he could save her, take her with him somehow, she would want nothing to do with him. "Well," he said, "it has been a great run, wouldn't you say? Your project has given me something that I can never thank you enough for. All of you. But it cannot last. It was never going to last. When this project ends, what I am going to be left with is life in a wheelchair, in a world that was partly destroyed by Project E. How is that fair? How can it be fair that you leave my world in ruins and give nothing in return? The thousands who have died, the countless people who have lost their loved ones, or their homes, deserve justice! Your people owe it to us. Ian and Jim killed my father! They killed my aunt and two of my neighborhood friends! Thousands of others. We will take back what was lost, and you will make sure that we get it."

Visitor stood with tears in his eyes, hidden only by his sunglasses, still looking down to his feet. This wasn't how he had imagined he would say his goodbyes.

It was again Gary who broke the silence. "You're not reversing the damage. You're going to bring similar damage to our universe instead. This is not justice you are serving. It is revenge," he said, looking furious. It was a look Lora had never seen on him before.

"Honestly, it may not be that bad," Visitor said, trying to downplay the severity of what was about to happen. "With luck, all that happens is that you'll see some weird stuff on TV tonight. But make no mistake, Jim sent me here to get what we need. And that is what I will do. It's our only chance, so I have no choice. Your best option is to just give us our forty-five minutes, and then all this—"

The hum of the beam suddenly faded into silence and its purple glow to darkness. Visitor was no longer present in the room. Gary's tennis ball remained unmoved, as its owner stood with his hand resting on the emergency stop button. "That asshole was going to destroy our universe," he said.

For a moment it was quiet. Everyone stared at Gary.

Randy looked up from the screens on the console. "Well, that was not even close to forty-five minutes," he said. "And it seems that the safety on The Slicer tripped. I thought we fixed that problem?"

After she took a quick look at the console screens, Lora confirmed his diagnosis. "Jarod?"

Jarod, who had remained uncharacteristically quiet, was glad to think about something less sensational than being threatened by someone from a different universe. "Yeah man. So, last time it was The Sharpener safety that tripped over a faulty part, remember? This is something completely different."

Everyone began to talk at the same time, trying to get to grips with everything that just happened.

"Randy?" Lora said, at first barely noticed over the noise. "What is wrong? Guys! What is wrong with Randy?"

Randy was lying face down on the console and wasn't moving, even when Lora touched his shoulder to gently shake him.

"No!" Lora cried out.

Gary and Dr. Shim came to help her get Randy upright and back into his chair. Jarod already had his phone out to call for help. Randy didn't appear to be breathing.

"Lay him down," Dr. Shim said. He and Gary placed Randy on his back on the floor, looking him over for any signs of injury, but there was nothing obvious wrong with him. "Please make some room. There's no pulse. He's not breathing."

Dr. Shim had required everyone who worked in his lab to complete CPR training. The only ones in that group here today were Gary and himself and both were on the floor with Randy, trying to bring him back.

"My phone is not working," Jarod said.

Lora was pacing back and forth behind Dr. Shim, not knowing what to do. She looked at her own phone, but it indicated no signal. "What the hell is happening?"

The doctor and Gary were frantically working on Randy.

"He's coming back!" the doctor called out.

"I have a pulse," said Gary, "It's weak."

Randy coughed and slowly opened his eyes a little. He moved one of his hands onto his stomach and moaned.

"Randy, boy! You almost died!" Gary said.

Lora kneeled beside the doctor, by Randy's head. She rubbed her hand on his forehead and said, "Randy, you scared me. Are you okay?" She looked at the doctor. "He's okay, right?"

Randy tried to speak but he managed barely a whisper. Lora leaned in closer to hear.

"My…," he said, swallowing before he could continue, "my phone shim—" He coughed again, but this time it sounded wet, and he brought up some blood that then trickled out from the corner of his mouth. Dr. Shim handed Lora a tissue, which she used to wipe Randy's chin. It seemed as if he was trying to speak, but then his whole body began to convulse. He coughed up more blood.

Dr. Shim said, "Jarod, did you make the call yet? We need help here!"

"No sir, I can't get a signal."

"No, me neither," Gary said, returning his own phone to his back pocket.

For a moment Randy's eyes opened wide, and he looked directly at Lora, who was still hovering over him. The convulsions slowed down enough to allow him to hold his gaze, staring into Lora's eyes.

"Randy? Please, don't do this to me. Stay with me," Lora whispered, imagining she could see he was doing better now.

He tried to speak again.

"Lora," he said, following it with a gurgling sound. He was breathing fast and shallow. "Help… Lab help… Thank you."

"Yes! Yes, I need you here with me. I will need your help. We're going to be famous, remember?" She tried to smile but couldn't. "Tom Holland. Stay with me, Randy. Look at me."

She watched a tear roll down the side of Randy's face. She looked at Gary, then the doctor. "Why is this happening? What is happening to him? Please help him!"

Dr. Shim put his hand on Randy's. Randy grimaced in response.

"There's something about his stomach," the doctor said.

Randy's convulsions had all but stopped, but he was shaking as if he was very cold. He tried to speak again. "Lora… I love… I wish more… time…" He coughed again, and more gurgling sounds bubbled up from his throat. "I… loved working…"

Suddenly all sounds coming from Randy stopped. All movements ceased. Silence.

Lora shrieked; a sound she had rarely ever made. It was a soul piercing cry that reverberated around the quiet lab and deeply affected everyone present.

Jarod was the first to speak. "Oh man! Is he dead? Did he just die for no reason?" His arms were flailing, as if looking for support. Dr. Shim got up from the floor. He grabbed Jarod's shoulders and looked him in the eyes, making sure he wasn't going to faint. Instead, Jarod burst out crying. Loud and fast sobs.

Gary looked up at them and nodded. "He's gone."

Dr. Shim wrapped an arm around Jarod and led him closer to the console for something to lean on.

"No, no, no," Lora said, as she was holding Randy's head in her lap. She cried. Gary remained on the floor, still holding Randy's wrist as if checking for a pulse. He looked over at Lora and gently placed a hand on her shoulder. Softly, he said to her, "There, there now."

JIM WATCHED IN HORROR as his console suddenly flashed error messages at him. Project E had been running for barely twenty minutes before it, on only the second haul, suddenly fell back into its usual habit of producing meaningless puffs of toxic gas in the chamber while testing the limits of the generators. The connection to the source universe was somehow no longer there.

He sprinted up the flights of stairs to the third floor and burst into the meeting room, where he saw Ed sitting in his wheelchair, leaning back as if he was trying to catch a nap.

"What the hell, Ed?" he yelled.

Ed would have jumped in his chair if that was possible for him to do. He dropped his phone on the floor.

A few minutes before, when Ed had found himself suddenly back in his wheelchair, he had quickly grabbed his phone from the large oval table in the center of the meeting room. He had to find out quickly why his visit was cut short. Immediately, the room at B-Site faded into that unsavory purple mist, while he welcomed the warm cozy feeling of floating near Lora in another world, close to the console where Randy was sitting. Gary still had his hand on the emergency stop button at the other console, so that cleared up his question. Ed felt stupid. He had been on a combined power and guilt trip as Visitor. He told them too much. Now, he had to make sure that these people would keep their end of the deal. Forty-five minutes of runtime, plus some overhead for restarting. How would he get a message to them? He searched for something he could move to draw their attention. Everyone in the room appeared to be in frantic discussion, except the boy at the console, whose attention was with the screens. Ed sensed the cellphone sitting at the edge of the console table. It was easy enough to move the phone a short distance on the table. That should get their attention. But no one even noticed the shimmering among the chaos of the moment. For his second attempt Ed thought he might instead move the device off the table into Randy's lap, so the boy would feel it even if he didn't see it. He focused all his attention on the phone again and then shifted his concentration to where he wanted it to be, just above Randy's lap.

The loud noise of someone crashing into the purple meeting room interrupted him.

"What the hell, Ed?" Jim yelled.

As Ed dropped the phone, he thought he sensed Randy getting up from his seat, maybe to press a button, just before the lab disappeared. For a few seconds Ed looked disoriented, squinting at the light in the room. Then, turning to Jim, he said, "You can't just do that when I'm on the phone! I need to focus!"

"What are you doing back here already?" Jim wanted to know. "That wasn't even close to long enough!"

"Well, there was always a chance that they weren't going to just cooperate. You expect them to just sit there and watch us destroy their world?"

"Why? What did you tell them, Ed?"

Jim was right, of course, but Ed ignored the question. "My dear old father hit the emergency stop button. I was working to make sure they will keep their end of the deal when you barged in here." Ed gestured at his phone. "It will normally take them about an hour or so to get the machine back up and running. They'll come through."

"They better."

"Did we get anything?" Ed asked.

Jim nodded. "It is working as expected. But we got only one run in, and it was only a small load. The first one is a little tricky because of timing, so it takes a little longer. We were just about to start the second run and then we would have been off to the races."

"Can I see it?"

"Sure," Jim said, picking up Ed's phone from the floor. "But right now, I think you should get back on your phone and make sure they're doing what you're expecting of them. It occurs to me you are putting an unwarranted amount of trust in these other-worldly scientists. Forget about them, Ed! We have millions of people here who will be better off if we get this right today. I'm going to need about a half hour to reset. You get me a new time. Do whatever it takes, Ed!"

Ed looked at Jim in a peculiar way.

"What is it?" Jim asked.

Ed pointed at the phone Jim was holding in his hand. "That doesn't bother you?"

"No, why? Here, get to it."

Ed took the phone and as Jim left, went back to looking like he was almost asleep.

Chapter Thirty-Five

D ART WAS PASSING the bus terminal at the train station. At one of the bus platforms a large white tour bus was parked, and a significant number of people were gathered to one side of it. Dart's sixth sense went into overdrive. A cold chill ran down his spine. *This is going to be bad.* He looked around for any signs of danger, but other than the size of the crowd and the seemingly heated discussions between the bus driver and some of the prospective passengers, everything looked normal. His observation conflicted with the feeling of imminent threat that was stronger than he had ever felt it. He moved closer to see and hear more clearly what was happening.

The bus driver was in discussion with the passengers. "There will be another bus here shortly. Nobody is going to be left behind. Don't worry folks, it is going to be a wonderful day today!"

It was in fact already a very nice day. A second, equally big white bus drove past Dart and turned into the bus depot. It parked behind the first one, and the crowd split roughly in half as people moved to gather by the second bus.

The second driver opened the front door and stepped out. "How are you today?" he said to the first person he saw. Then, louder, "All luggage must go in the luggage compartment. If you would please give me some room, I will open the hatches for you."

The driver of the first bus made a similar request to the crowd around him. Dart still couldn't see anything wrong, but his uneasiness was growing stronger regardless. He decided that whatever it was, it couldn't wait, and he made his way to the buses.

"What is *that*?" one of the passengers called out.

Dart looked, hoping that the woman had seen something out of the ordinary, but he found her pointing directly at himself.

The bus driver answered, "Oh him? He is our hero, Dart! Isn't that right, Dart?"

Some in the crowd seemed to know who he was and said hello, while others had obvious doubts about the man in the tight green outfit.

Dart reached the driver. "Hey. Is everything alright here? Something seems off to me."

The driver looked around him and then at Dart. "Too many people for one bus, that's all. Now that we finally have our second bus, I think we'll be on our way shortly."

Dart shook his head. "That's not it." He started working his way into the crowd, checking people's faces, checking their luggage, looking for anything out of the ordinary.

The driver made an announcement from behind him, "Once you have placed your luggage in the baggage area you can enter the bus through the front or rear doors and take any seat you like. Please take your time, no need to push and shove."

The crowd started shifting around Dart, toward the bus. He stepped out of the crowd and watched the first luggage being loaded. Similar activity occurred near the second bus. The doors of the second bus were still closed, so those who had deposited their luggage took a spot by the doors waiting for access. At the first bus, two people were now climbing on board through the rear doors. Everything looked normal. An older woman was climbing aboard at the front with the help of the driver. Dart felt his neck hairs raise. The tingle was not subtle today. It was screaming at him.

Dart ran toward the second bus to find its driver. "Does everything look normal to you? I feel something bad is happening."

The driver looked around and said, "All good here."

Dart almost had to doubt his sixth sense. He was never going to make that mistake again though and decided that he would take no chances today. "Do not open those doors. Just wait!" he said, turning around and running back to the first bus.

"You!" he called to the first driver. "Close those doors now. Don't let them in yet!"

"Dart, what are you talking about? These people are excited to go, and I am not about to disappoint them."

Dart pleaded with the driver. "Please! Please stop! Something is wrong!"

The driver could see that Dart was genuinely worried about something. "Alright folks," he said, as he boarded the bus, "excuse me!" He closed the rear doors and stepped back out as the front doors were closing. "Please wait, I'll be right with you," he said to the growing number of people who had stowed their baggage and were ready to board. "Now. What is this about?" he asked Dart.

"Something is wrong. It's bad, I can feel it."

The crowd was getting restless, as some of them overheard Dart's distress. Some people were gathering around him and the driver.

"Listen Dart, I appreciate your concern, but you'll have to be a little more specific than that."

"I can't. Not yet," Dart said.

Someone from the crowd asked, "Are we in danger?"

Dart didn't want to cause a panic, but his sense of impending doom was only getting more powerful. He hesitated. "Yes."

The message spread through the crowd quickly, and some people started backing away.

"Please, everyone!" Dart now yelled into the crowd. "Please all go to the train station and get inside! Go now! Just leave your stuff and run! Run!"

Only a handful of people broke away from the crowd and reluctantly began retreating toward the station, dragging their luggage with them.

The driver of the second bus made his way through the crowd and reached Dart.

"What the heck are you doing?" he asked Dart, and then, turning to his colleague, "What is he doing?"

The first driver grabbed Dart's arm, "Stop it Dart. You're scaring them!"

Dart shook his arm loose. "You don't understand. These people are going to die unless you get them inside. Right now!" Dart didn't know at all if that was true, but he could not take the risk. "Run! All of you!"

There were some muted screams now as the sense of danger, the beginnings of a panic, was spreading. A few people started running toward the station. *Good.*

A large cloud blocked the sun and the temperature seemed to instantly drop a few degrees. Until now the skies had been clear. The weather was turning rapidly. From a distance, the first sounds of thunder rolled in.

The second bus driver yelled at Dart now. "Dart! What are you on? Where is the danger you—"

Dart felt the ground move under his feet. One of the glass panels of the waiting area exploded loudly, and shattered glass sprayed on the pavement. The whole crowd seemed to synchronously take one step away from the buses as everyone adjusted their balance. The ground *was* moving! A few people fell to the ground. There were more screams now, and more people began to walk or run toward the station.

The first bus was leaning oddly into its driver-side front corner, as if it had sprung a tire. The driver made his way around the front of the bus to check what had happened. Another loud rumbling sound came from somewhere behind the second bus as the ground shook again, more intense this time. The empty bus swayed a little.

"Run! God damnit! Get inside!" Dart yelled. A roaring thunderclap helped get his point across. This time it worked. The whole crowd broke apart and people started running, or walking as fast as they could, away from the buses in the direction of the train station.

The driver returned and said, half out of breath, "The ground sank out from under the wheel. There's a hole underneath there. Was that an earthquake?"

The second bus tilted, producing loud creaking noises. People closest to it ran and screamed. The front wheels left the ground and the whole bus started sliding backward, angled into the ground. The sound was deafening. In just a few seconds the whole vehicle slid out of view, consumed by the Earth. The bus crashed down leaving nothing behind but a hole in the ground.

"Sinkhole! Sinkhole!" several people yelled.

Lightning brightly lit up the scene and was followed immediately by loud thunder. This storm was close.

Most of the crowd had now left and were on their way to the station. The ground was littered with luggage left behind. Large sections of pavement around the hole that had swallowed the second bus began cracking and tilting into the hole. Cracks were forming in the pavement all around. Another glass panel of the waiting area burst into pieces.

Dart looked at the driver and said, "Get these people out of here! I will see who's still on the bus." He had to raise his voice over the increasing noise of collapsing ground and thunder around them. "How do I open the doors?"

The driver ran to the front of the bus and stuck his hand under the bumper. The door opened.

"Now go!" Dart said as he approached the bus. He hesitated for a moment, but then decided to climb on board. Another thunderous roar sounded from directly beneath the bus and served to emphasize how questionable that decision was. The front of the bus tilted slightly further down. All four passengers were in the back, with two of them prying at the doors. Dart looked around the levers and buttons in the driver's area to find out which one would open the rear doors. The bus suddenly leaned hard to the left and then tilted further forward. The passengers screamed. The rear doors hissed open, and Dart made his way up the incline to the back of the bus.

"Get out of here and run for the train station. Don't stop for anything, just run!"

With the bus tilted forward as it was, the front now hovering over a gaping hole, the rear was the only way out. But it was up off the ground quite a bit, so getting out meant jumping. The first two passengers made quick work of it and were already running toward the station. Left, were the older woman who had needed help from the driver to get on the bus and a much younger woman wearing headphones. Dart suggested to the younger woman that she follow the two passengers who had already left, but she insisted that she would help get the older lady off the bus.

Dart turned to the older woman and asked, "How well can you walk?"

"I can walk fine. Dart, what is happening?"

The whole bus started vibrating, and a low rumbling sound rolled in from behind.

The younger woman said, "We need to move now. I think the hole behind us is closing in."

Dart agreed. "Let's get out of here fast."

The younger woman said her name was Lisa, and helped Dart get the older woman, Doreen, on her feet and to the door. The entire bus was slowly banking to the left, causing the right side to lift even higher off the ground. Dart jumped out and looked around. The waiting area on the platform had lost all its glass panels and looked distorted. It wouldn't be long before this entire area would collapse. He stretched out his arms and told Doreen to jump. "I will catch you. Jump now! We don't have much time!" The ground was unstable, and Dart had to continuously adjust his footing.

"I can't jump that far! My hip," Doreen said.

Dart reiterated the urgency of the situation. "You are going to die if you don't jump now! I promise, I will catch you!"

There was a near constant strobe of lightning now, accompanied with loud thunder from all directions. The sky was dark, but the grey clouds were still not shedding any rain and there was hardly any wind.

Lisa shouted, "Catch!" and then pushed Doreen, who yelped in wide-eyed alarm, hard out the door.

Dart caught the woman and immediately put his shoulder under her arm. Lisa jumped out of the bus and took the other shoulder. Together they dragged Doreen away from the bus. A signpost, next to the waiting area, disappeared into the ground. Cracks shot out through the pavement around them. Only a few steps further, a thunderous crash sounded from behind them. The bus was already gone. The two cavities that had devoured the buses were now merged into one massive hole that was still expanding. More and more of the pavement broke off, tilted toward the hole, and then fell in. Dart and Lisa ran as fast as they could, getting no help from Doreen. They felt the ground beneath their feet shake and fall away behind them.

"I can't, I'm losing my grip!" yelled Lisa. Dart was sure that if any of them fell, they would surely not make it.

"Faster!" Dart said, his eyes fixed on the train station building. He could feel he was doing most of the work by himself now. Then, Lisa fell and disappeared from his view. She screamed behind him. There was nothing he could do for her.

Someone came running toward them now. It was the first bus driver. The thundering sound was closing in, with the ground rapidly crumbling away behind Dart. Cracks in the pavement were shooting out before him.

When the driver reached them, Lisa suddenly sprinted past him, without her headphones now. *She made it!*

The driver took Lisa's place at Doreen's shoulder. "Go!" he yelled. Dart and the driver lifted Doreen off the ground entirely and ran as fast as they could with Lisa out in front of them. More people were coming out of the train station, calling urgently for them to run faster. It was working. The sounds of the pavement caving in finally receded behind them and the station was closing in fast. When the ground stopped moving under their feet they slowed down. They walked the rest of the distance, allowing Doreen to use her own feet again, under loud cheering from the small crowd outside the station doors. Dart looked back and saw the big hole that had now swallowed the entire platform and had expanded through another. The pavement around the hole was cracked all the way through several other platforms.

When they reached the building, Lisa offered Doreen her arm, to bring her inside.

"Thank you, Lisa, you did great," Dart said.

Inside, Dart addressed the crowd. "Someone, find this lady a seat!" A loud applause erupted. Many people were in tears. A lot of them were on their phones, trying to call loved ones or taking pictures. He could hear complaints about a lack of cellphone signal.

A man slapped Dart on his shoulder and said, "I don't know who you are, but you just saved all of our asses!" A woman grabbed Dart and hugged him. Others joined, offering Dart their gratitude.

"I'm Dart. This is what I do," he said. He felt great. This was the biggest job of his life. Outside he could now hear sirens. He began to excuse himself as two police cars and an ambulance parked in front of the door and two police officers made their way in. Dart greeted them and informed them that no one was hurt. A police officer in turn shared with him and the crowd that the storm had caused some type of outage that brought down virtually all communication lines, including cellphone service, throughout the city. Outside he saw many emergency vehicles surrounding the giant sinkhole. A Channel 56 News van was just pulling in as well. The storm dissipated as quickly as it had arrived. Besides a few fluffy white clouds, the skies were blue again, as if it never happened. Not a drop of rain had fallen. Dart turned to the crowd one last time and waved goodbye as he walked out the door, more applause sounding behind him.

CHAPTER THIRTY-SIX

"POOR KID," DR. SHIM SAID, as he covered Randy with a bright green, obnoxiously decorated blanket he had found in a storage room. No one had been successful in reaching the emergency services yet. Jarod had taken a seat at a desk, blankly staring out in front of him, while Lora, doing essentially the same, sat on the edge of the plateau with her legs dangling and a box of tissues sitting next to her. Lab rules didn't apply today.

When the box shimmered away from her side and reappeared onto the floor in front of her, Lora yelled, her voice reverberating around the room, "Leave me alone!" Everyone else looked up at her.

Dr. Shim asked, "He's back, is he?"

Lora nodded toward the tissue box. In the background, Jarod produced some poorly defined noises of discontent.

"Mr. Visitor's vexation at our cutting short his stay does not come as a surprise, I assume," Dr. Shim said.

"Man, I can't do this anymore," Jarod said, suddenly getting up from his seat. He headed toward the exit.

"Where are you going?"

There was no answer, but by the time Jarod reached the door, the doctor let out a cry, that sounded as if he was in pain. Dr. Shim had to grab on to the console nearest to him to hold himself upright. Jarod screamed, "Doc!" and came running back.

Lora covered her mouth with her hand as she watched in horror how Dr. Shim sat down in a chair that Gary pulled up. There was something sticking out of his foot. It protruded, at an angle and through his shoe, from the instep, and was lodged directly in the bone.

"What is that?" Jarod asked, with panic in his voice.

"It's a god-damned pen again!" the doctor yelled, sounding irritated more than in pain already.

"He can do this when he's not here?" Jarod asked in disbelief. "That's the thing he did to Ian!" He pointed over to Randy on the floor. "He did that too, didn't he?"

"I don't understand. Why is he doing this?" Lora asked, hopping off the plateau. *Did he really kill Randy?* "Oh my god… He has completely lost it!"

"Does this idiot know," Dr. Shim asked, in a sarcastic tone of voice uncharacteristic of him, "that if he kills us all off, there will be no one left to run this machine for him?"

"Why would he kill Randy?" Lora asked. "What did he do?"

"It would appear that Mr. Visitor's plan to save his world is rather more important to him than we are," Dr. Shim said. "I suppose, in a way, given his mission, that makes sense."

Gary approached Lora. "If it wasn't for me, Randy would still be alive." He sounded remorseful, but in that typical way of Gary.

After he had suffered through the traumatic loss of his wife, he lost much of his former capacity to empathize. "I am sorry. I thought I was saving the universe, but I acted before my turn and without consultation."

Lora stared at the blanket-covered body on the floor by the console. Internally, Lora agreed with Gary. Technically, he did get Randy killed. But it wasn't that simple, was it? "He was here because of me," she said, not sure if she was referring to Randy or Visitor. "If it wasn't for me, Randy would still be alive."

Gary simply nodded. "So, what do we do now? Run it again, like he told us to?"

Jarod protested. "Dude! You cannot seriously be thinking about bringing him back again… He's a freaking psychopath!"

All turned to Lora. "I agree, Jarod. There is no way we're bringing him back. He can go to hell for all I care. We need to get help for David… and for Randy…"

"When Jarod tried to leave, he went after my foot rather than Jarod's. Am I to infer that he can do this only to people who are in the vicinity of the machine?" Dr. Shim asked.

"No, David," Lora answered. "It's me. As crazy as it sounds, I'm quite certain that he can only do this near me."

"So, then just leave! You can send help and then we can all get out of here," Gary said.

The door to the foyer opened and Naomi entered the room. "Hello? Anyone in here?" she called.

Jarod looked wide-eyed at Lora. "What is she doing in here?"

Even though the cleaners had their own keycards to access the building, they weren't normally allowed to enter the quantum lab. Regardless, Naomi confidently walked further into the room, not giving the impression that she was unfamiliar with the environment. She came about halfway toward the group as Gary and Lora went to meet her. "Oh, hello. I was beginning to doubt there was anyone in the building. I'm looking for the keys to the cleaning supply room. They're supposed to be with the security guards at the desk, but there is no one there."

Everyone thought about ways in which Naomi's unexpected arrival might be of help. At the same time, they wanted her out of the lab as quickly as possible before she saw anything. Randy.

"Well, I'm afraid you'll have to come back later, when the guards are back," Gary, who had the keys in his pocket, said.

"Oh, okay. I just came to see if I left my reading glasses in there. I suppose it can wait until Monday. I have another pair at home."

"Yes, good idea," Lora said. "Is Matvei out there with you?"

"No, it's just me. I was about to go home myself, you see, but I thought I'd try to find my—" Suddenly, Naomi's eyes rolled back, and she dropped quietly, as if she fainted, and remained still on the floor.

Gary ran to her and turned her over on her back. "Oh god!"

"What the hell?" Jarod yelled.

Gary, with two fingers on Naomi's neck, said, "She's dead!"

Dr. Shim was trying to get up, but he couldn't put any weight on his injured foot and had to remain seated. Naomi was laying on the ground with her eyes and mouth open.

"Did he do that? Did the visitor kill Naomi too?" Jarod asked from behind Lora. "He did this, didn't he?"

"But how?" Gary asked.

Lora knew how. On a desk nearby there was liquid on the surface, some of it dripping off the edge. She pointed it out to Gary. "Alice's snow globe."

Jarod came to see as well. "I don't understand," he said.

The doctor, still in his seat, couldn't see what was going on, but he had heard enough. "He put the snow globe in her head, or in her chest maybe. And Randy has his own phone in his stomach."

Lora suddenly took off, running to the door. She ran quickly through the foyer, past the security desk where she opened the entry doors and went outside, off the path and into the grass. She screamed as hard as she could, drawing the attention of a few students on their way out of the campus gates. *How was I so stupid to trust him? His ridiculous outfit should have been enough of a warning!* The students looked over at her, but then kept going. For the moment there was no one else outside, and Lora walked onto the main campus road, contemplating if she should go into the main building to get help. She watched an older man walking his dog on the sidewalk, just passing the gates. The man stopped and fell face forward to the ground, never even looking in her direction. The dog barked loudly as it circled around its master, clearly confused by what had happened.

Lora began to cry. "Stop… Please…" she said, "Why are you doing this? I'm begging you… please, stop!" Behind her, Gary came out of the building, carrying Naomi's key card. He didn't need to ask what was going on as he stood beside Lora watching the dog.

"We have to run it again," Lora said. "He won't let us leave. He's not going to stop, Gary."

Gary nodded and led Lora back inside. "I am sorry," he said.

With the group reunited at The Shim, a calmness that might seem inappropriate for the circumstance came over them. They were about to resume their daily routine. If they wanted to make it through the day without random fatal implants in their bodies, if they wanted to go home, the path of least resistance was to grant Visitor his last walk.

"We've pissed him off bigtime," said Jarod.

"I'm sorry," Gary repeated. "I shouldn't have—"

"No, Gary," Lora said, "We're not going there. Right now, we have to make sure no one else dies today."

The group had accepted defeat.

"Before we do anything else," Dr. Shim said, "we must inform Mr. Visitor that we have received his message loud and clear and that we're working on bringing the machine back online. He does not need to apply any more of his persuasive measures."

Lora walked away and came back wheeling a mobile white-board. "Just write it on here. He can see it somehow."

Gary picked up a marker and started writing some profanity on the board, erasing it immediately to replace it with a simple message. "Calm down, we're on it," he wrote. He followed it with a few short details about why they needed some time to fix the safety on The Slicer.

Dr. Shim, not unfamiliar with leading a team through a tough crisis, talked to Lora, attempting to get her focused on her work again. "Mr. Visitor said that he believes there is a flaw with The Slicer, or that there is some sort of interference between it and Project E in his universe."

"He said a lot of things," Lora answered, without interest.

"Indeed. But is it not possible that we've already observed the effects of this interference in The Slicer data?"

Lora understood what he meant and thought for a moment. "Hmm. Yes, the discrepancies that we looked at together. That means that Ian and Jim have been interfering with my experiment whenever they successfully ran Project E, at B-Site. It caused The Slicer to somehow lose precision during the run, which then caused anomalies in Visitor's world. Leakage, as he called it. And those anomalies amounted to real changes in his universe, which I then had to compensate for, in The Slicer configuration."

"Exactly." Dr. Shim nodded as if he had always known this; a trait of his that Lora wasn't too keen on. "The question is, can we patch this weakness? If we do run it one more time, which it seems we are about to, we cannot stop them from taking from the multiverse as they please, but they can only take so much, limited by the volume capacity of Project E and the limited runtime of our machine. Maybe we can find a way to stop The Slicer from drifting during their ransacking, and so reduce the alleged devastation that Mr. Visitor expects we face."

"I don't think we have time to fix fundamental problems with the machine today," Jarod said.

"Lora," the doctor continued, ignoring Jarod, "how far did you get in finding a way to predict the duration of the experiment?"

"Um… I found some patterns that correlate with a long run or a short one. But I can't predict the duration with any sort of precision. Why?"

"Is there any chance that we can force the machine into a configuration that would guarantee us the shortest possible run? In your opinion?"

"No. I can't see how. We can only observe, not control."

Gary saw what Dr. Shim was getting at, and he had an alternative. "How soon after we start The Shim can you tell if it will be a long or a short run?" he asked Lora.

"It shows up in The Slicer data right away, but it is not something you can just see by looking at it. It's too much data to monitor by eye and the pattern is quite subtle. If we have a computer look for it in real time, I'd say we could detect these patterns almost immediately. A few milliseconds, maybe."

"Good. Then we can program this thing to abort the instant we detect a long run, and then restart immediately without shutting down. We repeat that until we find a short one." Gary stood, waiting for confirmation.

"We could reset the expansions, while keeping the beam running," said Lora. "We've never done that before."

Dr. Shim nodded. "I don't see why that wouldn't work. The beam is not going to be interrupted, so no calibration or alignment issues should occur. The environment remains stable. Just keep resetting the expansions until we get a short run prediction and then let it run its course."

The box of tissues, still on the floor, spontaneously relocated elsewhere, closer to where the doctor was sitting.

"Oh my god, he's annoying," Lora said.

Knowing that it would be inappropriate to laugh under the current circumstances, the doctor struggled to suppress a chuckle at the saucy remark.

"What about Randy? And Naomi? Are we just going to leave them there?" Jarod asked.

Gary answered, as only Gary would, "Of course not. Only until the phones are working again. Unless you want to carry them out of here yourself."

Another pen materialized on the floor, just in front of Dr. Shim's uninjured foot. It was a whiteboard marker this time. Lora picked it up and walked over to the board. She wrote, under Gary's previous message, "Working on it! Asshole!"

She turned to Jarod. "Can you please go fix the safety on The Slicer? I think we have no real choice but to run again unless we're willing to end up like Randy today. If we run the machine, we may still be here tomorrow to deal with whatever side-effects Visitor's plan has. We'll do whatever we can to shield The Slicer from interference, and to make the run as short as possible. Time is not on our side either. The longer we wait, the more we run the risk of being found out. If we get escorted out of here, we'll never get back in."

"I agree," said both Dr. Shim and Gary, leaving Jarod with no further say in the matter. Without an alternative proposal, and no desire to end up with random implants, he walked in the direction of the electronics lab to get his tools.

Lora called after him, "Jarod, we'll need some time to figure out if we can detect the interference and suppress it. So, please take a bit of extra time fixing the safety. I want Visitor to think it's difficult."

Jarod nodded. "It is."

"Gary, I'll send you some files with what information I gathered on the correlation between the data patterns and run duration. You can set up the program for resetting the expansions. I'll sit with David to think about the interference issue."

"He's doing it again," Gary said, pointing at three markers on the floor, that laid themselves out in a deliberate pattern resembling the number four. "What do you think that means?"

Lora checked her phone and said, "He wants to walk at four. That gives us less than fifty minutes."

Everyone in the room knew it would not be possible to find a feasible solution to the interference problem when the problem itself wasn't even understood. Meanwhile, they could hear the worrisome sounds of sirens in the background. A passer-by must have gotten word to the police about a dead man lying on the sidewalk. If they came to the Everett building, they would find a locked door and no one manning the security desk, so it wasn't all that likely they would interrupt the experiment.

When there were less than ten minutes to go before the deadline, Lora and Gary were at the consoles, going through the motions of getting The Shim ready for its final run, again. Gary was confident that the reset mechanism for the expansions would work, so Visitor's walk would be short, whatever that meant. Dr. Shim was still over at one of the desks that Lora had rolled his chair to, poring over lines of data as well as code to find some way to improve on the interference problem. They hadn't made much progress, as expected, but the doctor had made a few changes based on best guesses and hunches. No one had ever thought about running The Shim and Project E in parallel, and certainly not in separate universes, but Dr. Shim's intimate knowledge of both projects made him the only person who could even begin to do so in any meaningful way.

Lora walked past his desk on her way to the levers. "It's time, David. There's nothing more we can do."

The doctor seemed to be in a world of his own. He shook his head. "It is quite fascinating, isn't it? Interference caused by Project E appears to coax The Slicer into creating an additional slice, a side channel if you will. A connection is formed between Project E and another part of the multiverse where the materials that Project E was programmed to retrieve happen to exist in an environment that resembles the machine's chamber, allowing—"

"David! Our time is up," Lora said.

"Yes, but don't you understand what it is we just uncovered, Lora? Your Slicer configuration isn't just creating a channel between us and our intended target, but also an additional slice for which the conditions are unintentionally set by Project E. The Slicer is used by Project E to reduce its search area. But I expect this side channel to be imprecise at best, an unfocused view of a narrow slice. It is a coincidental effect of interference, not a carefully designed slice like ours. As a result, Project E is pulling in not just what it is told to, through the side channel, but also excess baggage from surrounding areas. Countless other universes."

Lora wasn't sure she followed what Dr. Shim was trying to explain, or why he thought he should do that now. "It doesn't matter. We—"

"And all this uninvited detritus is somehow being channeled away from Project E, toward the opposite end of our own intended slice. Our slice is acting as a waste disposal. If we were to run Project E on our side, all this extraneous matter coming in from the side channel is deflected away from us, while we get only what we ordered. That could explain the supernatural phenomena in Mr. Visitor's world. But if they run Project E on *their* side—"

"All that crap comes our way," Gary interjected.

"David! That's enough! There isn't any more time!"

The doctor pointed at the screen with a pen he held in his hand, a grimace on his face which could be indicative of his annoyance at being repeatedly interrupted or simply the pain he felt in his foot. "The changes we have made so far, are aimed at suppressing the side channel, without even knowing what exactly it is. Take this change here for example. It's quite possible that we will make too aggressive a correction when the side channel appears or if that extra slice is of an altogether different nature than we have assumed. I think that could have geographical consequences. It could also easily send The Slicer off course, possibly widening the slice and—"

A clunking sound interrupted him this time.

"It has to be now," Lora said with finality. She was over at the levers, and had pulled down the first one, activating The Slicer.

She had her phone in her hand looking at the time. Pulling down the second lever activated The Sharpener, indicated by a slew of little colored lights across both pods and on the consoles. She quietly counted down the seconds until four o'clock.

"I mean, it *could* work. We may have made it worse," said Dr. Shim, rather unhelpfully.

The third lever came down and the beam formed. The purple light, which had always instilled a sense of wonder in Lora, now seemed nauseating to her. *Distasteful, really.* A brief burst of clicking noises came from the machine that she had never heard before. She looked over at Gary, who was focused sharply on the screens of the console. Just behind his seat, lay the bright green blanket that covered most of Randy, only his lower legs and feet sticking out on one end. Where the purple light hit it, it looked dark and colorless, giving it a more appropriately sinister look than the tacky decorations it was anointed with.

Gary looked back around at Lora. "It worked. It reset seven times before settling on what promises to be a short run, hopefully not much over thirty minutes.

"Didn't he say he needed forty-five?" Jarod asked.

Lora shook her head. "He already got fifteen minutes earlier."

"Something is off," Dr. Shim said. "This thing could overcompensate when Project E comes online. If The Slicer drifts too far, we might lose it altogether. It could abort the run again."

Lora came back to the other console and confirmed with Gary that everything looked normal so far. "We can't change anything now, there is no time."

CHAPTER THIRTY-SEVEN

E D WAS FEELING TIRED, occasionally almost drifting into sleep, his phone sitting in his lap. He looked out the meeting room window down at Project E and tried to attract Jim's attention by tapping on the glass. The new time was set for four.

Earlier, when he sensed Jarod's attempt to leave the lab, Ed had to act quickly. Jarod had been too far away from Lora to clearly sense his location, or to safely approach him, so he couldn't target him accurately. Every attempt, thus far, at using his mind control as a persuasive measure, had catastrophic consequences for his target. He had been accurate enough, he thought, but his emotions, his anger, his impatience, or some external disturbance always got in the way. His power was easy to wield, the effort no different whether he wanted to move an object onto a table or into someone's head. But that ease of use came with a matching ease of making mistakes. Targeting the doctor's foot with a pen turned out to be his first success at using it in a non-fatal way and Ed was pleased with that.

Randy, the student, was unlucky. The phone was supposed to land neatly in his lap. That would have worked to attract the attention of him and the rest of the group. Instead, Ed's concentration was broken when Jim interrupted him, while at the same time Randy was unexpectedly getting up from his seat. With both Randy's lap moving and Ed's focus shifting, it was hard to say where the phone would end up. Ed didn't know until he came back to check. He watched as the student died in Lora's lap. That wasn't necessary. None of the people he had killed needed to die. It had served him no purpose. In fact, killing the student was counterproductive. That was not the kind of motivation this group of scientists needed to bring Visitor back to their world. All Ed had needed was to make sure they resumed after Gary's rude interruption of the experiment.

When Visitor killed Neil, it was arguably in self-defense. Then he killed Ian, which was unintentional, but not a big loss as far as Ed was concerned. *He deserved it.* Lora didn't know about the bartender, and she seemed to understand that Ian was a mistake. But she would never forgive him for accidentally killing her young lab assistant. Ed had crossed a line that he could never come back from. Effectively, he had just cut all ties with Lora. Now he had to observe the group and persuade them somehow to put Randy's death behind them and focus on the job at hand. *Do whatever it takes.*

These people technically didn't even exist. Not in his entire universe. Does that warrant killing someone in theirs? Probably not, but it just didn't feel as if it had the same gravity as killing someone who actually existed. A killing, using his special power, particularly when using the phone, felt more like witnessing a murder than committing one. What did Ian feel when he learned that he had killed thousands? *Nothing.* Because of Randy's misfortune, the cleaner and the passer-by had become *whatever it took* to get this project back on the rails.

Thirty seconds before four, the lights in the meeting room slightly dimmed and a loud, low frequency sound filled the air, vibrating Ed's seat. Project E was live. As the sound faded, a blue glow began to form underneath him. Ed's paralyzed legs began to float out in front of him, in anticipation of that jolt of pain that would shoot down from his back into his legs soon, restoring his ability to walk on his own two feet one last time. The ball formed, and Ed floated in the center, well clear of the chair now. It was such a blissful experience, seeing the world disappear behind this blue curtain of light, to make way for a better alternative. There was a short flickering in the sphere, which caused his body to re-orient rapidly a few times before the crackling sound started to fade as usual. As soon as the first sounds of traffic started to filter through, he knew where he would be. It was the alley across from Delaney's. He appeared at a strange angle, and too far up in the air, causing him to drop down hard on the pavers in a puddle of dirty water. He had never had such a rough entry into this world before.

Visitor got up and brushed himself off, annoyed with the wet stain on his pants and jacket. Then he shrugged and stomped hard in the puddle. Just another thing he had not been able to do since he was a young boy.

Jim would give Visitor fifteen minutes before starting the extractions again. This would give him time to get into the lab if that was necessary. Together they figured they would need about five minutes for the first extraction, followed by one or two every minute after that, depending on how quickly they could unload the chamber. At that rate, with an estimated fifteen successful extractions needed to get what they needed, the run would have to last a minimum of forty-five minutes. Everything after that was a welcome bonus. If the run lasted long enough, they might perform over a hundred extractions.

Visitor crossed the street and looked through the windows of Delaney's. Nothing much had changed in there, but it was still closed, with notices posted on the door.

There was a police car and an ambulance parked near the campus gate, looking as though they were just about finished and ready to leave. He wasn't worried too much, as he watched two other people entering the campus through the gates. When he walked up, he was stopped by a police officer who looked him over, as people tended to do when they saw him, but after he explained he hadn't seen anything regarding the dead man and his dog, and that he was expected in the university, they let him pass without any trouble. It seemed that getting away with murder was not hard in this universe.

The Everett building was locked, as usual, but there were still no security guards in the foyer. The lights were on. The two TVs were on as well, one showing news and one showing information about NMU. He could see the security desk and he knew from watching Lora earlier today where the button to open the door was. It was easy enough to move a tape dispenser that he could see sitting on the desk and drop it on top of the switch. The door opened and he walked in, continuing straight to the lab.

"I am happy to see you have all come to your senses," Visitor said when he arrived at The Shim. He looked at Dr. Shim's foot. "Ouch. I'm sorry about that. I blame him," he said, pointing at Jarod. Lora came forward and slapped him hard across the face.

Her hand was on its way for a second time when he grabbed her wrist. He held it tightly while fixing his sunglasses to sit straight on his face again.

"I deserved that, I suppose." He threw Lora's hand away from him. "Don't touch me again." Visitor stretched out his hand and a marker appeared just above it, dropping neatly into his palm. He walked over to the second console and placed the marker by the emergency stop button. "I will remain here to make sure no one gets any more ideas. This marker will go into your head if you try." Visitor made sure everyone understood him. "And for what it's worth, I didn't mean to harm the boy. Bad luck. You people really pissed me off, you know?" He turned to Gary, who just nodded. "Just like that god damned bartender."

Lora gasped and lost her footing, stumbling backward and ending up sitting on the floor, still backing away from Visitor.

"Neil," she whispered. "You killed Neil? Why?" She hardly recognized Visitor anymore. *I let a monster into this world.*

Visitor pointed his index finger at his neck and answered, "Because he shot me. He *killed* me! Did you know he had a gun hidden away under that bar? He killed me because I couldn't pay for my drink. I bled out on the floor and then I woke up in my wheelchair. Can you believe that? I can't be killed! I cannot die!"

"That sucks man," Jarod said.

"Bygones," Visitor replied. "All we have to do now is wait for this run to complete and then we can all go home. Sound good?"

In the silence that followed, there was a noise that resembled the creaking of floorboards, but louder, as if something was applying a large amount of pressure to the whole room. In the distance, dust was swirling down from some of the light fixtures. Lora could feel a tremor in the floor.

"Do you feel that?" she asked, not particularly directed at anyone.

Gary responded. "Whatever it is, we can't have it messing with the plateau. If that ball moves, this experiment is permanently over."

A loud cracking sound emanated from the direction of Ian's office, at the far end of the room. A cloud of dust rose from the area behind a stack of equipment that blocked most of the window to that room. The tremor subsided as the dust settled.

"What the hell?" Gary said.

Visitor gestured everyone to stay put. "That, my friends, is probably just the world coming to an end," he said, with a satisfied grin on his face. "Project E is back online."

Another, even more alarming sound now came from the direction of the foyer. It sounded like a man, screaming with hopeless despair, followed by things breaking. The door swung open so hard that the glass panel broke as the door recoiled from the doorstop. When it opened for a second time, the source of the scream stepped into the room. It was a slightly pudgy looking man, dressed in a green onesie that revealed only a part of his face. He screamed again and stomped his feet, almost like a child throwing a fit. As he stomped his way into the room, he kicked and thrashed at everything he passed. An office chair careened across the floor and crashed into a stack of boxes with lab equipment parts, sending them tumbling. He kicked at the individual boxes on his way to a workbench, not even noticing Naomi as he trudged past her.

He pummeled everything on the work surface, picking up small items and flinging them into the room while pounding on the larger items. "I saved a hundred people! A hundred! And still, they get it wrong. What will it take for these assholes to—" As he turned around, he froze on the spot when he noticed people looking at him, with one pair of eyes trying to peek at him from the floor behind them. The silence returned for a moment as everyone in the room tried to make sense of what was happening.

"Wh...," Visitor started. He looked around at the others before finishing. "What is that?" He pointed at the violent stranger.

"That's Dart, man. Everyone knows that," said Jarod.

"How did he get in here?" Lora whispered.

"Dartman?" Visitor burst out laughing. "*That* is Dartman?" He had heard of the infamous superhero in his own world, but since he didn't live in this city, he had never really known much about him. The appearance was disappointing.

"The name," said Dart, through his teeth, "is Dart!" He was seething with rage, his fists balled and his entire body tense, as if ready to launch himself. "I saved a busload... two busloads of people from falling to their deaths today!"

"Wonderful. You need to leave so badly," Visitor said.

"I am on TV! Right now, I am! It's all over the news. I was watching Channel 56 in the foyer just now. 'Dartman, Dartman, Dartman!' I told them exactly what to call me and they still manage to screw it up."

"Dartman, you need to leave. Now!"

Dart stomped his feet on the ground, his face red with anger. "Apologize! Now!" he yelled, his voice jumping up an octave or two. "I will not take any more abuse from anyone! Apologize, or I will shut you up permanently!"

Visitor lost his patience. The marker by the emergency stop button disappeared just as Dart started coming toward him, stomping hard and holding up his fists in front of him. Dart subtly moved his head aside just as the marker appeared, avoiding it so precisely that Visitor did a double take. It looked as if Dart had known exactly where to be to dodge it. Before Visitor knew, the crazy green man was right in front of him, and a tightly balled fist struck his chin. It sent Visitor flailing backward, stumbling, barely able to stay on his feet. When he regained his balance and straightened his sunglasses another fist was already on its way, accompanied by a loud scream from his green assailant. He quickly pulled his head away to the side and avoided a direct hit, instead catching the brunt of it with his shoulder.

"The name is Dart. Apologize, clown!" Dart screamed at him so loud it made his ears ring.

Visitor took the opportunity to take a swing at Dart, who, again masterfully, avoided the punch by ducking under it and then landing one of his own in Visitor's gut. It knocked the air right out of him, and he took another few steps backward to give himself time to recover. Dart wasn't waiting and followed him, ready to strike again. This time Visitor fended it off by blocking it with his arm. It allowed him to push Dart's chest with both hands, hard enough to send him stumbling, losing his balance. Dart fell over backward and landed hard on his butt, only slightly softening the landing with his hands. Visitor kicked him down, then kneeled on his chest, making sure to push his knee down hard, forcing the air out of Dart's lungs and readying himself to deal a well-aimed blow to his face.

"Dartman, it was nice not knowing you. Freak."

"No!" Lora yelled. "Don't hurt him!"

Visitor raised his arm and made a fist. Dart struggled to breathe and was clawing at anything within his reach. He managed to grab on to one of the pockets on the red jacket and yanked on it hard. The tough fabric ripped, and the pocket separated from the jacket. A cellphone came flying out, sliding away on the floor.

When Lora saw it, she suddenly knew what to do. She scrambled to her feet and jumped toward the phone. Visitor made a similar move, never even landing his punch, instead diving for the phone. His hand met Lora's on the phone, and he grabbed onto it firmly. Lora let out a short cry of pain as she tried to pull her hand with the phone out of his. But he was too strong. He squeezed a little harder to make that point, and it hurt, before he loosened his grip and pulled the phone out with his other hand.

"Thank you," he said, turning back to Dart. "Dartman, where do you think you're going?"

Dart had got back to his feet and screamed, kicking at one of the console tables. "The name—"

Another loud cracking sound came from the end of the room. A window broke and a single, loudly squawking crow flew into the lab. It flew a wide arc before landing on one of the light fixtures, unsettling more dust and still making a lot of noise.

"The name," Dart said, seemingly undeterred, but with slightly more restraint in his voice, possibly because the console table wasn't giving in much and he had hurt his foot, "is Dart, you red weirdo!"

A second crow flew into the hall, soon followed by two or three more. Each one adding to the noise. Once they had found their own perch to sit on, dozens more entered from wherever it was they came from.

"Dad… Gary, go close the window, will you?" Visitor said. "Don't even think about leaving."

As Gary walked away, Dart was stomping his feet again, swinging his fists randomly. He landed one on the console table that Gary had just vacated. Miraculously, nothing happened to The Shim, even though he had managed to put a crack in the surface and several buttons were now angled oddly out of the panel. Visitor shoved him hard, away from the panel.

"God, you're annoying!" Visitor yelled, pushing Dart again.

Dr. Shim, who had been quiet all this time, suddenly made a loud snorting noise, then apologized as if he had just sneezed.

Dart ended up facing away from the panel and trudged on to the next available desk, where he resumed smashing things to bits while screaming and cursing, competing with the incredible noise made by the now numerous birds. Visitor stood and summoned pens, pencils, pencil sharpeners and many small objects he didn't recognize as anything other than small enough to use, made them disappear and then reappear precisely where Dart was. Dart made a strange series of dance-like moves that looked almost unnatural, somehow evading almost everything that Visitor threw at him. But not everything. Dart screamed, which, so far, seemed to be the only kind of sound he made, and grabbed his leg. Something was protruding from just above his knee. He yanked it out and threw it at Visitor, only to continue bashing everything around him. He disappeared behind some equipment cabinets, continuing to make a lot of noise.

Visitor grabbed on to the edge of the console, his phone still firmly clasped in his hand. He had spent a tremendous amount of energy fending off Dart and moving all this stationery in his direction. With his free hand extended, he summoned another marker from the floor, caught it as it fell neatly into his palm and carefully propped it beside the emergency stop button as a replacement for spent ammo.

Dart reappeared from the other side of the cabinets holding a piece of wiring in his hand.

Lora cast a concerned look at Jarod, who had now sat down on the ground opposite her. "Don't we need that?"

"Dude, I just want to go home," was Jarod's only response.

Gary now returned from the other side of the room, looking a little lost.

"What is it, Gary?" Lora asked, having trouble being heard over the loud caws coming from the crows.

"It's… It's Ian's office. It's as if the whole thing has just disappeared. When you look inside, there is just nothing there. I was looking into the abyss. It's black as night in there."

"Is that where the god damned birds are coming from?" Visitor wanted to know.

"Yes. One of the windows is broken. I tried to cover it up. It smells putrid."

"That must be Ian's after shave," said Dr. Shim, surprising even himself.

"It shouldn't be much longer," Lora said to Jarod, as quietly as possible, nodding toward the beam.

Dart continued his rampage, now apparently wanting to climb onto the plateau, once again drawing the attention of everyone in the room.

"What the hell is the matter with this guy?" Visitor said, throwing his hands up in despair. "Hey, Dartman! Get off the table, you idiot!" He watched in horror as Dart began kicking at pod one. Pieces of material started coming off the side of it immediately and something started beeping urgently.

"He's destroying the machine!" Visitor yelled, panicking.

A similar panic came over both Lora and Gary.

All three started running to the plateau. As Visitor passed Dr. Shim in his seat, the doctor suddenly and with surgical precision stuck his foot, with the marker still embedded in it, out in front of him. Visitor tripped and keeled over forward with no way to stop himself. He landed hard on the floor, his phone briefly separating from his hand. But he grabbed it before anyone even had a chance to approach. His mouth was open, and he was making an odd-looking rotating motion with his lower jaw, apparently testing if it still worked after his chin had hit the floor.

Jarod, meanwhile, was moving toward Visitor. Possibly he was thinking he could overpower him.

Lora called after him, "No Jarod!"

Before Jarod even made it halfway the distance to where Visitor was on the ground, something appeared inside his upper arm. He screamed and immediately retreated. "Man, I was just trying to help!" he said, lying.

Visitor tried to get back on his feet, but he needed a moment to deal with the pain in his knees, hands, and chin.

"No, Dart!" Lora yelled.

Dart was now moving on from kicking the pod, stomping around on the plateau in the direction of the beam. Gary climbed on the plateau and attempted to block Dart from getting near it. Dart didn't need this interference and simply decked Gary with a single punch. Gary limply fell away, remaining still with his head hanging off the edge of the plateau.

"Gary!" Lora yelled.

Dart screamed at the beam right in front of his face. It looked like he was trying to alternatingly punch it with his fists and strangle it.

Lora watched his feet, now so close to the target object that it was almost inevitable that it would get trampled. She saw the damage done to pod one, which was not the pod they selected for this run, but she had no idea if the machine could even work if one pod was damaged while it was running. *Now would be an excellent time for The Shim to finish and move the ball.*

She looked back at Visitor, who was now sitting up, shaking his head, and about ready to get up on his feet. She had no choice.

The sound of the crows seemed to swell in anticipation. Lora jumped forward and ran fast at Visitor. As she flew by him, she delivered a firm kick to his chest, knocking him over on his back. He was down on the ground again, still clenching the phone in his fist.

Dart, screaming at the machine he was fighting, looked down, briefly sticking his head in the beam, casting a partial shadow over the target object. When he saw the ball, he took a step backward and looked at it curiously.

"Dart! No, please!"

Dart heard his name, and he looked over at the group. Both Jarod and Lora were waving their arms at him, while the man in the ridiculous red outfit was laying on the floor. They finally got the message, it seemed. They got his name right. Still, no apology from the man in red.

Dart pulled his right foot back, spread his arms in some sort of imitation of a soccer player and brought his foot forward again. He hit the ball perfectly and sent it flying fast and hard through the room. The hum of the beam changed in tone slightly, made more obvious by the curious and sudden silence of the crows, but it remained shining just as bright. Dart made a simulated crowd sound. *Goal!*

Lora was standing on Visitor's hand, which was still clasping the phone as Dart kicked the target object. Visitor began making a sound from his mouth, somewhat as if he was trying to sing, but with a very fast vibrato and no discernible trace of talent.

"Noooo, noooo, noooo," he sang. A blue glow started to appear beneath him, and somehow, he was beginning to float above the floor slightly.

Lora shifted her weight and adjusted her feet, so she could hold down his wrist with her left foot, while she used the other to trample the hand. She lifted her right foot and brought it back down on the fingers and the phone. Electric arcs danced around Visitor's body as he gained more elevation, his hand still firmly trapped under Lora's feet. She could feel the arcs brushing her feet and running up her legs. It looked extremely dangerous, but it was strangely pleasing, causing her goosebumps. Her foot rose again, and she brought it down harder this time. For just a moment, the hand let go of the phone. Lora kicked it away, out of reach for Visitor. She stepped away from him, feeling a resistance as if the blue light was pulling her in, or rather as if she wanted to stay in. Visitor's skin now had an odd transparency to it and his face looked contorted, without revealing if he was feeling pain or ecstasy. Surely, he had a broken finger or two.

His song continued, "Nooooo!"

Visitor started moving wildly, flinging his arms and legs around, seemingly trying to escape the strange electric apparition he was trapped in. What looked like random movements, soon turned out to be more directed, as he was suddenly near enough to the phone that he could grab it again, the electric arcs immediately embracing it as they had him.

Lora noticed a shimmering in the corner of her eye. She didn't hesitate and tried to kick the hand that held the phone as hard as she could. Another pen appeared in mid-air, where her leg had just passed through. He had just missed her. The blue light rapidly intensified and engulfed Visitor, concealing him from view completely. It was taking on a more spherical shape, and it was hard to tell where his hand had been only a moment ago. The shape briefly hovered still, giving the impression that Visitor was no longer inside, before it contracted rapidly until it disappeared with only a slight popping sound. A few arcs of light fizzled out over the floor.

"Did I get it?" Lora asked, sounding afraid. "Did we get his damned phone?"

Dr. Shim and Jarod both shook their heads. "I don't know, I didn't see it," Jarod said.

All eyes turned to the box of tissues. It sat still on the floor.

"I didn't feel it. Please tell me he is gone," Lora said.

Jarod got up. "I'll look for the phone, you go tend to Gary."

Lora nodded and got up as well. She asked Dr. Shim if he was alright. He was, so she turned to Gary, just as one of the whiteboard markers suddenly slid by across the floor. Lora screamed. "Oh no!" she yelled. She was so scared. With no way to bring Visitor back, now that the target object had moved, she knew he would have no use for her, or any of the group. The marker had missed her, but only just. She was shaking, her eyes rapidly tracking every small object near her.

"Sorry, that was me," Jarod said from beyond The Shim when he realized he had accidentally kicked a marker in Lora's direction.

The beam faded out and the hum died away as a subtle chime sounded from the console. The Shim was ready. The machine didn't know that the target object wasn't present anywhere near it, and that it had moved nothing. Lora looked over at where Randy was lying. "High five," she whispered.

Dart was wandering quietly around the hall confused about where he was and how he got there. He was looking for a way out, his usual quick exit strategy, but instead he ended up returning to the plateau after hitting a dead end. Gary had just opened his eyes again and blinked a few times before trying to sit up.

"That hurt," he said, rubbing his chin. "Is it over?"

Jarod came over when he heard Gary's voice. "Dude! Sleep well, did you?"

On his approach, Dart picked up something from the floor. He handed it to Lora, who was sitting on the plateau with Gary. Dart produced a murmuring sound that may have been an apology of some sort.

"Thank you. We just saved the world, Dart," Lora said.

Jarod and Gary wanted to protest but Lora put her finger to her lips, while showing them what Dart had given her. It was Visitor's phone, broken almost in half.

Lora heaved a sigh of relief, replacing the look of panic on her face with the beginnings of a smile. "It's over. He's gone."

"It's what I do," Dart mumbled.

Chapter Thirty-Eight

THE FIRST PERSON to exit the Everett building after the machine had stopped was Lora. She walked the path toward the main campus road and then stopped dead in her tracks as she witnessed firsthand one of the side effects of Project E's interference. She stared at two oversized horses walking calmly from the sidewalk onto campus, watching them slowly coming in through the gates. They were both white, their hair shiny and sparkling as if it could be made of glass. Down their legs, white transitioned into a soft pink and terminated in violet at their feet. And their feet seemed to be made of a pink glassy material. Their footsteps were barely audible, even on the pavement.

Jarod and Gary joined her a few minutes later.

"My god," Jarod whispered. "They are magnificent."

The surreal scene bestowed on Lora a tranquility she had rarely felt before. She welcomed it. In this blissful moment, all other thoughts and memories faded into the background, and she just stared. They all felt it. Gary almost lost his footing and had to sit down on the bench nearby.

On their foreheads, the animals had two protrusions made of a similar transparent material as their feet, arranged somewhat like a set of rhinoceros horns, but longer and further up. The longer Lora looked at the creatures, the less they looked like regular horses to her. They were larger overall, and their big eyes were more forward facing, and had a deep purple color. Their legs were proportionally longer as well, akin to a moose, maybe, or a giraffe. The animals moved with unbelievable elegance onto a patch of grass across from their entranced onlookers. Their long tails and manes had a hint of pink in them and when they caught the sun, looked almost like they were a source of light in themselves.

In the days that followed, the animals were captured, to become world famous residents of the city zoo. People lovingly referred to them as unicorns, which Lora thought was silly. Seeing as they had two horns, that should make them at least bicorn, but a new name would be more appropriate in her opinion.

Once communication channels had been restored, only a few hours after the events in the lab, reports started coming in of other animal sightings throughout the city. Bats were spotted emerging from the roof of a shopping mall and several people had reported finding snakes in their homes and gardens. The sighting of a tapir found roaming a parking garage generated a lot of headlines. It was unknown where the animal had come from. It certainly wasn't missing from any known zoo. Some people reported seeing animals that were known to be long extinct, but none of those were corroborated with evidence, and the animals were not seen again since their first encounter. The unicorns of NMU were the only two sighted creatures that didn't appear to have a known origin anywhere on Earth.

The modifications that Dr. Shim and Lora had made to The Slicer, intended to minimize the effects of interference from Project E, proved to be not entirely without result.

The first, unprotected, run of The Shim that day, had caused a series of sink holes across the globe, with the biggest one, coincidentally, forming not far from campus, at the bus terminal by the train station. Sheer luck, combined with the heroic efforts of Dart, had somehow prevented anyone from getting harmed in any of those incidents worldwide.

On the second run, the modifications had not eliminated the interference problem, but had nevertheless geographically limited the effects to just the wider surroundings of the university campus, which included most of the city and some suburban areas.

Those effects were not limited to exotic animal sightings. The police responded to calls from concerned residents who spotted a man wandering their neighborhood unclothed. They found him confused and unable to identify himself properly or explain where he had come from. After examination at an emergency room, the man was declared healthy. The last thing he remembered, before finding himself walking around stark naked in a part of town unfamiliar to him, was that he had been home alone when multiple strangers forced their way inside. He had a distinct memory of being stabbed multiple times, first in his living room and again after escaping into his garage. It wasn't long before the man was identified as Mark Somerville, known to have died over ten years ago as the victim of a violent crime. He was soon reunited with his family; a wife who had since remarried, and two now fully grown children.

Throughout the city there had been reports of what people believed to be paranormal activity. One-time sightings of deceased persons, apparitions of all sorts, ghostly sounds, strange lights and odd behaviors in both objects and animals. One family reported that they could all hear a specific radio station for several days without turning on the radio.

Near the convention center, with the Physics Advances convention in progress, a large monolithic structure had appeared that replaced most of a small park and the surrounding sidewalks, streets, and buildings. It came in the form of a huge, near perfect, cube of pure Rhenium, nearly thirty-two metric tons of it, towering thirty stories that dwarfed the surrounding buildings. The extremely valuable Rhenium deposit, its size matching almost the annual global production of the rare-earth metal, was welcomed by industry and scientists alike. It didn't come without a cost, as no one who lived in the replaced buildings, or happened to be at the site at the time of the structure's appearance, was heard from or seen again. That story took a backseat to the opportunities it opened for the local economy. Curiously, the statue of Dart still stood, its distended belly so close to the steeply rising metallic wall that barely a finger would fit in between.

While the experiment was in progress, the fountain in front of the library caught on fire. Witnesses to the event described it as a religious experience. With only marble and water to burn, the fire could neither be explained, nor extinguished. The flames slowly subsided over the course of several hours. The fountain briefly became a place of pilgrimage for certain religious groups, but the city, at the request of residents of surrounding buildings as well as the library, eventually decided to remove the fountain citing safety concerns.

Behind Lora and Jarod, Dart emerged from the Everett building with Doug and Rupinder, both still dressed in their radiation suits. Both guards were busily chatting, apparently very proud and impressed that they too now had been rescued by their superhero Dart. From there, the story of how Dart saved them, along with most of the scientists in the lab and the world at large, by defeating an evil villain, a fraudster posing as a future sponsor visiting the lab, spread quickly and effortlessly. Jarod, Gary and Lora agreed with Dr. Shim that this story suited them just fine and that the truth about what happened in the lab was best kept confidential. For once, and to the great satisfaction of Dart, the vast majority of published stories quoted the correct name for the superhero.

The mysterious deaths of Randy, Naomi and the poor stranger on the sidewalk, along with the disappearance of the diabolical imposter in the lab, were added to the long list of unexplained phenomena of the day. Eventually, even the bizarre murders of Ian and Neil were attributed to the man in the red suit who Dart had defeated.

LIFE AT THE UNIVERSITY quickly resumed. Just days after the events in the lab, Dr. Shim, quickly adapting to the use of a cane, was put in charge of overseeing the activities in the Everett building while the university looked for a suitable candidate to replace Ian Byrne with. As Jim Ferguson had gone missing, along with the diamonds he and Ian had allegedly conjured up, the doctor found himself pressured by other investors to make haste with the relocation of The Shim. Meanwhile he proposed to resurrect Project E to study the possibility of a new version of The Slicer that could be installed as an expansion directly onto Project E. He became convinced that it should be possible to run Project E independently and without side effects, if the side-channel created by the interference could be properly studied, isolated, character-ized and finally reproduced by this new expansion. He needed Lora's expertise on The Slicer, but for the moment at least, she disagreed with Dr. Shim that Project E should even be pursued any further.

Unsurprisingly, no such hesitation was present with investors, who lined up to back both projects. Consequently, the university also offered little protest. Some investors suggested that Lora should be given the lab leader role at B-Site to oversee either, or even both, of these new projects. She declined, citing her desire to explore other venues.

For the time being, Lora spent most of her days at home. She needed time to recover and struggled to make sense of the losses she suffered. Occasionally she visited the university to speak with Dr. Shim, or Jarod if he had time, or just to go for a walk in the park. Delaney's had reopened, but she still found it difficult to go there.

Gary retired and never returned to the lab. For the second time in his life, he was having great trouble with feelings of guilt over someone's death. He retreated into solitude to work through it, as he had when his wife had died, and he allowed himself no contact with the others in the group.

Dr. Shim had begun preparations for a third project at the NMU lab, concerning research into the, as yet unexplained, void that had supplanted the interior of Ian Byrne's former office. It was the doctor's intention to run that project with only students and he hoped Lora might supervise it once she resumed work and until she was ready to help him with Project E. The area around Ian's office had already been isolated from the rest of the lab and some initial experiments were being carried out under his supervision, as there were concerns that the phenomenon could be temporary. So far, the doctor thought those experiments had very unsatisfactory results. It appeared that no signals could travel out of the void. Any measuring devices, electronic or mechanical, simply didn't register anything when inserted into the emptiness. Anything that entered the void untethered was immediately and irretrievably lost. Using ropes, cables, or chains, it was possible to dip objects into the nothingness and retrieve them, but they emerged unaltered, carrying no record of what happened inside. One of the students, invited by Dr. Shim to help define research goals and future projects, had been curious and recalcitrant enough to slip his own hand into the void. Upon insertion, he later told doctors, he felt nothing. It was as if his hand had no longer existed. Sadly, for the student, that feeling did not end when he retrieved his hand. The extremity was still present, and looked completely normal, but he could no longer feel it or use it.

Attempts to determine what the void was made of yielded nothing. Despite a definite foul smell perceived in the area around the office, extracted samples from the atmosphere within the void were indiscernible from regular office air, including even trace amounts of Ian's after shave. All insertions and attempted extractions were carried out through a newly constructed access port. It was put in the place of the hole in the window through which a murder of crows had previously entered the lab. It had yielded no other creatures or objects since. Students had suggested that one of the captured crows should be offered back into the void, but the university had forbidden any form of animal testing. It was likely that the birds, who upon close inspection appeared to be perfectly ordinary crows, were soon going to be released. Airflow into and out of the access port was found to be unremarkable as well, consistent with the office still being there. Equally unsuccessful were attempts to gauge the size of the void. The only way to perform such measurements was using passive tools, such as long sticks, measuring tapes, ropes, or strings. But so far, the only conclusion was that it was larger, in all directions, than any of the tools used, and certainly bigger than the former office. Nothing had been found inside the void, not even an end to it. Inspired by his collection of hazmat suits, Dr. Shim was now thinking about the design of gear suitable for sending a tethered and protected human observer into his predecessor's former office.

Epilogue

THE ELECTRONICS LAB had returned to its originally intended purpose now that The Shim was being removed from the lab. Jarod was happy to be working with students in his lab again, even though he was still often occupied helping with the dismantling of The Shim. Today, there were no students, but he found a welcome visitor in his lab. Lora had been nosing around the workbenches, with some of her old curiosity, as she waited for him to have a chat. He was happy to see her in the lab more often lately, more interested in what was going on there. When she dropped by unannounced like this, she usually just liked to talk to him about books she was reading, but today she subtly hinted that she might soon begin her work as supervisor for the void research project.

"It will be great to have you back here with us, boss," Jarod said.

Dr. Shim was ready to retreat from the lab again after he found Ian's successor in a woman from out of town with an impressive resume. She had fulfilled leadership roles at a few large commercial companies ranging from insurance to pharmaceutical. Lora was sure that Hannah Simmons, who was already building a reputation for herself as a tough negotiator, would be a formidable opponent in future arguments and, in that way, a worthy substitute for Ian.

When Jarod was called away to address a problem in the lab, she sat on one of the highchairs by a workbench, debating internally whether she should wait for him to return, or just go home. She brought out her phone to check the time. It was still early. For no other reason than to have something to look at, she opened a drawer and rummaged through it. Nothing but electronic parts, many of which she didn't recognize. The next drawer contained a bunch of baggies, each with more complicated looking parts. It wasn't any more interesting to her. Just as she closed it, she noticed one of the baggies had her name on it. She picked up the bag and read the full label out loud. "Lora, weirdo phone." A crude smiley face was drawn below. Lora smiled. On closer inspection she realized these were the parts from Visitor's phone that Jarod had saved for her. *Hmm, I wonder…*

Jarod wasn't coming back, she knew, after she had spent two full hours trying to fit the parts from the bag into her own phone. Just to see what would happen, you know?

"Y OU'RE DOING VERY WELL, Mr. Sutherland. If you keep this up, I'll soon be saying goodbye to you as you walk out the door. I'm very proud of you!"

Ed was annoyed by the incessant positive attitude of his physical therapist. Since his surgeries, this woman had been helping him to learn how to walk. It was a gruesomely slow process, but eventually, they had assured him, with enough training and the right medical care, he should one day be able to walk short distances, independently, without a walker or crutches. One day. In the meantime, he was struggling, hanging on to two bars, requiring all the strength in his arms to keep him there and receiving praise whenever he managed to move one foot in front of the other. *I'm doing great!*

He and Jim had made quite the name for themselves. Even though they didn't extract nearly as much as they wanted out of Project E before that angry green man had terminated the experiment, it was still enough to have a considerable global impact. They had already made significant contributions all over the world, including funding a successful effort for stopping some of the larger permanent earthquakes using a novel acoustics-based approach. That was only the beginning. They were working with aid organizations, schools and universities, scientists, politicians, and a host of commercial companies to make real and lasting changes that would improve the lives of billions around the globe. It wouldn't be the paradise they had envisioned, but they were determined to make it count. It was a delicate operation, trying to make sure that all the new materials and funds did not cause disruptions to the economy.

Of course, they had considerably benefited from it on a personal level. Jim, the do-gooder, was now one of the richest men on the planet, and Ed wasn't too far behind him in terms of wealth. It had opened doors for Ed. It had given him a real chance at going for a walk in his own world. One day.

Ed could hear a door open behind him but couldn't see who had entered. It must have been someone important because the room fell quiet. There were no footsteps, just a soft rustling of fabric, but Ed was suddenly overwhelmed with a familiar feeling. It was that feeling of warmth and comfort, a feeling of well-being he knew from only one other place. The place where everything around him was in sharp focus.

His therapist wasn't saying anything, and he could no longer feel her presence behind him. Was she even there anymore? *Did she leave?* With his arms getting tired he tried to look behind him again, but then someone walked – or rather floated – into his view. She was wearing immaculate white dress pants and a white top, covered mostly with a stylish, bright red jacket. She moved in a way that seemed impossibly elegant, gliding forward as if her feet were never quite touching the ground. When she turned to him, her eyes hidden, as she looked down to the floor, Ed's heart skipped a beat, and he almost lost his grip on the bars.

Her appearance was surreal, as if he could see her more clearly than anything else in the room. Ed began to tremble. The warmth and comfort he knew from floating close to her was accompanied by the fear he had felt when he had strayed too far. He couldn't take his eyes off her. There was a brightness to her, a vibrancy, and an exquisite level of detail in her face that made everything else in the room seem irrelevant. It felt extremely dangerous to look away.

Then she tilted up her head and looked at him. All of reality faded into the background until there was only her. She had captured him. Ed wasn't sure if his mouth was open or closed.

She was beautiful.

Her eyes, filled simultaneously with a deep-rooted sadness for those whom she had lost, and a well-founded hatred for the man responsible, and in whose very soul they now peered, almost took his breath away. They were all that mattered now. She could see everything. He felt her going through him, effortlessly, as if she was skimming a book.

"Lora? How…" Ed stammered. Beads of sweat had formed on his forehead as he struggled to keep himself upright on the bars. But when his arms finally gave out, he did not fall. He stood, unable to move, unable to speak, held up by nothing but her intense stare. His eyes were locked onto hers, and he could not even blink to break the gaze. He felt insignificant. He *was*. She was incredibly strong.

When she finally spoke, her lips did not move, her voice instead manifesting only inside Ed's head. Gentle, but trembling with anger. Soft, but crystal clear. Instantly, Ed knew this was his last day.

ALCO LAMMERS

In one life, he built a career as an embedded software engineer in The Netherlands, working on cutting edge technology that might someday change the world. In another, he was a signed electronic dance music producer, crafting beats for nearly a decade. He has a keen interest in music and the natural sciences. Some rather improbable events propelled him into his next adventure as an author. It just goes to show that you don't need a multiverse to live a multitude of lives. Alco currently resides near Halifax, in Nova Scotia, Canada.